# The Bitter and the Sweet

## The Winds of Freedom: Book III

Beth Kanell

# Acknowledgments

A pandemic increases a writer's frequent solitude. Moreover, I wrote this book after the death of my chief research partner and forever-loved husband David Kanell. It was slowed by needing to sell our home and create a new one on raw and mistreated land. I did my best to live up to what Dave would have expected and celebrated. His research files and the Vermont portion of his library accompany me. The love lives on.

I am grateful for the amazing research, support, question-answering, and reassurance that accompanied me in writing *The Bitter and the Sweet.* My read-along team, whose expectant presence keeps me writing daily, for this book was Lois Allen, who also watched for typing errors, and Jean Linderman. Cheryl Minden provided essential encouragement, as did Linda Goldstein. I always knew that Lynn Troy and Gerard W. Lamothe expected the next chapter!

Research on "North Upton" and 1854 depended on countless books, articles, and the actual newspapers of the time. Fran and Bert Fissette consulted on horses and conveyances—any mistakes are mine, though. Kathy and Jeffrey Parsonnet helped solve a final knot of plot. For her morning emails of history that linked so many of us through the difficult pandemic period and often lit new areas of research for me, I thank Natalie Kinsey-Warnock. Stephen Mihm's book *A Nation of Counterfeiters: Capitalists, Con Men, and the Making of the United States* provided invaluable details on the role of counterfeit money along the Canada border of this part of Vermont.

Last but not least, for always sharing new versions of hope and energy, thank you, Kiril Savino, Mike Minden, and Sarah Lancy Minden.

# Foreword

**The History Behind *The Bitter and the Sweet***

Readers of the preceding volumes in the Winds of Freedom series, *The Long Shadow* and *This Ardent Flame*, already know that North Upton is based on the real Vermont village of North Danville. The inn building and the farm remain; so do the kindessses of the people. The actual churches and parsonage do not have the geographic relationship I've built here, but the farms and the former inn still focus the center of the village.

This is a work of fiction, and only the politicians named represent historic individuals. Eli Thayer really did create an organization to send New Englanders west, bringing their vote so that the new states being carved from the Kansas Territory could be free states—that is, states that banned slavery. Most people in Vermont favored his effort and were determined to rid America of its "founding sin" that horrified Vermonters so deeply.

The reformed leader of counterfeiters along the US/Canada border region was, in real life, a man named Seneca Paige. It's known that he stammered, and I gave that characteristic to Foster Pierce in this story, in part to honor Mr. Paige himself. On his cemetery stone in Bakersfield, Vermont, is carved this: "His Loss will be felt by many; particularly by the poor. He was truly the poor man's friend." I remain very curious about his actual life, including his decades of crime, his clear ties to religion, and his eventual position representing his region of Canada in that nation's Parliament. My character of Foster Pierce represents only a guess at what he may have seemed like, to a young woman of that time.

The copper mines, ah, the copper mines. Remember that the historic settlement of America by Europeans, and some Asians, and captured Africans and their descendants, drew its power from the rewards of the land. Those determined to farm or ranch uprooted the Native Americans who had a very different relationship with the earth, and for a time, the settlers' pride in generating food and homes erased their awareness of tragic side effects. But mining opened gashes in the planet's surface that were far more obvious. Today the Vermont copper mines where Isaiah Hutchinson performed assays—especially the Elizabeth Mine—are only just being declared "sort of" safe, after more than 20 years and $90 million spent by the Environmental Protection Agency on the segment in Strafford, where the worst environmental damage occurred.

I knew there were copper mines in Canada, too—I drove past the turnoffs to them, many years ago—but when I noticed their geographic overlap with the towns among the "Eastern Townships" of Quebec that became counterfeiter havens in the early 1800s, I had to put them together into this novel. Yes, there really is gold up there and in Vermont, much of it so-called "placer gold," the kind you get from panning a stream. More on that, at another time. You did notice Isaiah Hutchinson's investment, I hope.

The 1850s were such a complicated time in Vermont. Their themes were often propelled by women and by religious leaders: an end to enslavement, some way to tame the alcohol use that often brutalized families, and a voice for women via the vote. Here among the Green Mountains, hope that these could be accomplished without violence persisted through that decade. The very real mill family that supported the growth of St. Johnsbury, which I have named the Gilmans, exhibited a mix of approaches to all of these issues. I was startled to discover how much that family would lose if the nation entered a civil war, and I deeply respect the choices they eventually supported.

A book like this depends on constant research, from fabric names to human names—I borrow from my own family names back then—to the strands of political forces and belief. Two books were especially important to me this time: *A Nation of Counterfeiters: Capitalists, Con Men, and the Making of the United States* by Stephen Mihm who kindly emailed responses to some questions, and *The Half Has Never Been Told: Slavery and the Making of American Capitalism* by Edward E. Baptist. Also vital were *Frontier Crossroads: The Evolution of Newport Vermont* by Emily M. Nelson, and insights from Andrew Delbanco's *The War Before the War: Fugitive Slaves and the Struggle for America's Soul from the Revolution to the Civil War.*

Small local historical societies, here and in Canada, provided much evidence and valued maps; the Vermont Historical Society and the Center for Research on Vermont answered questions and offered resources. Thank you.

# From the End of This Ardent Flame

I stumbled at first. It was necessary to speak aloud to Almyra especially, while catching as much detail as I could in my hands. Other than in the strange intimate language Caroline and I shared, I didn't have practice in speaking two languages at once. Or so it felt, as the grandfather clock in the distant parlor began to chime the hour, and time itself ran short and urgent.

"People are dying each day under the Slave Power's brutal force," I started. "Families are torn apart. Sarah's is only one. There are more than three million Africans enslaved in America now."

Caroline asked for the number to be repeated. Almyra marveled. "Millions?"

"Three millions," I confirmed. "And we who treasure freedom need to reach out and end the slaveholding, the torture, the killing. Together."

"How?" my friends demanded as one.

"Together," I repeated. The American Anti-Slavery Society; the legislators fighting to right the laws and Constitution; the surging ocean of persons drawn to action by Mr. Thaddeus Stevens, Mr. William Seward, Miss Lucretia Mott, the sisters Grimké. Miss Farrow brought a tintype of Frederick Douglass to show them, and two of his books. I turned the conversation back to the moral roots we all knew were right: No more slaveholding.

"How?" asked Caroline again, with her face enforcing the message of her hands. "How does a teacher take part? Two teachers heading west? How does a girl?" She placed a hand on Almyra's, gripped it as if to protect her.

Almyra said, "A minister to be. Perhaps I will even read law. Tell her, Alice."

I did, as quickly as my fingers could. Caroline cast a glance of fresh respect and affection at Almryra, who returned the hand clasp and leaned forward for a quick short embrace.

Miss Farrow rapped gently on the table for attention. "Caroline, Alice, I believe your journey will take you through Albany. We have things to send to the ladies there, and to Mr. Douglass. I'll start stitching them inside comforters and such, so you can carry them without risk. Almyra, we need you most of all now."

Almyra nodded eagerly. "When do I start?"

"Today," said Miss Farrow. "Mr. Eli Thayer is about to stir up a revolution of his own, if I'm seeing the future clearly. And I believe I must be. You'll begin to make the lists of people willing to head to the territories and fight with the ballot to contain and defeat the Slave Power. The time is coming rapidly, and we must prepare and be strong."

I romanticized it for a moment. "An ardent flame of freedom will seize this land, won't it?"

Miss Farrow said bluntly, "It has already started to burn. And we, my friends, are carrying the matches forward."

Almyra beamed. "I've always wanted to make things right," she said plainly. "Go west, Alice, Caroline. I'm here. And I'm staying to take hold."

Miss Farrow leaned forward and grasped all our hands in hers. "To take hold," she repeated. "To make things right. To follow the call of justice, wherever it will lead."

"Amen," I murmured, spelling it with my fingers as I spoke. "Amen."

## ~ 1 ~

Spring rain battered the house in torrents. The roof shook, and the brick walls, even with their plastered interior and cloth covering, exhaled a cold dampness in the sitting room. April weather, truly? Or November?

Almyra Alexander stared with gloom at the half page she'd written. The text from Ephesians seemed straightforward enough, and she didn't want to ask her uncle, the minister, how he'd used it for his own sermon. "In love He predestined us to be adopted as His sons." She understood that a sermon based on this text should declare hope for the sinner and a demand for better lives.

But in the dimness of the moment, her own response refused to come to the page.

A rattle from outside took her swiftly to the window where she rubbed a circle clean on the rippled glass. Someone calling at the house? She longed for distraction.

But it was only the clatter of the mud-spattered stage carriage conveying passengers and mail. It entered the village and proceeded directly to the inn, where her friend Caroline's brother Matthew would feed and water the horses and receive any traveler wishing to stay longer in North Upton. As for the mail, Almyra knew the stage driver would send it to the general store. If there were a letter for her from Caroline or Alice, she'd receive it when her uncle brought it home. Lately she chose not to visit the store herself without another woman or her uncle at her side; something in the nature of the men who lingered there for afternoons concerned her, even frightened her a bit, truth be told.

"A wise daughter depends on the women around her to uphold her," she said aloud. It sounded rather pretentious, but she inked it onto her page to consider later. Sons, that was the trouble with the Bible verse. It only treated sons.

Almyra sighed. Her aunt, assembling a ham pie in the adjacent kitchen, called out. "Between sighing and pacing, I gather you're not making much progress, my dear. Come to the kitchen and have some tea. I've some scraps of pie crust for you to sugar and bake, and maybe a little sweetening will do you good."

Almyra wiped the nib of her pen and capped the inkwell at her table. She longed for a proper desk on which to draft sermons and inscribe letters. Still, this table all her own, for schoolwork and study, gave her deep pleasure. She straightened the unfinished page and promised herself she'd return to it shortly.

Steam filmed the kitchen's two windows, and a marvelous aroma teased at Alymyra's nostrils. "Oh aunt," she exclaimed, "you'll have me faint with hunger, long before supper's served."

Her aunt beamed, and urged, "Go ahead, sugar these scraps at the side while I set the pie into the oven."

The reassuring warmth of the cookstove and the glow of a kerosene lamp emphasized the cozy room. Almyra marveled at the change in her aunt over the past two years, from someone both stern and shy, and downright miserly in her cooking, to a cheerful and accomplished cook, earning praise both at home and at community gatherings. All since Almyra had chosen to live here, after the death of her own mother in Boston.

"Adoption," she whispered to herself. That must be the key to addressing the text. Not so much the word "sons," but the meaning of adoption and the affection invoked.

The scrape of boots outside the door announced her uncle's arrival from his afternoon visits to homes in the village. Mrs. Alexander, Almyra's aunt, swiftly wiped her hands on a cloth and untied her apron to greet her husband.

"Heaven bless the cook," the Rev. Alexander enthused as he handed his dripping wet cloak to his wife and brushed a hand affectionately to her cheek. "My dear, I must include the enchantment of a bustling kitchen in one of my Sunday mentions, I believe." He twinkled at Almyra, one hand hiding something behind his back that rustled enticingly. "If I allow you, niece, to peruse the latest Harper's Magazine before I do, will I earn a cup of tea and some of those sugared piecrust morsels I see you preparing?"

In haste, Almyra passed the tray of uncooked treats to her aunt, to slip into the top of the oven and laughed as she wiped her own hands. "I'd give you my own share of them as well, Uncle, for that shining opportunity."

"Shining opportunity," her uncle repeated. "A nice turn of phrase, young lady. From your sermon preparation?"

"Not at all," Almyra confirmed. "You may take it for your own. Now, Uncle, that Harper's Magazine, if you please!"

With much laughter, the magazine changed hands. Almyra read aloud, "The Grinnell Expedition. And something on robbers of Le Mauvais Pas, as well as life in Abyssinia. But nothing on the war, is there?"

Her uncle gazed gravely at her. "In the Crimean peninsula? No, child, we'll have to find that news in the newspaper later in the week. Is there some reason for your concern?"

Almyra shook her head, dark curls bouncing. "It just seems so important, with such strife over the Holy Land itself."

Mrs. Alexander interrupted this serious turn of conversation. "For myself, I'd rather look at the fashion pages. No, no, I am only jesting. You both know it's the library notices I crave to examine. When you're ready to retire to your desk, Almyra, kindly leave the magazine in my hands."

The gentle household competition over preparing a sermon from the weekly Bible text—the Reverend Alexander for his congregation on the next Sunday, and Almyra for her growing stack of writings to present, sooner or later, to a seminary admission board—gave all the household much to discuss. Again, Almyra reflected on how things had changed since her two best friends in this northern Vermont village, Alice Sanborn and Caroline Clark, had departed for the western frontier, where the fierce fight for free or slave states took shape.

Almyra longed to be with them. Or at least receive fresh letters.

"Tush," she scolded herself under her breath. She must work at her own path to righteousness. If she had a pulpit of her own, she might shape the course of people's thinking toward an end to slavery, and urgently, to also end the wicked use of intoxicating beverages.

As if she'd drawn the thought out of the very air, she heard her uncle shift to a tone of deep concern as he said to his wife, "Another of the Hall daughters seems to have relocated to the Clark inn this winter. I stopped to call and met her over the noon dinner there. She can't be more than fourteen years old, and, far too much like her mother, I fear."

Oh my. Another addition to the inn's assortment of women who were "no better than they should be," as the village ladies said.

Almyra wondered, *Would a woman minister owe a visit to women whose growing notoriety was making a scandal of the village? And if she should go to pay a call, whom should she take with her?*

Lost in her own thought, she left the kitchen, repeating aloud the word she wanted to pursue in the next portion of her sermon: Adoption. Not, of course, the sort that people thought of in terms of the nearby Poor Farm. But something closer, and perhaps more fraught with risk and heartache.

She touched the locket hanging at her throat, seated herself at the table, and dipped the pen freshly into the ink. A woman might work for the Kingdom of Heaven in many ways.

From the kitchen behind her, the sound of the door and a gust of cold air suggested her uncle might have left again. But instead, a new voice called out. "Eliphalet Alexander, you old fox, you. I couldn't believe it when the innkeeper said I'd find you in this village, of all places. Mrs. Alexander, your servant, ma'am, Jonathan Stoddard at your service. Late of the Mexican War, and now of Seward's forces, yet a man of peace, and delighted to make your long-overdue acquaintance."

Almyra bolted toward the kitchen, then slowed to ensure a ladylike entrance. Seward's forces? Surely a jest. And yet, was the fight for Abolition flaming up, right here in North Upton, Vermont?

She met the gaze of the grizzled, sharp-eyed visitor directly, and dropped a half curtsey before crossing the room to him and offering a greeting. "Of Seward's forces?" She turned to her uncle, who seemed struck speechless for the moment. "Uncle, will you introduce your guest?"

Almyra's uncle clutched the hand of their newly arrived guest, his face a study in incredulity and delight. "Jonathan! What brings you to North Upton? No, don't speak to that as yet. Tell me how I shall say your rank to my wife and niece—Major Stoddard, is it?"

*Heavens*, Almyra thought, *this man occupies half the kitchen*. Not that he did in reality, but the atmosphere of him, his bold merriment and outflung arms in a greatcoat that steamed from the oven's heat. And laughing, slapping her uncle on the shoulder in a way entirely foreign to how anyone else greeted the town's treasured minister.

"Eliphalet, you force me to blush and confess to having achieved a colonel's rank by the end of hostilities, but plain Mister Stoddard is sufficient, I assure you." A hand gesture of dismissal didn't fool Almyra; the man clearly wore responsibility and action closer than his cloak.

Nor did her uncle accept the modest disclaimer. "Indeed, I should have guessed as much. My dear wife Charlotte Alexander, and my niece Almyra," said her beaming uncle, "may I present to you Colonel Jonathan Stoddard, whom I last witnessed at the age of seventeen, riding toward Boston on one of the finest horses of the county."

"Gad sakes, Eliphalet, that was no county horse, but a fine specimen from the stables in Randolph," the big man teased in return, as he disengaged his hand, swept off his coat, and made a gallant bow toward Almyra's aunt. "Mrs. Alexander, your humble servant, and honored to make the acquaintance of the gracious helpmeet of my oldest friend. And Miss Alexander, at your service," he concluded, tilting a nod toward Almyra with a kind smile, a bit gentler than the one he'd entered with.

He turned back to Almyra's uncle. "We've a great deal to exchange, to discover each other's route to this moment," he added. "And I fear we're hindering the preparation of an astonishingly good meal. Might we step aside and allow the ladies to continue their noble efforts?"

"You'll join us for supper, I trust, Colonel Stoddard," Almyra's aunt urged, blushing. "Eliphalet, there's ample for your friend, and more, should you wish to invite another one or two from the village."

Oh, how clever of her aunt to think ahead. Often a guest from "away" meant others should stop in and take part in conversation. Almyra dove to the oven to pull out her well-toasted sugared scraps as the men stepped toward the front parlor. She heard her uncle ask something in a low voice, then call back, "No others arriving this evening, my dear. Give us three-quarters of an hour and we'll rejoin you for the meal."

Without need for further decisions, Almyra began to set the table with the good silver, while her aunt drew out two relishes to spoon into serving dishes and set a compote of pears at a side table.

The familiar routine of preparation let Almyra think again of the words that Colonel Stoddard had used: "Seward's forces," he'd said. William Seward, the U.S. senator from New York, held a powerful position in supporting a route to abolish slavery in the nation's Territories, as well as in the South, where the Slave Power thrived so far unhindered. And this very village of North Upton knew something more because a Seward organizer, the young Solomon McBride, had conducted secret message services here, even conveying papers from a local mill owner so that fugitives headed north could have documents to keep them safe as they fled.

Without meaning to, Almyra thumped a dish overly loudly onto the table, and her aunt clucked a warning. "Sorry, Aunt," she said quickly. "My thoughts were elsewhere."

"With Alice Sanborn, I dare say," her aunt agreed. "But what's done is done, and I'm sure Colonel Stoddard has nothing to do with the McBride boy. Almyra, when the places are all laid, you may go repair your hair if you so choose."

Almyra nodded her thanks, both for the opportunity to "primp" a little for company supper, and for her aunt's ready understanding. Solomon McBride, who'd also claimed to be "Seward's man" and surely continued to labor for that cause, had badly misled Alice Sanborn, Almyra's first friend in this small village. And that was part of why

Alice had left to go West, with another young woman, Caroline, nearly two years ago now.

Almyra bit her lip, thinking, *What would Alice and Caroline ask this guest? What should she discover?* She bolted up the steep steps to her attic bedroom, to brush her curls and refasten them into a pair of ivory combs. The latest letter from her father, now close to the frontier himself in the surging new city of Chicago, sat on the dressing table awaiting a reply. Almyra scolded herself for sloth, and determined to start a letter back, by candlelight if need be, before she slept tonight.

What had happened to the quiet country life she'd witnessed in North Upton when she'd first arrived for a short stay with her aunt and uncle? Suddenly everyone seemed connected to the bustling frontier, as well as the fierce politics of Abolition.

Footsteps downstairs spun her into action again, and she navigated the stairs with care, to keep her skirts in place and her ankles modestly hidden. If only she had a stiffer crinoline. The ones she'd brought from Boston had long since gone limp and crushed, and in North Upton, all the girls made do with woolen petticoats instead, gathered and tucked. Best not to think of such vanities, however.

At her aunt's gesture, she stepped directly toward her chair, where her uncle waited courteously to assist her. The others already sat at the table, and her uncle led a moment of thanksgiving to the Lord before seating himself at the head of the table.

Almyra yearned to move the conversation directly to matters of moral and national interest, but politely waited for her aunt's questions on Colonel Stoddard's parents, wife, children, and indeed grandchildren, to all have suitable replies. The colonel in turn asked about her studies and lifted his brows appreciatively at her progress toward entering a seminary.

However, when she added that she hoped to become an ordained minister, he turned to Almyra's uncle instead, frowning. "Is that possible?"

Her uncle paused for longer than Almyra liked but gave a slow nod. "The Free Will Baptists ordained a woman year ago, though she didn't hold the pulpit long. Became married," he added succinctly. "The Universalists continue to talk about it, but it's still not a reality. At a guess, the Wesleyan Methodist denomination may reach the decision soonest. Although not in New England at first, but in the West where there is such need." He eyed Almyra. "There are easier paths," he suggested. "And some of them would not limit your effectiveness after you marry."

Almyra drew a long breath. She didn't wish to argue, especially with a guest at the table. She opted for conciliation. "Of course, Uncle. And I am fortunate to have your guidance." After all, her uncle encouraged her sermon drafts so she could hardly complain that he held her back from what she intended.

She recalled her plan to seek other information. "Colonel Stoddard," she began, "will you not tell us about your role for Senator Seward's labor? And how goes the movement toward abolition in the wider realm of varied states?"

Their guest looked enquiringly at Almyra's aunt. "Would that be a conversation for your table, ma'am?"

Aunt Ida nodded graciously. "Of course. At our table, Colonel, we must often take up the moral and Godly standing of the nation, as Almyra and I find much interest in supporting my husband's leadership in this area."

"In that case." The Colonel pressed his chair back a bit from the table. "First off, a bit of news that I shared already with Eliphalet before the meal. A number of us gathered in Ripon, Wisconsin, two weeks back and have proposed a new political party. We take the moniker of Republican for it and propose that it stand against the disastrous Nebraska Act, which as you may know was acted upon in the House on the twenty-first of last month. There is unfortunately every reason to expect its further passage and final form to take against us in the weeks ahead. So," he looked around the table, "we must step forward, to prevent further expansion of slavery and to reform the economic underpinnings of this great nation."

Almyra drew a deep breath. At last, an organization to raise the banner of moral correction. She struggled to find words fit for the occasion. Her uncle cheerfully forged ahead. "Such grace and power from our finest men," he praised. "May God bless your efforts,

Stoddard, and those of the men working with you. You'll stay until Sunday, of course, to speak with my congregation?"

"I wish I could," the colonel said. "But Seward has me on a ten-state tour, spreading word of the new party and seeding the possibilities." To Almyra and her aunt's puzzled looks, he added, "We need candidates for the next round of elections, and a plan to see them into office. Every vote matters and every voice for justice must speak."

A sermon began to unfold in Almyra's thoughts. "The rocks and stones themselves must speak," she pictured as its centerpiece. She checked to see whether her uncle also noticed the possibility. No, he didn't look toward her.

"Stoddard," he said instead, "you won't leave before the afternoon stage tomorrow, no doubt. Let me gather a few kindred souls, and perhaps my wife will provide some morning tea and gingerbread for them, to meet here and listen to you directly. It's lambing season, mind you, but I dare say I could draw half a dozen men."

"Done," the colonel agreed.

Almyra and her aunt exchanged glances: Gingerbread to be started this evening, then, as well as other preparations. And it should have been laundry day in the morning; clearly, that would have to wait. Moments later, the men departed for the tavern at the other end of the village. Almyra knew her uncle wouldn't stay there long and surely would not indulge in any intoxicating beverage, either. She recalled what he'd said earlier, about one of the Hall daughters. Living at the tavern, where Matthew Clark struggled to earn his living despite the anti-liquor laws? How could that be? And why wouldn't Almyra have seen this girl around the village, even walking to school or the store, if she lived here now?

"Hands to work, hearts to God," she reminded herself, and joined her aunt in preparing to wash the plates and cutlery, to clear space for starting the gingerbread.

"Almyra," her aunt pointed back toward the table, "did the colonel leave something beneath his chair?"

"Oh dear! It's a glove."

"See whether you can catch your uncle, just call from the doorway, dear one."

The rain hadn't ceased. Almyra leaned out into the chill darkness. "Uncle! Colonel Stoddard."

She saw them by the glow of the covered lantern her uncle carried, but they didn't hear her over the splashing raindrops. Irritated, she stamped her feet into a pair of boots by the door, flung a cloak over herself, and hastened down the muddy roadway, careful not to slip on the patches of remaining ice where the snowroller had packed it.

When she reached the men, she offered the glove quickly to her uncle, avoiding his friend's inquisitive look, bobbed her head, and turned for home at once. Her uncle raised the lantern high enough to shed some light for her return to the house. Just as she neared home, she caught a movement at the other side of the road and made speed to reach her own doorway. Skunk out prowling? An early raccoon?

In a flicker of light as her uncle and Colonel Stoddard resumed their direction, she realized the creature in motion was a person: a small girl, wrapped in layers of shawls, sliding away quickly and headed, like the men, toward the tavern.

Almyra paused to watch, but the rain closed off all sight of the child. One of the Hall daughters?

Pondering what might be expected of the Good Samaritan or any other neighbor, and what a woman ordained to the ministry might take as her duty, Almyra hung the damp cloak to dry.

"If you are wearing boots over your slippers, would you step to the cellar for cream before you take them off? We'll need to sour some overnight." Her aunt sounded harried.

"Yes, Aunt, of course."

The moment to speak about the child passed, and it wasn't until she'd shed her skirt, brushed it out and hung it to dry, and undone her petticoats that Almyra brought it back to mind. "The Lord is my Shepherd," she prayed, and hoped the little girl was dry and safe, and doing the same.

~ 3 ~

By morning the hard rain had ceased, though the continued chill and drizzle annoyed Almyra. Her aunt chattered cheerfully over the various fixings, with breakfast out of the way and the fixings for two pans of gingerbread laid out. Fresh-baked Sally Lunn sat to one side, along with the low wide bowl where bread dough continued to rise.

Aunt Alexander counted off the provisions again and exclaimed. "Almyra, we've only three eggs, and the doubled receipt calls for six. Speed to the Sanborns for an extra dozen, would you? Have them set to our account, and make sure Mr. Sanborn has heard about the gathering with the colonel. He wouldn't want to miss it."

Almyra donned her short jacket tucked at the waist and the woolen cloak, still damp from the night before. Egg basket on one arm, she hurried down North Upton's main throughfare, trying to step only where the ground was still frozen so as not to splash mud and manure on her garments. At half past seven, most neighbors were still tending to animals, though none kept as many as the Sanborns.

She didn't bother rapping at the house door, but tramped straight to the barn, where one door hung partway open and the mingled sounds of cattle, sheep, and a bold rooster reached her. So did the rich odor of a barn that hadn't been shoveled out since November. To protect her skirt hem, she paused and rolled her waistband one turn—enough to keep the skirt from dragging in the animal soil, but not enough to show the tops of her short boots.

"Mrs. Sanborn? It's Almyra, are you here?" She leaned into the dim recesses of the barn, unsure which way to walk.

In response to her voice, calls from the poultry rose louder, off to the left, and she stepped hesitantly toward a pen enclosed by lathing that reached the low ceiling. She called again, "Mrs. Sanborn?"

A small dark form ran toward her. Almyra squealed and dodged sideways, thinking it was a sheep or dog, then realizing from the motion that it must be a child. As it ran past her, she realized the child's legs, awkwardly propelled forward in flapping boots, were half bared by a skirt bunched up for speed. Only the wide basket for the eggs stopped her from trying to catch the small fleeing girl.

Mrs. Sanborn, Alice's mother, followed at a more sedate pace, a pail of cream dangling from one arm and the other extended to stop her. "Almyra, my dear, you mustn't come into the barn in that lovely skirt of yours. Come with me to the kitchen and we'll find what you need. I'm sure your aunt sent you for something for her baking — is it butter you want, or maple sugar?"

"Only a dozen eggs," Almyra replied, turning and following Mrs. Sanborn out into the much better light of the cloudy morning. "Would you have sufficient?"

"I can give you eight," came the calm response. "The girls are laying again, but not yet up to what they will be. Will that do?"

A few minutes later, after agreeing to come for another four eggs later, Almyra remembered the second part of her errand. "Ma'am, my aunt asked me to make sure Mr. Sanborn has heard there's to be a gathering with my uncle's old friend, Colonel Stoddard, at our home at half-past ten this morning. I hope your husband can join the others. I'm sure there will be much to discuss."

Mrs. Sanborn's sympathetic smile, so much like Alice's that it made Almyra miss her friend more than ever, confirmed that she understood how much and how long such discussion might be. She said only, "Indeed. He'll be in attendance. Let your aunt know I've set aside some extra woolen yarn this week, should she have need for more."

"Yes, ma'am." Almyra turned back at the doorway. "Was that one of the Hall daughters coming from the barn just before I saw you?"

"Oh!" Mrs. Sanborn pulled off a muffler and dusted her hands. "That child. She's nearly lived in the barn all winter. I'm sure she should be enrolled in school, but they say she's too young. Not that I believe it for a minute."

"Then she didn't just arrive in the village recently?"

"Heavens, no. She arrived with her mother at the new year. Mrs. Hall is cook and barmaid and such, for Matthew's tavern, now that he has such lively custom from the stage passengers and more."

Almyra inquired further. "Perhaps there's a second daughter, then? I did hear word of one who'd just arrived."

Hands on her hips, Alice's mother frowned. "That would be the third one. Susannah I believe. Her father sent her here last week. The eldest is Jane, of course. You will have seen her on Sundays with her mother. Then Susannah, who is fourteen and a bit more, I think. And the youngster, Polly, claims to be but five, though I'd guess she's closer to seven. At any rate, the Hall boys are all still on their farm on Fairbanks Mountain. Horses," she added briefly.

Almyra knew nearly nothing about horses, so she didn't ask more. Instead she confirmed: "So Mrs. Hall would be living at the inn with her three daughters then, is that correct? And the older two would be of school age?"

There was a pause that she didn't understand, and then Mrs. Sanborn said, "I can only manage one wild child at a time here, you know. We shall have to hope the inn remains a quiet place, without undue influence on the others." She flicked a long apron into place, knotting the ties. "Do give your aunt my greeting, Almyra. Do you need anything else?"

Accepting the clear dismissal, Almyra repeated her thanks and exited the warm kitchen, back into the cold drizzle and mist. It wouldn't harm the eggs in her basket. She walked briskly down the farm lane and eyed the joined structures of Matthew Clark's home and inn.

As she angled onto the village road, she caught a glimpse of a face at the inn window, a child's wide stare. She lifted a hand to wave, and the watcher vanished.

Almyra sped up, thinking of her aunt waiting for the eggs. She must ask: Had her uncle paid a pastoral call on the female portion of the Hall family? Or was it a task for her aunt? If so, she'd seek permission to go along. It wasn't only the wild child that interested her, but she didn't have time to think it through further.

There was no time for deep conversation when she reached home, with her aunt in a flurry, the table to be set, a hot afternoon dinner needing preparation at the back of the stove for later on, and the entrancing scent of butter melted and browned, ready for the gingerbread batter to be whipped together. Nonetheless, as she scrubbed and cut up carrots and potatoes, carefully setting aside any winter-spoilt portions, Almyra began to tell her aunt about the three Hall sisters and their mother at the inn.

"Dear merciful heaven, three daughters? With the men who drink there each night? Oh, I know," Mrs. Alexander added, "there's only cider that can be served now. But that's bad enough, and who's to say those menfolk don't add a bit of something stronger when they can? Not even in school, the little one?"

Almyra nodded as she began to peel an onion. It had long green stems out one end, a sign of spring.

"Aunt, how does one make a pastoral call on owners of a tavern?"

"During the morning, of course. Why do you ask?"

Adding the vegetables to the neckbones already in the kettle and checking that her aunt had already seasoned the stock, Almyra answered, "It does seem that someone should visit, to see that all's well there. And yet, would that be seen to approve the strong drink that may be provided? Or any other," she phrased it carefully, "any other evening activity that a tavern may offer?"

"Such as gambling? No, a morning call can't show approval of any of that. I'm sure Eliphalet has made a visit over the winter, of course."

"Of course," Almyra agreed. Yet in turn, she wondered whether the Halls, Mrs. Hall and her daughters, would have been included in her uncle's visit. She rather thought not. Perhaps she should invite the younger daughters to a church social or some such event. Ideas swirled, with her curiosity pressing them forward.

Just short of ten, as the gingerbreads emerged from the oven and a full iron kettle of water began to simmer, a knock at the door and a call of, "Letters, Mrs. Alexander," startled them both.

Almyra leapt toward the boy at the door, accepting two letters and a newspaper tied with string. She set them on the sideboard, then realized one of the envelopes bore her own name, franked by the judge who lived off in St. Johnsbury. It must be from Miss Farrow, the dark-skinned woman who lived and worked there, and who from time to time expected Almyra's assistance related to the cause of abolition.

Thoughts of this necessary labor shamed her for a moment. Here she was, her mind upon the small concerns of a country village, when she should be applying all her efforts to that noble cause in whatever way she could.

In this confused state, it took a moment for her to realize her uncle had just entered the house with two other men in tow, one of them Colonel Stoddard.

Her aunt bobbed a half bow from the waist, alerting Almyra to the importance of the unfamiliar third man, who also had a military erectness to his narrow shoulders.

"Captain Young," her aunt said. "We are so pleased to have you here. And Colonel Stoddard. Permit me to introduce my niece, Almyra Alexander."

Almyra extended a hand to the stranger, who gave a graceful half knee, such as she hadn't seen since she'd lived in Boston. She looked up into a gentle face with dark brown eyes that seemed to ask a dozen questions at once, in the kindest way.

But the only thing this new acquaintance said aloud was, "My very great pleasure. I understand you know my colleague in town, Dr. Jewett? Perhaps we can converse later."

Dr. Jewett. That was the leader in town of the anti-slavery group, the man that Miss Farrow trusted most securely. Almyra bit back any direct mention, saying instead in her best Boston manner, "I would be most pleased, sir, to hear from you later." She received a tray from her aunt, bearing a steaming pot of tea, and turned to carry it to the table.

Now she burned to open the letter from Miss Farrow. Was there a connection? Would she soon be working toward a meaningful change in the nation and its sinful enslavement of so many?

She forced herself to take a new breath and led the way to the table in the front room as her aunt began to slice into the fragrant cakes of fresh-baked gingerbread.

$$\sim 4 \sim$$

By the time they had all settled, eight men sat around the big table and two more in chairs to the side. Almyra wished she could see the faces of the two officers, but they faced away from her toward her uncle at the other end of the room. With her aunt's hand gentle but firm on her arm, she backed away into the kitchen.

"They will talk more freely if they are not looking at ladies," Aunt Charlotte murmured, drawing her further around the corner. "This is not a moment to stand up for rights, but rather to sit down and learn," she added. Her mischievous smile assured Almyra that permission to eavesdrop had been granted.

With mending on her lap, needle slow but steady, stitches small and careful, Almyra concentrated on listening over the soft bubbling of hot water in the big kettle and the intermittent crackling and settling within the cookstove's firebox. She wanted every detail of Colonel Stoddard's news of the new political party. Surely Mr. Seward, for whom the Colonel said he worked, would be one of its leaders. Yet that seemed not to be the case. She set aside her puzzlement for the moment to listen even more carefully. Yes, the Republican Party would honor Thomas Jefferson and his pure ideas. Most of all, though, it would oppose any expansion of chattel slavery into the new territories being opened and organized to the west: Kansas and Nebraska.

Aunt Charlotte's face glowed, though she was perhaps influenced by the heat of the stove. Almyra willed the word "abolition" to emerge in the conversation. Let it be so. But the Colonel spoke more about opposition to the Native American Party and its attacks on Catholics and other immigrants.

Almyra whispered, "The Irish?"

Her aunt nodded but lifted a finger to call for silence. Now the men were talking about a Jewish man, a Mr. Levin, a leader of the Native American Party and suspected of corruption. Almyra stared at her aunt, who gave a small shrug.

A new voice cut across. It must be Captain Young, the one who'd mentioned Dr. Jewett, the local leader for the abolition cause. He'd lowered his voice but spoke so clearly that Almyra had no difficulty following.

"We are all in hopes of drawing the Free Soilers, with former Whigs also empassioned about the shameful repeal of the Missouri Compromise, and of course, all those already opposed to chattel slavery. And Frémont may take the reins at some point. But we have a difficulty, gentlemen, on which we hope to enlist your assistance."

Several of the men were already agreeing to help on whatever it was, but Almyra noted that Mr. Sanborn's farm-gruff voice cut through. "Let's hear what it is, first."

There was a general thumping of chair legs as people rearranged themselves. Almyra's aunt winced, no doubt picturing some harm to her treasured floor rug.

If possible, Captain Young spoke in an even lower voice. Aunt Charlotte rose on tiptoe to quietly move the kettle off the heat of the stove, to hush its burble.

"Naturally, the party's treasury must be carefully nurtured, to support the effort and the candidates. But already, even in these infant days, we are seeing counterfeit currency among the donated funds, most particularly those sent to us from New England, especially Boston but also, yes, New Hampshire and Vermont." The man paused for a breath. Small sounds of dismay erupted from the room. Then he continued, "The party has paid an investigator, a Scotsman, Alan Pinkerton, and he's told us to look along the Canada border for the source of the bad funds. It seems there was a ring of counterfeiters, not far north of the border?"

Almyra's uncle quashed the question. "Foster Pierce, of course, but that was years ago. Surely he's too old for such idiocy now. He's a government leader in the Parliament up north, I've read."

The captain didn't hesitate. "Such movements have their inheritors. We'll be sending others north to see. Meanwhile, I understand you have a bank here in Upton at the county seat. Are any of you directors of the bank?"

Mr. Sanborn cut in, "It's Ephraim Paddock you'll want to talk with. He's both a director of the bank, and a lawyer, sometimes even a judge. In St. Johnsbury."

Almyra drew a sharp inward breath, lifting her hand to her mouth to quench the sound. Judge Paddock, Miss Farrow, Almyra's own mentor in the women's movement locally for abolition, had worked for the judge and still shared his home, with her own quarters. Almyra had never described in detail to her aunt the request Miss Farrow had made of her—to step forward in some of the political work herself, to the degree that she could.

Her aunt looked a query at her, and Almyra lifted a hand to wave the moment aside. This was not the time for explanations; she needed to hear the captain's reply.

"I'll go to see your Justice Paddock this very evening, if Colonel Stoddard can find me a horse," he declared. "Will one of you write me a letter of introduction? There's no time to lose in alerting every institution managing currency. A fresh wave of counterfeiting, aimed at a particular party could crush our labor before it's fairly begun."

Almyra made a gesture of apology to her aunt and tiptoed to the sideboard. She brought the letter from Miss Farrow back to her seat, lifting it a moment to show her aunt, then carefully unfolded the missive. Written on a half sheet of paper, to best suit its length, the brief message gave little detail: *"A—Corresp. rec'v'd here from yr friends in the West. Kindly reply with soonest date to arrive here for considerat'n. Y'rs most truly. R. Farrow."*

From the front room, several voices continued to cross with details of horses and arrangements. Aunt Charlotte held out a hand, and Almyra handed the scrap of paper across.

Her thoughts spun. Her "friends in the West" must be Alice and Caroline. She had no others who would correspond with her. Why would they not write directly to her, however? Was there something that must pass through Miss Farrow's hands first, something about ensuring someone's safety? Or—her pulse leapt with the connection— could it be also something involving Dr. Jewett and his network of informants? That could be what the captain had hinted at in his greeting to her. Oh, how ridiculous, to press possible pieces into patterns when she must be missing several.

Aunt Charlotte gestured urgently toward the front room. The men had formed a plan. Mr. Sanborn proposed to accompany Captain Young to town the next morning, though the Captain would ride the stage, and Mr. Sanborn would take one of his own horses. Another one or two from the village might accompany them.

Aunt Charlotte pointed to the kettle. She lifted one eyebrow meaningfully.

Almyra rose, straightened her skirts, and entered the men's gathering with a half-smile and a bob of her head. "May I freshen the teapot for you, Uncle?"

"Yes, yes of course. And send your aunt in here a moment, if you please, Almyra."

Captain Young rose from the table without explanation and followed her back to the kitchen, while Aunt Charlotte responded to the summons she'd clearly heard. Almyra refilled the teapot, set it to one side of the stove, and said very quietly, "I should fetch more sugar from the pantry, but it's on such a high shelf."

"I would be glad to assist," the captain murmured. He followed her around the corner into the cool side room, where the shelves were crammed with crocks of foodstuffs.

Almyra lifted a small paper sack from the shelf in front of her. "My mistake," she apologized. "Not such a high shelf, after all."

"The Gilmans," the captain interjected quickly, "do they travel often to Canada? Would you be aware? Do the women talk with each other?"

"Best to ask Miss Farrow that," Almyra said with surprise. "Word might not come out to this village. Or ask the stage driver, who'd likely hear more about where the horses are driven, as well as the north-bound stage itself."

"Damnation. Your pardon, miss. I should have asked Samuel before this. I hadn't thought of it." He paused, then added, "He's my brother's son. Does he always manage the stage? Do you know his next arrival?"

"Tomorrow morning, eastward, I believe. That's the stage you were all talking about riding."

"Then I'll sit on the upper bench with him, outside, and see what I can learn. Doctor Jewett said you're helping Miss Farrow."
It was a statement, not a question, but she nodded anyway.

"For the moment, remind her to watch any north-bound stage, and to keep note of who travels on them. Can you do this? It will be safer and quieter to keep the message among the ladies," he emphasized, then swiftly lifted a heavy copper basin and carried it out into the kitchen, a gesture of pretended assistance.

Almyra made sure her word of thanks rang clearly enough to be heard, as the captain returned to the front room and she lifted the fresh pot of tea, with a cloth to shield her hands from the heat of it.

Circling the table, and refreshing the men's cups, she heard only forecasts of more rain and concern about the mill race. Her aunt passed more gingerbread as the talk turned to horses.

If it hadn't been for the captain's strange message, Almyra wouldn't have noticed when Mr. Sanborn mentioned, "The livery up in Lyndon's lost two more horses to the Canada route. Word is, they were stolen for payment of obligations across the border, where a bank note no longer has value."

This mysterious phrase made no sense to her, but she repeated it to herself in order to report it later to Miss Farrow, with the message about riders going north. What did this have to do with the political movements of the moment? She wished it were all more clear. And when could she herself travel to St. Johnsbury?

When the men filed out, twenty minutes later, Uncle Eliphalet stood at the door a moment, watching, before turning to Almyra and saying briskly, "Your aunt says you were asking about my pastoral visit to Matthew Clark at the tavern. Why is that, niece?"

She took a quick breath to reorient her thinking. "I wondered, Uncle, whether your visit would have included the Hall women working there. And if not, might I have your permission to visit them to see that all is well?"

"Of course not," her uncle snapped. "Women at a tavern? Why should you concern yourself with such women?"

"There are children there," Almyra countered swiftly. "It's one way to draw them toward the church." She backed off from his irate and reddened face, but persisted. "Our Lord would have gone to them."

Uncle Eliphalet scrubbed his hands vigorously over his eyes. From behind them he muttered, in a quieter tone, "No doubt our Lord would even have dined with them. But you are not a prophet or savior, my dear." He looked straight into her face as he added, "Nor a minister of the Word. Not yet. This is why you must enroll in seminary, child."

"I'm not a child, Uncle." She didn't dare look sideways at her aunt. It would not do, to encourage any friction between man and wife. If her point was to hold, she'd have to make it on her own. "And there's no need for me to enter the tavern, I'm sure. I'll take a loaf of bread to the house entrance and look for a seat in the kitchen. It's the right thing to do. There are three children, Uncle." She couldn't help pleading just a bit.

"So I've heard," Uncle Eliphalet sighed. He shot a look to his wife, and whatever he saw, it made his shoulders settle. He crossed his arms, gave Almyra a long look, and said, "For one hour only. And directly home to give your aunt a full report. Better yet, take her with you."

"Oh, thank you. And …." But she could tell from his face there should be no "and." She'd have to ask about a trip to Miss Farrow at another time. "My thanks," she repeated. "I will go directly after our dinner."

At last she turned toward Aunt Charlotte, who rewarded her with a smile, and the two of them began to organize the afternoon meal together.

~ 5 ~

The eaves of the house dripped steadily along thickened icicles. Bold April sunshine heated her face. Almyra closed her eyes to enjoy it, and waited just outside the door, a little chilled but glad to escape the closeness of the house. She could already catch the thick scent of manure, which would strengthen as the village road thawed over the next few weeks. Boston's aroma would be likewise heavy on animal dung now, but with an overglaze of salt sea, and far more human waste than in this little village.

On mornings like this, Almyra admitted she much preferred country air to city. She wondered how her father managed, a widower in the close society of "the City on a Hill." Even his letters, when he traveled, did not reveal much of his actual circumstance, and the ones from Boston said only pleasant greetings with little substance. Like my own to him, she reminded herself.

Then she hushed her own thoughts to appreciate the sun's warmth further.

At last the scrape of the kitchen door spoke to her aunt stepping outside. The two of them examined each other critically, looking for untied laces, stray curls, or dragging gaps in any bit of skirt hem. Almyra reached out to smooth Aunt Charlotte's tatted lace collar just a bit and adjust the woolen shawl's folds.

"You see, my dear, a loving glance is far more helpful than a polished looking-glass," her aunt reminded her gently.

It was one of the few frictions between them: Almyra's beloved silver-backed hand mirror lay captive in her aunt's chest of clothing, to prevent the besetting sin of vanity.

Out of affection, Almyra said only, "Is my cap set straight, Aunt?"

An approving nod and smile warmed the day further. Almyra linked one arm in Aunt Charlotte's and raised a covered basket of baked goods with her other hand. "Forth, good Christians," she teased lightly.

By mutual agreement, they crossed to the sunnier side of the road. Matthew Clark's tavern anchored the other end of the village, so they might as well make the most of the weather and perhaps a bit less depth of mud.

They passed the rutted track to the Sanborn home, where last year Almyra had spent many happy hours, until her friends Alice Sanborn and Caroline Clark had headed West. A memory of appreciative looks from Alice's much older brothers, the prospectors Charles and John, heated her cheeks. At least if her aunt noticed, this moment of blushing would be blamed on the brisk outdoor air.

Ahead, almost before she was ready, hunched the linked structures of the Clark home, the tavern, and the rebuilt stables that served as livery for travelers and stage alike.

Letting go of her aunt's arm, she felt for her skirt and twitched it to lie more smoothly over her petticoats. She heard her aunt whisper, "Which door?"

"The house door," Almyra decided. "Uncle said we weren't to go to the tavern, and only Matthew is likely to be in the stables."

They picked their way across the ridges of half-thawed mud and reached the house door, then knocked and waited. A loud voice, high-pitched, called out, and Almyra guessed they were being told to enter. She clenched the latch and pressed forward, her aunt following half a step behind. Awkward with the basket on her arm, she scraped the mud from her soles at the doorframe as best she could.

"Mrs. Hall?" Her words seemed caught among the overloaded pegs of outer garments crowding around her, but the scent and clatter of the cookstove and another unintelligible voice made it plain where the women of the house must be. She opted to hold her own shawl in place and edged forward.

A girl in her teens, in an oversized and smudged apron, met them at the entry into the large kitchen. "Oh! We were expecting the stage, but not yet. You're not travelers, are you?"

Almyra shook her head. "We live at the other end of the village. We've brought some gingerbread from our own baking and wondered whether we might be able to sit with you and your mother for a few minutes, to get acquainted."

The girl looked both excited and dubious. "We're making haste, you see, as the stage passengers arrive famished most days. My mother's in the tavern, setting a hot posset on the hearth. I'll ask."

She pressed past them in the crowded hallway and through the next door of the passage to the tavern. Almyra could hear her already calling out as the door swung closed.

Her aunt nudged her and nodded toward the kitchen. "Best to go forward," she noted.

So the two of them stepped beyond the passageway, into what had been, when Matthew's mother lived there, a fresh and welcoming kitchen space with a small sitting room just beyond. But at the moment, it appeared shockingly unprepared for any sort of guest at all.

A kettle of stew bubbled too vigorously on the cookstove, spattering and hissing onto the hot iron around it and adding scorched gravy to the room's stale aromas. To one side, a pan of biscuit perched precariously, too close to the fire. Without thinking, Almyra set her basket down, wrapped a hand in a layer of her shawl, and reached out to adjust both pans and prevent further damage.

From under the table, hidden by the legs of the benches, a child scrabbled toward her. "Mam says never to touch the stove when she's not in the kitchen," a rough little voice proclaimed, ending with a rattling cough.

Aunt Charlotte, about to settle herself on a stiff wooden chair, gave a startled gasp. Almyra bent low to look into the grubby face. "And your mother is quite right, and you are a good child for obeying her," she praised. Girl child? Boy? The short hair and flattened skirt gave little clue, but a doll clutched tight suggested a girl. Almyra continued, "But I am much older than you, and I know how to cook safely. Most children call me Myra, you know. What's your name?"

The child ducked its face into the doll and did not reply. Aunt Charlotte, with an air of playing an infant game, teased, "I think his name is Isaac."

That was all it took. The little one scrambled out. "I am not a boy. My hair is growing out from the fever. And my name is Polly." Another coughing fit followed.

Almyra looked around her. Clearly a spoonful of honey was called for, and chamomile tea.

But before she could begin such ministrations, footsteps from the passageway made her pull back and stand beside her aunt, a careful smile in place, ready to apologize for visiting on impulse and to make polite conversation.

Instead, with the barest of small inclinations forward—not quite a bow, nor even a curtsy—a short, stout woman in a faded linsey-woolsey dress, rather dated in cut, said at once, "Jane says you brought gingerbread. Is there enough to fill a serving plate?"

"Yes, I believe so," Almyra responded. "Shall I set it onto one and cut it into slices?"

"Yes please, if you'd be so kind. Polly tipped her cup of milk onto mine, and," the bustling woman said with a quick smile, "though it will do nicely for her supper later, it's not fit for travelers from the stage. Dear merciful heaven, the biscuit. Oh, thank goodness, someone's set it to the side."

Almyra didn't see a need to say that she'd meddled, but set to work instead, as her aunt gathered her own draped shawl and Almyra's to hang over the chair. "What shall I do?" Aunt Charlotte asked, as if this were a perfectly normal way to visit.

"Slice the graham bread, if you please, onto another plate. And Jane, fetch the butter from the cellar."

That set of cellar steps, to Almyra, would always be frightening, since she knew Alice Sanborn's friend Jerusha had died from a fall on them. But she hushed her reflection and focused on neat slices of the gingerbread while listening.

"I take it the stage is running early," Aunt Charlotte commented.

"Yes, indeed, one of the lads just rode through and let Matthew know. Mercy, I've no manners to speak of today, but you're the minister's wife, I'm sure of that, and of course I'm Missus Hall from over near East Village. You'll know my nephew, Sam Young, the stage driver, I'm sure."

"A very fine young man," said Almyra's aunt, her sleeves already rolled, a loaf of graham bread in her hands. "And is Matthew also a nephew of yours?"

"Heavens, no. It was Sam who told us he needed help with the tavern, though, and Jane and Susannah came over with me at midwinter. Polly stayed with my mother, of course, but the fever's been at the farm, and I thought it best she come here for the spring. Polly, come out from under there, this minute. Lord save us, the child's a ragamuffin today. Here, take my handkerchief." An exclamation followed as Mrs. Hall dove toward her bubbling kettle of stew and circled a wooden spoon through it.

Almyra wondered where Susannah was—clearly not in the kitchen at the moment. She had no chance to ask, however, as Mrs. Hall gathered all of them and the prepared foodstuffs, set a stack of wooden bowls into the hands of the girl who must be Jane, and shooed them into the passage to the tavern.

So much for Uncle's requirement that they stay out of the tavern itself, Almyra thought. She caught her aunt's eye and a small shrug of "what else can we do?" The curious parade of Hall women and callers pressed forward.

The tavern itself surprised Almyra. As a location where men drank spirits in the evening, banned or not, she'd expected it to be shabby, even soiled. Instead it had the freshness of a wide parlor, with a long trestle table and benches. She supposed the corner counter might provide illicit beverages at night, but there was no sign of any just now.

The wide front door swung open as three men pressed into the room. One of them was Captain Young, another Mr. Sanborn, and the third, why of course, it was Matthew. How his shoulders had broadened over the winter. He tossed her a merry smile while inviting the other men to take part in the foodstuffs. "The stage will pause here for a good twenty minutes, for the travelers to do the same," he reminded them. He snatched a chunk of gingerbread for himself and turned back toward the doorway. "I've a horse to prepare, so you'll pardon me."

A youth met him at the doorway. "It's done, Matthew. I've got the bridle on him, and he's hitched and ready."

Almyra stared. The voice said right away that the speaker was a girl, though the short hair and Irish cap denied it, and that garment reaching nearly to the ground must be a Turkish dress. She'd never seen one off the pages of a ladies' journal before. Pantaloons. Were these the fashion now in Boston, perhaps? Had she fallen behind the styles?

"Susannah, my dear, come say good morning to the minister's wife and," Mrs. Hall hesitated, gesturing to Almyra.

"His niece, ma'am, Almyra Alexander. I'm pleased to meet you all."

Mrs. Hall beamed. "You see, Susannah, there are others your age in this village, you just need to make time away from the stables to meet them. Oh, don't mind her pantaloons, Mrs. Alexander, please. She's taken to assisting Matthew in the mornings, and she'll be back in her petticoats in a few hours."

Susannah did not appear pleased at that notion, Almyra saw. She stepped forward, a hand extended. To curtsey would emphasize the other girl's lack of proper skirts. "I'm so sorry we haven't met before."

The thumps and jingling of the stage arriving interrupted all conversation, and Captain Young and the other men rose from their recently filled bowls, to greet the handful of people stepping noisily into the tavern. Almyra found herself dishing up stew, while her aunt passed platters among all the men now crowding the table. Only men, with all the women serving. For an instant she wondered how she might use this, too, in a sermon.

Behind her, Mrs. Hall exclaimed, "Saints alive, where's Polly got to? Susannah, go make sure she hasn't slipped into the stage or the stable. That child will be the death of me."

Almyra took up a dish of butter and worked her way over to Captain Young. Leaning close, she offered the thick golden spread, and whispered, "Would you tell Miss Farrow for me, I'll be there before a week has passed?"

Sharp eyes met hers, and the man nodded. Whatever he knew about Miss Farrow's network kept him from asking further. He made a show of accepting the butter and passing it along, then reminded her, "Should you hear of anyone going north, get word to me right away. Doctor Jewett can reach me, or your Miss Farrow. Don't put anything on paper to me directly, though, do you hear?"

Almyra nodded in turn and lifted an empty dish, saying only, "Of course, I'll be glad to fetch more bread."

Sam Young, the driver, who hadn't taken time to sit down, poked his head outside, a wedge of buttered bread in one hand. He turned back to the guests and said, "Two minutes more, gentlemen. Time's a-wasting."

Hastily stuffed last mouthfuls, fistfuls of handkerchief-wrapped morsels, and a clatter of some pennies into a bowl held by Mrs. Hall raised the hoorah of noise further, and the Hall daughter in pantaloons accompanied the surge of men out the door, passing along almost-forgotten cloaks and staffs. The sudden silence, broken only by the hiss of the fire to one side of the room, made Almyra shake her head in amazement.

"And there's our Polly," Mrs. Hall proclaimed, drawing the young child from under yet another table. "To the kitchen with you, imp. Ladies, if you'd be so kind as to help me carry back all these servers and such, I'm sure there's some tea we can indulge in, before washing up and starting all over again."

Her aunt's cheerful countenance guided Almyra's acceptance of this very unusual way to treat morning callers, and she began to stack plates.

Mrs. Hall stirred her fingers through the dish of pennies, and exclaimed in annoyance, "Here's another of those leaden items. I declare, those men should all know better. Well, Matthew will have to see what he can do. Dear merciful heavens." She set the dish behind the corner bar and ,with a clearly reluctant Jane assisting, joined Almyra and Aunt Charlotte in seizing the gravy-slick bowls and small remainders of food.

Back in the kitchen, Almyra took a longer look around. More had changed than just the general level of tidiness she'd known here when Matthew's mother held pride of place. A multitude of bundled herbs hung from every beam, and the sharp scent of fermented spirits lingered, too.

Surely the Hall women, so quick to mention the Deity, could not be fermenting spirits of their own? A row of corked bottles along a wooden shelf made her even more suspicious, but she had no way to ask her aunt without revealing an unseemly curiosity.

Instead, she listened more closely to what the older women were saying.

~ 6 ~

Ever practical, Aunt Charlotte first asked Mrs. Hall whether the tavern business expected more guests in this day, and what was needed for them. "Will the men in tavern at the noon hour also be wanting a meal?"

"Not them," the round-faced woman snorted, as she poured hot water from the kettle into a pail in the wooden dry sink at the far end of the kitchen. "Mind you, it would do Old Mo some good to eat solid food, instead of his," she hesitated, clearly trimming her words, "his mugs of cider. He's nothing but a stinking skeleton with an endless thirst."

Almyra choked back a laugh. That description of Old Mo, who trudged daily between North Upton and Upton Center, cut close enough to the truth. She'd once asked her uncle whether he might encourage Old Mo to come to church, and Uncle Eliphalet in shock had told her, "There'd be no congregants willing to stay in the room with him. For the sake of dozens of other souls, never invite Moses to partake in my church."

When she'd pursued the topic with her uncle another time, wondering whether God's commandments meant they should try to teach the old reprobate some of the Holy Book, her uncle spoke plainly: "When a man has washed away both his mind and his heart with hard liquor, there's little point grappling for his soul. Say a prayer for him, niece, and leave him alone." She'd been happy to oblige.

Now she marveled at Aunt Charlotte's relaxed conversation with a woman who worked in a tavern. Wasn't this like Our Lord talking with Mary Magdalene? No, shame on that thought. Her aunt was no holy personage, not even a minister herself, and Mrs. Hall, despite the location of her labors, surely did not appear to be what Almyra envisioned as a woman of low habits. Nor were the daughters immoral in appearance. Unless, of course, you found pantaloons shocking, which no doubt her uncle would.

Mrs. Hall's explanations of her obligations included feeding a full meal to the stable crew at noon, and providing an early supper to all, so that Matthew could focus on meeting the trade in the evening.

"Most days, that allows time for Jane to go gathering herbs in the afternoon, though I'm always a-scramble for time to bottle the infusions, of course. You must take some of my newest formulation with you, to sample its effects." In a lower voice she added, "I have something for female complaints as well, if that's called for."

Polly, hiding under the table again, began to cough in paroxysm, and Almyra set down the bowls she'd been wiping in order to crouch at floor level, careful of her own skirts. "Come out," she coaxed, "and sit at the table. Your mama is sure to have something for that cough."

Mrs. Hall nodded. "Jane, give Polly a spoonful of honey, and see if she'll drink more chamomile tea. I'll be putting her back to bed if she keeps coughing so."

This appeared to be a threat. The child scrambled out and up, scowling, and extended her tongue for a dose of honey on the spoon already in Jane's fist.

Almyra stepped closer to the shelves of stoppered bottles. Some had labels pasted to them; some had lengths of string instead, tied to the necks of both clear and brown bottles of various heights. She asked, "How can you tell what is in each one?"

Jane yielded control of the honeyed spoon to Polly, who sucked noisily on it. The older girl, at a guess a year or so older than Almyra, stepped close to her and pointed. "By the number of times the string wraps around," she explained. "There's no sense wasting labels if they're not needed. Mother and I know which is which. Look, this one's in a brown bottle with five loops of string, so it's calomel. A purge," she added. "More loops of string, more caution. You mustn't dose with too much, and you mustn't lick your fingers after handling it, either."

Quickly pulling her hands back and tucking them under her arms, Almyra pressed, "Are many of these dangerous, then?"

"You'll be calling your own garden dangerous," Jane smiled. "There's more that can hurt you in the petals and leaves around you. Look, the boxes over here are from the plants we've dried."

Each bore a label, though the handwriting bore small evidence of grace, Almyra thought. Whoever penned the words could spell, after a fashion, but must not have much schooling. Elegance of the pen came with practice. Some of these were even marked with chalk or a pencil lead.

She said slowly, watching Jane's expressive face, "Many women in Scripture were healers, you know. Even midwives, like Puah and Shiphrah."

Those bright brown eyes crinkled with mirth. "Every woman's a healer if she chooses," Jane replied. "Mother's taught us that, but I'm the only one of her daughters to embrace the art of it. Well, you've seen Susannah." Scorn curled the otherwise charming lips.

"We each have our own path," Almyra corrected gently. "You've chosen a fine one. Will you dose little Polly today with one of these?"

Laughter in return brought a hot blush to Almyra. She'd clearly said something foolish.

Mrs. Hall called across from the dry sink, "Jane's learned well that there's no cause for strong medicine if ordinary care will do. Mind the kettle, Jane, it's close enough to boiling to make your sister's tea. Now Polly," catching the child by the arm, "if you wish to stay out of your bedchamber, you'll drink your tea right off."

Inspiration struck Almyra. "I could tell you a Bible story while you sip your tea," she coaxed. "Is there one you especially like?"

A sharp cough preceded a damp smile. "Noah and the animals," the child replied.

Feeling the slight breathlessness that she associated with having found the Lord's path in a situation, Almyra settled on the opposing bench at the table, and began, "Noah was a righteous man who walked with God. He had three sons, Shem, Ham, and Japheth."

"What were the names of his little girls?" the child asked.

"Oh," Almyra said, "Noah had no little girls. But he had a special task to do that the Lord God himself provided. And I think you know what that special task was, don't you?"

A slight nod of approval from her aunt assured Almyra that she'd chosen well for the moment, and at least this way she felt her visit qualified as a pastoral one. But this example need not confine her to

Sunday School teaching. Well, she would fight that battle later if need be. For now, she encouraged the child to make sounds of the animals as she named them. Jane too seemed drawn by the story, and Almyra felt a hint of power in the moment. This, this was how a minister might gain the loyalty of one's own flock, even through the little children. "Suffer little children to come unto Me," a whisper echoed within her.

Across the room, the older women continued to wipe the dishes and converse in lower voices. About raising children? About the tavern? About Temperance, and its sister demand, abolition? Almyra ached to know. However, with determination, she narrowed her focus to her own two listeners, pacing the tale's twists and discoveries, until the very rainbow itself and the great covenant. "Whenever the rainbow appears in the clouds," she finally narrated, "God will see it and remember, and will care for all the living creatures of every kind on the earth."

Like a finale, the connecting door from the house to the tavern banged open and Almyra knew it must be Susannah calling out, "Matthew says he'll be late for dinner, Ma." The door scraped as it closed again, and Almyra saw her aunt nod toward their shawls.

"We'll be off, then," Aunt Charlotte told Mrs. Hall. "I'm sure you're wanting to get on with your cooking, and I've a husband at the other end of the village who'll think he's ill-treated if I'm not ready with his own at noon."

"That's how men are, always ready to watch the clock." Mrs. Hall chuckled. "Though I think they watch with their bellies more often than their eyes. It's been a pleasure to get acquainted, and I'll have that list for you by evening. Susannah can bring it to you, I'm sure."

With a round of small bows, they said farewell, and Almyra followed her aunt away from the low-slung buildings, her thoughts still caught up in the unexpected usefulness of a Bible story. They linked arms again, though the mud was no worse than earlier.

Halfway home, her aunt tugged at Almyra's elbow. "A penny for your thoughts," she teased. "You're never this silent, my dear."

"Oh, I'm sorry, Aunt. A penny—not a leaded one, as Mrs. Hall found in her bowl this morning, I trust!"

More seriously, Aunt Charlotte said, "I expected you'd ask me about the list she's sending."

"Indeed, I'm so sorry for thinking on other routes. What list is that, indeed?"

"A list of simples she needs from town." Aunt Charlotte nudged sideways, then caught Almyra from slipping. "Let us watch our footing, in every sense. Mrs. Hall needs a few things, some items Doctor Jewett is holding for her. And I assured her you'd be only too happy to collect them. When you and I ride to town tomorrow."

This final phrase penetrated Almyra's distraction at last. "To town, tomorrow? You and I, Aunt?"

At the beaming smile and nod that confirmed the statement, all her urgencies and inquiries melded as one. "Doctor Jewett? Tomorrow? And I shall see Miss Farrow, shall I not?"

Her aunt corrected her gently. "You and I together shall pay a call on Miss Farrow, indeed. We have so much to accomplish. I suggest, my dear, that you spend some time this afternoon composing a list of your own, lest we miss some critical item, and I shall do the same."

The correspondence Miss Farrow held, which must be from Caroline and Alice. Tomorrow she'd know what that was all about. In her haste to get home and begin her list, Almyra almost toppled the two of them into a slippery mound of steaming sheep manure at the side of the road. "Oh, spring at last," she exulted.

How had she ever thought that life in this little village would stifle her, or remove her from her goals? At this moment, everything seemed possible.

$$\sim 7 \sim$$

Far more snow had melted in St. Johnsbury, with its bustle of commerce and schooling, and of course, the town stood at less of a height than North Upton. In addition to the earthy aromas of melting and spring, Almyra witnessed attractive displays of summer bonnets and gowns in shop windows.

Mr. Sanborn had brought them to town with his buggy and horse, assisting them to climb down from the high step of the conveyance. Then he'd left them at the head of the main street by the elegant buildings of the Academy and driven himself toward the river-side portion of town where men's businesses and supplies clustered.

Walking arm in arm, Almyra and her aunt strolled along the walkway to Dr. Jewett's house. The boards across the muddy ground were of great assistance in protecting their shoes and hems. A bell in the door let them announce their arrival, and a woman in wide bombazine skirts greeted them.

Aunt Charlotte offered a slight bow, and Almyra followed suit. A brief introduction confirmed that Mrs. Briggs, the housekeeper, knew Aunt Charlotte's sister Cicely. "And the doctor said you'd be calling today. He has your packets himself, as I believe he wishes to instruct you on the uses of some of the items," Mrs. Briggs continued, as she escorted them to the parlor that opened into the medical office. "Please do convey my regards to your dear husband," she concluded with a vague smile, before bustling away.

Dr. Jewett had already risen to greet them. For once, no other guests sat with him; it appeared he'd been writing notes in a large bound book, and he wiped his pen and set it to the side.

"My goodness," he said with twinkling eyes, "am I to understand you're collecting supplies for North Upton's own dispensary under Mrs. Hall's creative care? How kind of you, my dear." He made as if to kiss Aunt Charlotte's glove hand.

She laughed and batted the gesture aside. "You know quite well I'm actually in the service of my niece in her efforts to promote justice." Everyone became more solemn, for ever since the printing of Mrs. Stowe's "Uncle Tom's Cabin," the horrors of the South's "peculiar institution" of enslavement seemed a constant presence. Almyra felt a familiar wave of guilt, that she herself could not take more effective action toward abolition. Youth and New England distance worked against her aims. Still, she had pledged herself to the effort, to work with Miss Farrow, Dr. Jewett, and others around them, while Caroline and Alice had gone West to do their part.

She took her turn to speak. "Sir, we are calling on Miss Farrow today. Are there messages we can convey for you, or other ways we can be of assistance?"

The doctor combed his fingers through his beard, gazing thoughtfully at her. "I wonder, Miss Alexander, whether your travels might take you to Peacham in the near future. Miss Martha Johnson is very much in need of more local connections, so to speak. You have perhaps heard something of her father Leonard and her uncle Oliver."

Almyra shivered at the names of Peacham's most outspoken abolitionists. She gave an eager nod. "I might visit to seek knowledge of the Peacham Academy," she proposed. "I'm sure that can be helpful in my studies for the ministry. I will write to Miss Johnson and ask for a night's lodging." At her side, her aunt nodded agreement.

Dr. Jewett beamed. "Nicely planned, and quickly. Would that all my patients could seize upon the moment the way you do. Now then, here are the packets for Mrs. Hall. I've written directions for her, so there's no need for me to explain to you, but should anyone ask, of course that's what we have just discussed. The dangers of calomel, for example." He raised an eyebrow.

"Indeed," Almyra agreed. "Miss Jane Hall mentioned something of the sort to me yesterday."

"Good, good. As we say often in my dispensary, never lick your fingers."

Minutes later, her satchel now considerably heavier, Almyra assisted her aunt down the steps and board walkway, and north along the main street. She could see better through the shop windows from here and wrestled to repress her own covetous desire for the newest modes of skirts and trims.

Aunt Charlotte understood. "Let us stretch our pennies, Almyra. We need not purchase trims here. If we write to my sister in Boston, she can procure for us a few that are even more the mode, and send the packet by post, I'm sure. Study what you like, and we will employ our needles and update two or three of your best items."

That sufficed to turn their stroll into a merry one, laden with observations and notions, until they walked past the last in the row of the shops and entered the park-side area where the home of Judge Paddock and his housekeeper Miss Farrow towered over the brown edges of a formal garden not yet greened up.

An ostentatious four-wheeled brougham with matching bay horses passed them as they turned toward the inspiring brick mansion with its many draped windows. The driver's dark skin showed between his cap and the muffler wound around his neck. The sight reminded Almyra that most of the Africans in this region seemed to work with livery stables, something to ask Miss Farrow about.

She paused for a moment and confirmed the brougham took the northward turn. To her aunt's questioning look, she said only, "Someone asked me to take note of travel northward." But this was not a stage. Should she inquire about it?

They followed an ornate brick path, a bit slick with patches of ice, to the rear of the mansion, and Miss Farrow welcomed them into the immense kitchen with its beehive oven, multiple pantries, and the unmistakable aroma of a dried-apple pie freshly baked.

"Captain Young assured me he'd delivered my message," Miss Farrow explained. Almyra noted that Miss Farrow's dress, a deep rose wool, draped beautifully and admirably suited the warm dark tones of her face and hands. "And I was sure no pie would go to waste, whether you arrived today or later in the week. Come, I know you wish to read this letter at once, Almyra, and your aunt and I will enjoy our tea in the meantime."

It was indeed a letter addressed to both Miss Farrow and Almyra, from Alice and Caroline—Almyra recognized the two forms of cursive crossing and re-crossing the page. What she must discover at once, however, was the reason for its arrival here, rather than via North Upton.

She skimmed across the affectionate greetings and small news about frontier life, which she could read again at her leisure. The back of the first sheet reached the meat of the message:

"Mr. Thayer stopped here last night as he investigates a route to send settlers from New England in this direction. He reports the Mass'ts Emigrant Aid Society to be chartered in late April. And, captures of Freemen escalate under the terrible Fugitive laws. M's Farrow we beg you at once to send word of both, to Sarah and her brother, but also to the family in Coventry and all else who may be in peril."

Almyra seized on the threat to their friend Sarah, whose family remained enslaved—only her brother so far had joined her in liberty, and both resided outside Quechee where so many livery stables furnished welcome and employment to freed blacks whose skills embraced horses and their management. She stammered, "Have you, will you, how can we …?"

Miss Farrow patted her hand. "Done, child. There are many benefits to life in a railroad town. My part of this is accomplished, and you may take the letter with you now. Don't fear for Sarah. She is secure and happy. She writes when she can."

With a tender smile, Miss Farrow slid a short stack of pages across to Almyra to read what Sarah had written in recent weeks. The distraction kept her out of the women's conversation, although she managed to consume two broad wedges of pie as well as some hard cheese while reading. Ah, it was good to know that Sarah shared her daily discoveries and pleasures with their mentor here.

Suddenly, she realized Aunt Charlotte was gathering her things and preparing to depart. Time to meet Mr. Sanborn already? The hall clock, visible through the doorway, showed half past two. Goodness.

Almyra suddenly remembered her other mission. "Miss Farrow, about Captain Young—do you know him well?"

"Not particularly, but his courtesy with messages has been much valued," Miss Farrow responded.

"He asked me to give you another message: to ask you to watch for northward travel, and to let him know what you observe," Almyra said.

"Did he say why?"

"Not in any detail." Had the captain said more? "Oh, I have been remiss, Miss Farrow. I'm quite sure he especially wanted to know about any of the Gilman family proceeding north." The Gilmans, as St. Johnsbury's most wealthy family, gave generously to all civic causes, including resettlement of freed Africans into African nations.

This evidently startled Miss Farrow, but she only said, "I will inquire, and then write to you, and perhaps leave a note with Doctor Jewett also, depending on what evidence there is."

In haste, the visit concluded, with the letter from the westward wilds of Illinois tucked into Almyra's reticule for later enjoyment. However, it was not until she and her aunt were seated again in Mr. Sanborn's buggy that she realized she should have mentioned her planned Peacham trip to Miss Farrow.

Well, she would write it in a letter when she reached home. There could not be much loss in a day or two of delay in communicating about this. Almyra braced her increasingly shaken frame against the backboard of her seat, then leaned forward to kiss her aunt's soft cheek in thanks for this excursion, and more.

$$\sim 8 \sim$$

A sudden warming, a scattering of garden blooms, and an announcement of the district schools about to open for the season, all these pressed forward in  bright spring urgency. Almyra, however, tied to the seasons of the church, could not advance forward in her plan to visit the Johnson family in Peacham.

When she and her aunt arrived back in North Upton village after their hours in town, they'd found the house cold and empty. The almost expected death of Mr. Worden, a retired merchant who'd suffered a terrible carcinoma for the past three years, called for immediate action. There were family members to comfort, others to house as they arrived for a funeral service at the home and food to prepare. Of course, whenever Uncle Eliphalet reached home, he barricaded himself in his study preparing his texts for the other services ahead: Good Friday afternoon, Easter morning, and an evening service for Easter Sunday as well.

Almyra struggled to at least make notes of her own for appropriate sermons, but her uncle had no time to discuss anything with her, beyond the surface conversation of each day's mealtimes. He did delegate one piece of writing to her, but she could hardly value such a task, authoring a single paragraph commending the charity collection made by the Sabbath school during Lent.

At last, the Monday following Easter allowed the three of them to linger over the breakfast table.

"Uncle," Almyra began tentatively, "I would like to travel to Peacham later in the week."

Uncle Eliphalet rubbed his forehead. "I doubt that I'll have the time to take you to the academy this week, my dear. Can you not gain whatever you need by letter? I'm sure the grammar school is opening, as are all the others."

"I have done so, sir, for the most part. But I should like to see the village and the school premises, should they be open."

"Yes, well, hmm." He turned to Aunt Charlotte. "What about the two of you traveling together? Is there a family where you might stay overnight? One of your cousins perhaps?"

At nearly twenty miles, the drive in one direction would be enough for a day, and still allow time for her business. If only Martha Johnson were one of her aunt's cousins. Almyra meant to remain dignified but allowed her eyes to beseech her aunt.

Clearly, Aunt Charlotte had already thought this through further. "I've written to an old friend there, Miss Cranston, who is a milliner. She will make Almyra welcome, and I have some items to send to her, and she in turn has some fabric for me. However," her aunt turned to Almyra, "between the ladies' circle and the spring tasks here in the house, this is not the best week for me to travel."

Almyra fought to repress her own disappointment. "Of course, Aunt. And you must tell me what tasks here you wish my assistance with. I'm sure my visit to Peacham can wait." Though she felt she'd promised Dr. Jewett to go there soon.

Aunt Charlotte cut in crisply, "But I require my fabric almost at once, so you must travel with a hired conveyance, I think. Best make haste to clear the table and walk to the Clark place before any stage pulls in so you can ask about their livery service and a buggy to take you there and back. Careful with that platter, my dear."

A few minutes later, spirits marvelously lifted, Almyra walked briskly along the nearly dry side of the road. She had never arranged for hire of a buggy before. She wondered what it would cost, and who would drive her. Matthew? Surely he needed to stay at his tavern. Then who?

Across the road the windows of Mr. Wilson's store gleamed, freshly washed, though the light bouncing from the glass prevented her from seeing through it. Usually, only a few men lingered through the morning hours, but Almyra kept her gaze forward, anyway. Only in the ladies' circle could one betray curiosity, or, of course, if one were actually a minister of the Gospel. Thinking of this amazing possibility passed the time, and she found herself at the other end of the village quickly.

Mrs. Hall stopped her vigorous sweeping as Almyra came closer. The door into the house stood open behind her. None of the girls were in sight.

"Are you looking for my Jane, Miss Alexander? Or has your mother sent you with a message for me?"

"Neither one." Almyra blushed. "I'm to see about hiring a buggy and horse for tomorrow to go off to Peacham in the morning, then back again the next day."

"A buggy, is it? And do you know how to drive horses, may I ask?"

"No, ma'am." Almyra felt more heat in her face. "I'm to ask about a driver, also. I'm afraid that's not one of my skills."

With hands on hips, Mrs. Hall considered Almyra a long moment, then said, "Come around to the livery stable with me. Mind your footing. The pathway's still deep in mud, so walk along the edge."

As they circled around toward the horse stables, a flash of movement caught Almyra's eye. It was the young child, Polly, peering from an upper door to the hay mow and then ducking out of sight. There was no need to tattle on the little girl. Surely her mother must know where the child played. Straw in the girl's hair come evening must reveal her adventures.

Instead, Almyra hid her own smile and watched her footing. The ground sucked at her shoes, wet and thick with standing water and mud well mixed with thawing manure.

She followed her guide into the shadows of the stable and caught a whiff of animal urine that bit at the back of her nose and throat. A handkerchief to her face for a moment let her recover. In the shadows, there seemed several people moving around.

Her eyes adjusted and she saw both Matthew and the middle daughter, Susannah grooming horses. Each animal stood with a tether of some sort from the leather bands around its face. Seen like this, standing on the ground near them, instead of riding in a carriage, they seemed enormous and unpredictable. Almyra drew back toward the doorway.

The conversation was quick, abrupt, and in short phrases. It seemed to involve some disagreement. Finally Mrs. Hall turned and walked toward her.

"If you can wait til the Friday southbound stage, you can ride with Sammy's brother Alonzo, who's making the trip. Peacham's not on any of the regular stage routes, but Matthew says he believe Alonzo is carrying the post there. And return the next Tuesday. That's the best we can do for you. Perhaps you'd like to discuss it with your aunt? The price is fifty cents each way."

Almyra couldn't help wincing. The cost seemed very high for what was in some ways an indulgence. And she did not wish at all to wait until Friday, and then be away from home for so long, including the Sabbath.

From the shadows, another person came forward. It was Susannah herself, in the awkward and scandalous-looking pantaloons. "Can you ride a horse?"

"Yes, of course," Almyra replied. She'd ridden in Boston around the green on a pony. Even as she answered, she half wished she'd said no.

The young woman seemed to see the doubt in her face. "Been a while, no doubt. I haven't seen you on any mount here in the village, have I? Matthew, and Mother, I'll lead her on horseback tomorrow, and back the next day, for half the cost."

Matthew began to argue about putting up two horses in Peacham overnight, and seemed to be in the right. But Mrs. Hall, watching everyone at once somehow, stepped in and ended the discussion."Once you've given a price, you don't back off. Fifty cents for the round trip, no staying overnight, but you'll need to carry your lunch and supper with you. I've no extra to be spending on another person's food right now."

With relief, Almyra announced, "I'll pack a basket for both of us, for both meals. Let me help."

"Satchel," Susannah corrected her. "Riding on a saddle, you'll want a satchel, not a basket. Best be here at half past seven tomorrow morning. I'll have the horses ready. And if you own a hoop or crinoline, leave it at home. Wool petticoats only."

To her relief, Aunt Charlotte made no demur about the proposed journey, saying only, "Then let us postpone the business with my Miss Cranston until later in the spring, when we have a carriage or wagon. For tomorrow, you must assemble double the woolen petticoats, my dear, for the horse stays warm by moving, but you'll be tossed in cold air all the way. And your winter jacket with at least two shawls, one to pull up over your cap. No, a bonnet will simply not do to keep you from catching your death of cold. Your uncle and I used to travel on horseback when we were young."

This startling announcement came in the midst of setting out a light supper for all, and Almyra had no chance to ask more. But she promised herself to inquire further, when time permitted.

In the chilly morning at half past seven, the air so cold she could see every puff of her breath, Almyra stared at the broad-hipped animal Susannah offered her, which never seemed to stop moving some part of itself. The lone stirrup dangled at about the height of her waist. At eye level, a horn-shaped protuberance erupted upward from the side saddle. A pommel. She understood the idea. Her right leg must wrap around that thing—what was it called—and her left would catch in the stirrup. But her skirts were sure to swirl and catch as she struggled into this strange seat.

Pride must not deter her. She said politely to her companion, "I'm afraid I've never ridden a horse with a side saddle, only on a pony. Would you kindly show me how to manage?"

Surely there was a way. Susannah herself wore heavy skirts today, much more mannerly than the pantaloons. How irritating—Almyra felt a tear of frustration, but she brushed it aside to watch Susannah demonstrate how to step upward, rise, and swing her body. And Susannah did this without even climbing up on the block first to reach the stirrup.

That, of course, was not going to work for Almyra. She stepped up onto the wooden perch and let Susannah bring the horse close to her. The animal aroma seemed overwhelming. But there was no time to fuss. Lifting her skirted right leg, she grappled up onto the seat, startled at the pressure of the odd post supporting her there, and struggling to tuck the extra fabric between herself and the curiously hard leather saddle.

Mrs. Hall stepped out of the house to examine the result and tugged firmly to make the seating more secure. "Give her the reins, now, Sukey, and let's see how she holds them."

Reins? This part she'd seen many times. She accepted the knotted straps of leather and drew her spine erect, left hand lifted politely to let the leathers drape.

Mrs. Hall chuckled. "I guess you do know your reins for a town promenade. But you can lower your arm now, or you'll wear it out before you've gone a mile. Best take hold of the reins in both hands to start with. Hold your horse back a bit now, Miss Alexander, so Susannah can fix the tether before she mounts her own. Here, this must be your satchel, I'll strap it behind you. There you go."

A few minutes later, with a broad bay horse in front of her own, and the embarrassing tether linking them, Almyra wobbled as her own horse began to walk. Its footsteps rocked her and she clutched at the saddle with her right hand. Susannah called over to her, "You hold with your legs, even on this sort of saddle. Try to curl your upper leg closer, and brace your other foot against the stirrup iron. Yes, that's better. We'll go slowly for a bit, until you're well seated. Just let me know when you're ready to trot for a while."

Riding through North Upton, Almyra felt as though half the village men watched her, whether standing outside the store or mending fences. She dared not try to lift a hand in greeting, or even to nod her head. All of her body felt afraid, and she clenched both legs more tightly, following Susannah's instruction.

As the road took a wide curve, the farms to either side opened drab brown vistas with just a hint of green in the fields. They passed along a column of tall elms, the river rushing to one side of them, and the sun at last offering some warmth.

Susannah announced calmly, "We'll trot for a while, or we'll be forever getting there. Let the horse do the work. Treat him like a dance partner, give way a bit."

Since the only dance partners Almyra had experienced were stiff boys in her long-ago ballroom dancing lessons, this advice was not really of much help. Moreover, trotting threatened to hurl her from the horse with every second bounce. The layers of skirt and petticoats beneath her could not provide sufficient cushion, either.

All at once, Susannah lifted an arm, pointing toward the noisy river. A family of gray foxes stood on the bank, watching them. The marvel of it reminded Almyra that this ride meant more than discomfort and trepidation. Many women would not ever be allowed to do this. And just look at the glory of the Lord's morning!

Whether joy or distraction, the moment brought relief, and with relaxed muscles, a better sort of sway in her seat. The more she remembered to use her legs, the more secure she felt.

After about half an hour more, woodsmoke and cacophony signaled the village of Upton Center, not far ahead. Susannah slowed the horses to a steady walk, and turned aside onto a narrower lane. "We can avoid the Green and having so many carriages around us, this way," she called over her shoulder.

On the one hand, this felt disappointing. After all, the Green bustled with business and neighbors making errands into cheerful social visits, and one always met good conversation there, as well as news to bring home. On the other hand, what if her skirt now hung crooked, or her petticoats showed their edges? Almyra sighed. Perhaps it was better not to be much observed at the moment.

More than an hour later, mostly spent trotting, a fresh wave of woodsmoke meant they'd soon reach the outskirts of South Upton where Mr. Greenbank's enormous mill took power from Joe's Brook, at this time of year a torrent more like a river than a brook. Almyra strained to sit more erectly. She could see fresh alertness in the set of Susannah's shoulders, too.

At the wooden bridge with its peaked roof, two farm wagons piled high with wool were waiting to cross, while an empty wagon came through from the further side. From her "halloo" calls and cheerful waving arm, Susannah seemed to know the sheep farmers. Or did one simply greet everyone, out here?

Before Almyra could summon words to ask without seeming foolish, the knot of wagons loosened and someone gestured for Susannah to proceed, leading Almyra's horse. At least this time Almyra managed to smile and nod at each of the drivers. As they crossed the bridge, the horses struck hollow thuds with their feet, and the waters beneath roared. Thank goodness for firm ground on the other side.

Susannah gestured, then walked her horse into the yard of a small dooryard with livery stable, an improvised tavern far less impressive than the one in North Upton, but busy, mostly with people on foot and some cheerful shouting. The nearby woolen mill was responsible, and Almyra looked around with interest.

With a graceful twist and slide, Susannah left her saddle and looked expectantly at Almyra. Was there a block to step onto? No. Oh dear.

Stiff and clumsy and concerned about her petticoats, Almyra did what she could to unlock one leg from the pommel and somehow jump with the other. She stumbled on the ground, then grabbed at the dangling reins, and the horse shook its head in complaint as the bit yanked on its mouth.

"I am so sorry," Almyra gasped to the animal, while also grabbing at the saddle to keep upright. Understandably, the horse began to back away from her. She handed the reins to Susannah, who took over, reassuring the horse while scowling toward Almyra.

"Just keep a loose hold on the reins when you slide down like that."

"I know, I didn't think. I won't do it again. I'm sorry."

But it took until their meal was spread out on a small table inside, with two mugs of hot posset that Almyra quickly paid for, for Susannah to cease frowning. Indeed, as she opened her satchel, her assorted sandwiches of ham and potted meat and the paper of sugar cookies resulted in wide eyes and quick consumption. Almyra ate quickly herself to secure a share of the repast she'd packed the night before.

After a long swallow of the hot beverage, she dared to ask, "Do we need to water and feed our horses? How does this go?"

Susannah shrugged. "I know most of the boys who work here. My brothers come through with the post. So they're taking care for us. It's the same as I'd do for them." Grudgingly, she added, "For someone who's new to riding a sidesaddle, you managed well enough."

"Thank you. How much farther is it to Peacham?"

"Barely four miles to the grammar school, but it's all uphill, and a busy road. So we'll walk the horses. Close to an hour's walk, most likely. And I can't use the tether, so you'll have to follow me on your own."

Almyra flinched. She hoped her horse had forgiven her clumsiness and would respond willingly to her hands on the reins. If she were the horse, she might not be pleased.

But the last stretch was uneventful, until they finally reached Peacham Green, where Almyra saw a dark-faced driver on a waiting wagon, and called out impulsively, "Franklin! Is that you?"

~ 9 ~

The young man perched on the wagon bench tipped his head to one side in a polite but definite reply, "Good afternoon, but I'm not Franklin, whoever that might be, ma'am. Are you seeking such a person?"

Susannah clicked softly to her horse as she eased to a halt between Almyra and the youth. After a moment of appraising him, she turned toward Almyra. "Are you? Seeking someone named Franklin?"

Embarrassed, Almyra shook her head. "No, I'm sorry, I just thought—well, I know someone named Franklin who looks something like … I mean, he's also young and," she kept hesitating, not saying the word "African." She lurched past the moment and said instead, "It was foolish of me. Franklin's missing most of a leg, so there's clearly not such a resemblance. I beg your pardon," she added directly to the young man. "My name is Almyra Alexander, and this is my, umm, my neighbor Susannah Hall. And your name is?"

For a moment she'd seen a flash of recognition in his eyes, under the thatch of stiff black hair and the hat that almost captured it. But what he said was, "Benjamin Blake, ma'am. Not Benjamin Franklin, I'm afraid. Though wouldn't it be a fine thing to be a clever inventor and politician like himself." He nodded toward the building closest to him. "That would be Mister Jasper Blake's home. If you might be seeking him."

"No, I'm not," Almyra said, confused. She looked to Susannah for confirmation. "We're here to see Mister Leonard Johnson."

A burst of surprise crossed the man's face. He tipped his hat back some, to look more directly at Almyra and Susannah, then said calmly, "You'll need to be turning back, then, I'm afraid. The farm on Centre Street was Ziba Johnson's, but Leonard and his family are farming out toward Danville. Though I believe that cart by the store," he nodded ahead, "might be Miss Martha Johnson. So long as you are here already, you might begin accordingly."

Susannah finally spoke up. "Thank you, Mister Blake. And you yourself would be from?"

The question felt bold, hanging in the air, but also ordinary. Everyone always said where they lived, where they'd come from. With her misidentification of the man as Franklin, brother of a girl who'd lived in North Upton named Sarah, Almyra expected to hear either West Upton—where Sarah's brother Franklin stayed for a while, tending horses—or Woodstock, where an entire village of Negro people thrived around a collection of livery stables and such.

Instead, after a long pause, Benjamin Blake replied, "Potton, ma'am. Potton, in Lower Canada." He added, "Across the border from North Troy, about fifty miles north of here."

Almyra couldn't hold back. "So far away? But why are you here in Peacham?"

As Susannah laughed aloud, Almyra blushed. Susannah rescued her from one more rude moment, however, by drawling, "My friend here is as curious as a cat. No need to answer at length, friend. We'll look for Miss Johnson at the store."

"She's tall and fair, so you'll see her right off," Benjamin noted, nodding. "And they say that curiosity killed the cat, but satisfaction cured it. I work on Mister Jasper Blake's farm north of the border, and I've brought some of his winter wheat down for a better grind of flour than we have up north. Your servant, ma'am, and yours," he gave Almyra half a bow from his seated position and let his hat settle forward again, half a smile dancing on his lips.

Susannah's horse, urged with a slap of the reins, headed along the green toward an obviously busy store, and Almyra, face hot, allowed her own mount to follow as she held herself upright with all her aching muscles. She could see the graceful buildings of Peacham Academy beyond the store. There might not be time, though, to approach them more closely. Focus on the most important tasks, she reminded herself.

Several conveyances stood near the wide plank walkway of the store. Almyra's horse skittered sideways, unwilling to step close to them. Hitched horses stamped and huffed, with a great deal of unpredictable motion and sound.

Susannah turned back toward Almyra and called out, "Just walk him around the green. I'll be right back out." Her lithe lift from the side saddle belied the long ride, and without any notable effort, Susannah led her own mount to a granite post, knotted the tether rope through an iron ring, and swung up toward the door, which was already opening. The movement provided one more disturbance for Almyra's own horse, which swung sideways and began a slow trot down the road.

"No, no," Almyra called to the animal, then finally remembered to use the reins the way she'd done in the city, years ago. By the time she had some semblance of control and had returned to the green, Susannah stood outside again with another woman in a capacious skirt, clearly draped over several crinolines or perhaps a set of hoops. Envious and curious in equal measure, Almyra rode as close as she dared and raised a hand in greeting.

The other woman looked as young as Susannah, close enough in age to Almyra, and rather than lift her own hand in reply, she simply nodded, in a brimmed straw hat with neat black ribbon. Hand gestures suggested she was explaining a route to Susannah. With her mount twitching again from all the cacophony, Almyra allowed the horse to side-step past the others, then did her best to turn the animal again, just in time to follow both a trim little wagon with several people in it, and Susannah on horseback, down the main street in the direction they'd arrived.

Please, she thought, let this be only a short distance. Her right leg burned with chafing from the saddle post, and her left foot felt nearly numb.

The horse seemed more than willing to follow the others, and kept up a steady, if lurching, trot. Down one hill, up the next, downhill again toward a small river. Were they riding all the way back to Greenbanks Hollow? At a small mill on her left, clearly built for grain, stood a buggy and two farm wagons, horses still hitched, heads hanging. To the right a large pond, nearly free of winter ice, glowed in the midday sunshine.

The road began to rise again, as Almyra struggled to hold the chafed skin of her upper leg away from the saddle post. Abruptly, her horse swung to the right, and she grappled for her balance.

At last, two young men in the blue smocks of farm labor walked out of a small stable, one speaking with their hostess and the other reaching for the bridle of Susannah's mount. Almyra spotted a block to dismount upon  and coaxed her horse toward it. Her swing off the saddle stung and tore at both her legs, the right leg burning, the left nearly numb from pushing against the stirrup for so long. But she grasped her skirts in time to avoid an unseemly display, wobbled a moment on the block, then climbed down to lead her horse, or be led by it, more like, toward a watering trough.

After a flurry of greetings with an older couple, clearly Miss Johnson's parents, everyone except the laborers gathered around a heavy dining table, where Almyra gratefully accepted tea and some cold meats and biscuit.

The merry conversation about nearby neighbors and friends, most of them not familiar to Almyra, finally paused, and Miss Johnson asked, "Miss Alexander, I understand you've come in response to my request to Doctor Jewett. Are you sure you will be able to get everything to him safely?"

What did she mean? Almyra lifted her chin and said, "Doctor Jewett only mentioned that you wished for some local connection, ma'am. I don't understand."

The low chuckles around the table made her blush. Susannah said, "I've no need to hear this sort of business. I'll visit the stables and see to our horses. If there's cake, save me some." She strode out of the room as if she wore pantaloons, her skirts swishing with authority.

The older gentleman, Mr. Leonard Johnson, leaned forward and explained: "You've been entrapped in our indirect language, I'm afraid. To us, a request for such connection is notice to the doctor that we have items for him. You know what we mean by that, I presume?"

Almyra thought of what her friends Alice and Caroline had transported the previous year. "Papers?" she guessed. "Documents for people seeking their freedom? Letters of manumission or apprenticeship?"

Mrs. Johnson, who'd been mostly silent, shook her head sadly. "That's far too risky now with the enforcement of the Fugitive Slave Act. Anyone headed north is going up Lake Champlain or by the seacoast, in a great hurry. Or else simply settling at Rokeby." She added, "The Quaker farm, in Ferrisburgh."

How would a Boston-bred girl know where that was, anyway? Irritated at appearing so ignorant in front of strangers, Almyra pressed what seemed to be the main point. "Then what is it that you need carried to Doctor Jewett? How can I assist you?"

Miss Martha Johnson said bluntly, "Money. Printed bills, of course, but also specie. The doctor makes sure it reaches Boston, to pay for shelter and cargo fees on the ships there. If you have two saddlebags, we'll place the bundles into them along with ladies' garments atop. Thus far, those have been the most powerful incentive for searches to cease should someone catch word that you're transporting something for our group." She smiled at Almyra's shock. "Most men are quite unwilling to pull out drawers and garters and such, in public, you know."

"I should imagine so," Almyra admitted. "But why don't you simply carry the funds to St. Johnsbury yourself? Why do you need me for the task?"

The Johnsons seemed surprised. "My dear child," Mr. Johnson said, "setting aside our need to run the farm, there's no sense in being obvious about these things. We make an effort to change transport as often as possible, as long as someone trustworthy can be found. And Martha, of course, must ride to Hardwick tomorrow so that she can receive word from the minister there on what's needed to our west. Also, to meet with my brother Oliver, if time permits."

"Of course," Almyra said politely, as Martha nodded without looking up from papers in front of her. Almyra didn't see any reason she should have known about any of that. These people had no idea how to talk with strangers, she reflected. Well, if needs must—she would tackle this task anyway.

She added aloud, "Our satchels are near to empty. Most likely Susannah may wish to pack them herself, as the horses know her best. Are there any letters you'll need carried by hand as well?"

Mrs. Johnson brushed a hand against her husband's arm. "That might be wise," she said. "I've heard Jasper Blake is assisting in the post office. And you know what that means."

This time Almyra decided to ask. "I've only just heard Mr. Blake's name today, at the Green, when we met a young African there who said he worked on the Jasper Blake farm in Lower Canada. How does he come to assist at the post office here, and what does that mean for your letters?"

"Why, he owns land in Peacham as well as up north." Mr. Johnson thumped a fist on the table, making the china cups rattle. "And a bigger two-faced hypocrite you'll never meet. Talking abolition here in Peacham, when he's been a slave owner himself, three times over."

"What! In the South?"

"No, child, in Canada, of course. Dear merciful heavens, it won't even be twenty years until this summer, since the British Commonwealth set aside slavery."

Almyra stared at the man. "But the Africans run to Canada."

"Yes, of course, now they do. But Jasper Blake owned two Africans and an Abenaki women as slaves north of the border."

His wife cut in, "Martha, if Miss Alexander met an African from the Blake farm today, would that be one of Isaac and Harriet's sons?"

"Bertrand, or Benjamin," Miss Martha Johnson confirmed, still not looking up.

"Benjamin," Almyra said. "That's what he said, Benjamin Blake. But I don't understand. Does that mean he is the son of this Jasper Blake and an African slave?"

"No, no, just Isaac and Harriet's son, not Jasper's. This isn't the South, you know. Jasper wouldn't lie with a slave, I'm sure."

Mrs. Johnson's blunt language shocked Almyra, but she needed another answer. "Then why does he have the surname Blake?"

Now Miss Johnson did look up. "Because it was given to Isaac when Jasper Blake claimed to own him, of course."

Almyra had never felt so ignorant in all her life. Her cheeks hot, her eyes damp with embarrassment, she made one more effort. "How can the people of Peacham allow such a man to hold land here? I should think it would be called disgraceful."

After a startled silence, Mrs. Johnson said to her daughter Martha, "I like this one. She has good sense. Make sure to tell the minister in Hardwick just what she said. And now," her voice turned brisk, "let's load your parcels while my husband scratches a few notes to be carried by hand, a very wise precaution. Martha, the key, if you please."

From that point, everything happened quickly: Mrs. Johnson and her daughter opened a locked chest, withdrawing two leather pouches bound in string, which Martha Johnson covered with a tea cloth and carried to the stable. The laborers stood outside with Susannah, apparently talking about horses. Almyra noted Susannah's stance, leaning against a post as if she still wore those shocking pantaloons, and laughing aloud with the men. It distressed her—but she told herself to button her own lip and wait to discuss the matter with Aunt Charlotte. For now, Susannah's skill with horses mattered more than such coarse manners.

As Susannah stepped across and secured the bundles, without curiosity, Almyra realized she'd have to ride another few hours on the uneasy perch. Perhaps it added some dismay to her voice as she said farewell to her hosts, for Mrs. Johnson leaned close to whisper, "This is how we women make a difference in the battle for the right, you know."

Almyra forced a smile and nod. "Of course," she said, satisfied to turn the tables. "My uncle is a minister too, you know. And I have a sermon to write, this evening."

She knew it wasn't very high-minded, but it cheered her to see Mrs. Johnson pull back and look surprised. Briskly, she climbed the block again and allowed Susannah to lead the horse into position. She had only a brief moment to tuck her petticoats into a thicker bunch between her thigh and the saddle post, before the animals began to move toward the road.

"Thank you for your hospitality," she called over her shoulder. She heard Susannah say the same. Then, with a cluck from Susannah and a slap of reins, the horses lurched into a trot, toward the turn for Greenbanks Hollow and the long road back to North Upton.

Almyra tried to consider topics for her next sermon, to take her mind off the jolting ride. "Precious as rubies" came to mind, and she considered also the Jubilee, which should release all slaves from their masters. A thread of ideas began to form—only to be interrupted by a sudden question in her thought. *What about those counterfeits that the men had discussed with Colonel Young? Did the pouches in her satchels contain forged bills of tender? How would she know—and if they did, was she guilty in conveying them onward?*

She had so many questions to ask Aunt Charlotte and her uncle. So many.

~ 10 ~

"You were boastful and spoke an untruth, Almyra, about writing your sermon in the evening," she scolded herself as she eased carefully out from her bedcovers the next morning. Arriving home when only the faintest light still glowed from the sky the night before, she'd promised her aunt she would describe the day's events the next morning and limped through the kitchen with barely enough strength to brush her skirts free of dust and horsehair and tumble into bed.

At least this morning she reached the kitchen in good time, setting the firebox quickly alight and pumping water for both the iron kettle for tea and a tureen for oat porridge. The more she moved, the less everything hurt.

Aunt Charlotte, sailing in a few minutes later, beamed with pleasure. "Now, my dear, there's yesterday's graham bread and half a mutton pie as well. Your uncle will return from his walk by the time the meal's hot and ready, and then you shall recount your journey."

The ride across country made the least of her tale. Sitting at the table together, what Almyra had learned about Mr. Blake, his recently enslaved servants, his anti-Abolition stance and position as the postmaster, all seemed far more urgent to convey. Her aunt's shocked exclamations and her uncle's steadily more solemn visage confirmed the importance of her news.

"Nonetheless," Uncle Eliphalet pronounced at last, "you have completed the circle of acquaintance and information that Doctor Jewett asked of you. You may write to him without fear of the postmaster here in North Upton. Or the stage driver who'll carry your letter."

Almyra understood she was being teased. Mr. Weeks, the postmaster, was an ardent abolitionist himself, and of course Sam Young, who drove the stage, observed firsthand the conditions of the handful of free black persons who'd passed through or stayed in the area, as well as the arrival of Sarah Johnson to the village when she'd been a small child. No doubt her letters would be safe from local prying, but that didn't mean she could be careless.

"Oh! Uncle, I've neglected to tell you. Miss Martha Johnson didn't wish only to make my acquaintance. She sent two parcels with me that I'm to convey to Doctor Jewett myself."

Aunt Charlotte frowned. "They can't be very large, as you only carried your satchel into the house with you last night. Why couldn't she simply send them with the post?"

Almyra lowered her voice. "They are funds for the labor against the South's continued machinations, I believe. Bills and specie—they have some considerable weight, from the coins."

Her uncle pursed his lips. "I don't like it," he said slowly. "Not the parcel carrying, mind you. I've no quarrel with a favor for a neighbor, in a moral cause. But currency has become such a questionable substance. You'll note that I've never accepted a seat among the bank's directors. One mustn't provide an easy route for those who confuse Mammon with blessings."

Mammon. Almyra knew the portion from the Book of Matthew, of course, including "Lay not up for yourselves treasures upon earth, where moth and rust doth corrupt, and where thieves break through and steal." It ended with, "Ye cannot serve God and Mammon." But what did that mean for her uncle? she pondered.

She asked cautiously, feeling her way, "Will people associate the funds with you, if they know I've taken part in conveying them?"

Aunt Charlotte's small moan of dismay echoed her uncle's long exhalation. "Niece," he said slowly, "let me at least examine these funds and be sure we are not delivering false documents to the good doctor. I will ask young Matthew to come and look at them with me. I believe he subscribes to a publication that describes the most common forgeries. This, at least, we can do, before you carry someone else's problems to town."

For the sake of discretion, Matthew and Uncle Eliphalet settled in the "study" to examine the contents of the two bundles Miss Johnson had provided. Almyra considered begging for a seat at the desk as well, then realized this would abandon her aunt to the kitchen, an unfair situation. With reluctance, she tied an apron about herself and buckled down to sweeping and scrubbing, as her aunt cleaned the pantry shelves and called out the items that needed replenishing. Soda for baking, extra vinegar for early pickling, graham flour.

The mention of graham flour reminded Almyra of what Benjamin Blake had said, "Aunt, he brought wheat from Lower Canada, from the Blake farm there, to be milled in Peacham."

Aunt Charlotte wrinkled her nose in puzzlement. "In springtime? Surely most milling's done in late autumn or early winter. Spring is for planting."

That notion hadn't occurred to Almyra. Abruptly, she set her broom against a table and rapped on the door to the study. "Uncle," she said with excitement, "what if errands from the farms across in Canada could be a way to carry forged instruments into commerce here?" She'd heard mention of a Canadian forgery, she was sure of it, but it would be imprudent to suggest she'd been listening to the earlier conversation with Colonel Young.

Uncle Eliphalet only grunted in response, thumbing bills and inspecting them, but Matthew exclaimed, "Why not?" He eyed her appreciatively, and she blushed, then backed out to resume her tasks. Perhaps it was a leap of reasoning, yet if this Mister Jasper Blake's moral flaws extended to enslaving Africans and Natives, what would stop him from participating in a ring of counterfeiters? And how better to injure the Abolition movement, than to seed it with forged money that would collapse upon receipt at any knowledgeable banking enterprise?

The problem to solve next must be how to speak again with Benjamin Blake. But would he admit to her that his employer across the border in Canada sent him on morally wrong errands? Surely such an admission could put him in danger. And what right did she have to place any person in danger, especially one barely distanced from the horrors of enslavement? No, there must be some other way.

Her studies of the Gospel said little about women and their labors. Still, it seemed unsurprising that as she wiped clean the last items of cutlery from the noon meal, an idea blossomed in her thoughts, as though the morning's work had woken her mind. *Susannah, she thought. I must talk with Susannah.*

In the light of this fresh awakening, she saw clearly what to do, and a few minutes later, she fetched from her chamber two neatly hemmed handkerchiefs. She carried them to the kitchen. The voices of her uncle and Matthew issued in low exchanges beyond the closed door to the study. Still counting, she presumed.

"Might I take a few minutes to carry these to Susannah Hall? I couldn't help but notice that she did not have one with her the day we rode to Peacham," she said quietly to her aunt.

Aunt Charlotte made a sympathetic sound. "Of course, Almyra. And here, take a paper of cookies for those children. I'm sure Mrs. Hall rarely bakes small treats for them, as she must feed such a crowd twice each day."

A hint of guilt at her double intention nagged at Almyra as she briskly walked down the village road avoiding the worst mud and feeling a sharp breeze on her cheeks. But wasn't it the Lord's own work, "to seek justice and love mercy"? She must keep her goal foremost in her thoughts: to discover the source of the counterfeit specie, or even printed bills of commerce, that could damage the prospects of all abolitionist efforts of the region.

She made a swift delivery of the sweets to Mrs. Hall in the inn's kitchen and saw them set aside for later. Should she offer to help with meal preparations? No, she told herself firmly, stay with the work you've chosen. Her comment that she needed to speak with Susannah raised no curiosity among the others. Mrs. Hall simply nodded toward the door to the inn, and said, "She's likely in the stables. Jane, mind that kettle, it won't stir itself, girl."

The wide room of the inn stood dim and quiet. Almyra passed through and out the next door again, pausing only a moment to twitch up her skirts. The closer she'd come to the stable, the more risk of soiling them.

Outside the livery building, roped to a granite hitching post, two horses tugged at a small pile of hay in a rack. The thick aroma of the stables set her to sneezing. In response, a voice from the darkened horse shed called out, "God bless you."

Susannah, in her usual Turkish pantaloons, stepped out into the sunlight. "Oh, you again. Come to look for another ride to Peacham, have you? You're walking better than I thought you might, considering."

Almyra blushed. "I'm in no hurry to ride again," she admitted, "at least not yet. But I wondered, do the riders bound for Canada come through here? Is there a stage for them?"

"Goes through Hardwick, not Upton. Then Glover, Barton, Brownington, Derby," she rattled off. "That's the Canada line, Derby."

Frowning, Almyra asked, "How far is that from here? Hardwick, I mean?"

"Fifteen, sixteen miles, over Stannard Mountain." Susannah eyed Almyra curiously. "You want to ride to Hardwick now?"

"No, no, I'm only—that is, I am trying to understand more of the geography, now that I'm not going back to Boston." She recalled the handkerchiefs she'd brought, and handed them to Susannah, saying in slight mistruth, "My aunt told me to share these, since I have more than I need of them. Spring sorting, you know."

Ignoring this excuse, though pocketing the handkerchiefs swiftly, Susannah continued, "You're thinking of that colored man in Peacham that you spoke with? But he didn't ride the stage, did he? He took himself there from those Canada farms, I'd wager. The mountain roads are still all mud, you know. Most likely he drove along the river route, to St. Johnsbury and then west."

"With a load of wheat for milling, he said," Almyra point out. "That would be the route he'd take?"

"Nobody mills wheat this time of year." Susannah frowned. "You're sure he said wheat?"

"Perhaps I am mistaken. He had a wagon in Peacham, though, didn't he?"

"That's no sign of anything. He could have been driving it around the farm there, and stopped in the village. No," Susannah decided, "chances are if he just came down from Canada this past week, he rode a horse, not pulling anything. Now, I've stables to shovel. Was that something you were wanting to learn, also?"

Almyra grabbed at her skirts and backed away. "No, I don't believe so, but thank you. I should get back to my aunt. But do you think ...," she hesitated, then decided not to ask at all. It was obvious that

Benjamin Blake wouldn't come over to North Upton's inn or ride the stage that stopped here. She'd have to send a letter. Awkwardly, she finished her sentence, "Do you think the mountain roads will dry out soon?"

Over a shoulder, Susannah replied, "Heaven only knows."

All the way back home, Almyra puzzled over the new information. Had she misunderstood what the man in Peacham had told her? Yet what if her notion of forged currency from Canada held true—it could easily be carried in saddlebags or a satchel on horseback. A wagon from Canada would not be needed.

As she approached her aunt and uncle's house—her own home, she reminded herself—Matthew came hurrying out the kitchen door. Almyra stepped out of his way as he tossed a wide grin her way. "Stage," he called out simply, escalating his pace to a jog as he reached the road.

The kitchen stood empty. Almyra hurried toward Aunt Charlotte and Uncle Eliphalet, around the corner in the study. She asked immediately, "Were the funds proper?"

Her uncle's nod reassured her, and she paused to catch her breath. "Aunt, Mrs. Hall was pleased to receive the cookies, she set them aside right away for her children."

Aunt Charlotte beamed. Almyra asked, "When might I carry the packets to Doctor Jewett, then?"

Uncle Eliphalet shook his head. "I'll take them myself, niece. It's not to deprive you of a visit to town, but your aunt reminds me that you can't continue your studies if you're out and about too often, and I have business in St. Johnsbury on Friday." Seeing her disappointment, he added kindly, "There will be another errand for you soon, I'm sure, my dear. Scripture tells us, of course, that the Lord is the one who makes the plans. 'In all thy ways acknowledge Him, and He shall direct thy paths.'"

"Of course, Uncle," Almyra responded. She bit back any hint that she'd rather direct her own paths.

Perhaps Aunt Charlotte noticed, however, for she laid an arm over Almyra's shoulder and said, "I shall continue to note the supplies we must refresh, child. At the very least, we'll need to visit Upton Center next week. In the meanwhile, I release you to your books and papers."

It took enormous effort to settle at her table and confront her half-written sermon for the week. After all, now that the church calendar had passed Easter Sunday, what could be distinctive in the fifty days til Pentecost? Lambing had ended and fieldwork must wait for warmer, more settled weather. Almyra thumbed her leather-bound Concordance to the Holy Scriptures and examined several passages about planting and harvest. No, of course wheat would not be milled in the springtime. And surely not seeded yet, either, at this muddy, chilly time of year. The mystery kept slipping back into her thoughts.

A rap at the kitchen door distracted her further. Aunt Charlotte greeted someone briefly, then came back into the kitchen and brought Almyra a much-inked, part-torn envelope, franked from Hartland, Vermont, and addressed to "Miss A. Alexander, The Parsonage, Upton." The sender's mark of "N." for North had blurred, and the post must have gone astray, to be brought to the north village a day later. She opened it carefully, puzzled by the half-familiar handwriting, and looked quickly to the signature. Sarah! This old friend of Alice's, who wrote so often to Miss Farrow, had never sent Almyra a letter before. Was it because of the warning Miss Farrow had passed along from Alice and Caroline?

Reading hastily to discover what the now-grown sister of Franklin Johnson wished to tell her, she exclaimed aloud, "Alice Sanborn's brother John. One of the pair who went West to the Territories—Sarah says he is in Vermont and will travel to North Upton next week. Oh Aunt, we shall hear his news of Alice and Caroline, and of the Kansas frontier."

"There, my dear, you see? Now, isn't it a blessing that you're not planning some journey to St. Johnsbury, when you need instead to press even further forward on your labors? Tis the best way to prepare for distractions ahead. Doubtless a visit from one of the Sanborn lads will set the village all to visiting, and we'll have laundry and baking all confused as well." Clucking her tongue in concern, Aunt Charlotte patted Almyra's shoulder, then returned to the stove, rehearsing tasks aloud.

All at once her wardrobe called more urgently than her sermon. Almyra slid quietly up the stairs to examine her sadly crushed crinolines and her two walking dresses where she'd recently added fabric to the edges of the skirts, to lengthen them.  At such a distance from Boston, she felt she often made do. But still,

Abolition. Temperance. Justice. Ministering to the poor.

An inner chant of such noble topics drove her back to her writing. Half her thoughts kept darting away, though, as she wondered, *What should she wear when John Sanborn came to call?*

Between her labor and her distractions, she almost missed noting, out the propped-open window of the steamy kitchen, the view of little Polly Hall scuttling along the roadside, an air of haste and secrecy about her once again.

## ~ 11 ~

The week ahead proved contentious and disturbed, but not because John Sanborn's visit loomed ahead. Instead, North Upton shook with each day's news from the halls of Congress, as the papers reported Illinois Senator Stephen Douglas crowing over the terrible new Act of Congress, one that repealed the line drawn against slavery in the Territories—specifically, the enormous Kansas Territory. Editor Horace Greeley called the success evidence of a dark power in the nation. Every Northern man of the cloth, and even some Southern ones, it seemed, heard the call to respond to the forces spreading slavery across the nation.

Almyra found patience nearly impossible to practice. Men from the village, and beyond, gathered noisily in her uncle's study or at the kitchen table, and some expressed hope that Vermont's own governor would travel to the nation's capital in protest. Would her new brother-in-law, Simon, who carried messages for the noted Abolitionist William Seward, pay a visit to the North Upton once again?

Despite such distractions, she ached for John Sanborn to arrive—to seek his news about the Territory, whether slavery could be halted there, and about Alice and Caroline. She felt a surging eagerness at the notion of hearing about them, face to face with Alice's older brother.

Confronting her own impatience Thursday morning, she reviewed the virtues she aimed to achieve on her way to the ministry. Surely she must release such overly strong anticipation, become calm, take root in the warmth of the Lord's word.

"Is that why some women never marry?" She hadn't meant to say it aloud, but her aunt turned from a half-wiped window pane and regarded her curiously. Almyra added, "I only wondered whether one might remain more calm, more settled in the ministry, if one remained detached from emotional passions. And surely, love of man and wife must engender passion of the spirit, not only the body."

Aunt Charlotte nodded. "In many marriages, perhaps even most, I believe that is so. But there is no need to discuss it, my dear. It is a gift of the Lord, a blessing, but each of us has such abundant blessings already. We need not clamor to receive everything possible." Her head tipped to one side and with a questioning look she added, "Indeed, you know already, Almyra, a woman who marries does not continue in the ministry. If you are considering married life, consider whether your years of study and learning would be wasted on a mere year or two in a vocation."

"Vocation comes from *vocare*, the Latin verb for call, or summon," Almyra responded at once. "I am convinced this is my summoned path, Aunt."

"Then I am sore afraid that you must not expect to marry, at least for quite a number of years. Perhaps in your thirties, when you have labored in the fields of the Lord for some time."

"Thirties. How old I would be then," Almyra mused. "What sort of man might marry a woman of that age? Not for love, perhaps, but for a helpmeet? Oh, perhaps a man who'd lost a wife to childbearing. How sad."

Almyra caught a glimpse of a half-hidden smile as Aunt Charlotte resumed work. For herself, she frowned instead. This was important. Any discussion she had with, say, Captain Young, or Matthew, or Alice's brothers, must be dignified and correct. She must discipline herself now, and in the years to come.

She took a moment to envision herself speaking with a congregation in a village church, or even in a city, and resolved to think on this whenever enthusiasm might mislead her in the future. And to apply such serious consideration to her gowns, as well, no matter how that notion might sting. More black bombazine, ugh. Just when the Boston season must be erupting in bright gowns and marvelous hats.

A sharp rap at the kitchen door interrupted her thoughts. Aunt Charlotte cocked her head to one side, peering through a window, and said, "Almyra, why don't you answer this? I believe it's that young woman who rode with you to Peacham."

Susannah. Perhaps she had news of Benjamin Blake after all?

Opening the door swiftly, Almyra flinched at the ripe odor of horses and realized Susannah, in her mannish attire, must have run straight from the stables, muddy boots and all. Before she could gesture toward the iron boot scraper, however, Susannah was already speaking.

"I can't come in, I need to find Mrs. Sanborn. Quickly. Is she here? Her husband thought she might be up this end of the village."

"Not here," Almyra replied. "Perhaps at the store?"

"Not there."

"The schoolhouse, then? How can I help?"

Without response, Susannah turned and bolted toward the curve of the road where the track to the schoolhouse cut in. A bit enviously, Almyra noticed that Susannah could nearly run in the Turkish pantaloons. Though of course she'd lost all semblance of ladylike motion. What a shame!

Closing the door behind her, she met her aunt's questioning gaze. "Susannah only wishes to find Mrs. Sanborn. I wonder why?"

"Childbirth," her aunt guessed. "Since Mrs. Clark's departure, Mrs. Sanborn is the best at helping. But who could be ready? I haven't seen any indication of someone staying indoors over the winter. Have you?"

Almyra shook her head. Not that she'd really been watching for such things. "Could it be William Sanborn's wife is bearing again? She rarely comes out of her home anyway, so we might not notice."

Aunt Charlotte shook her head. "If it were Helen, Abigail would already be at her side. No, but it could be someone at the inn. A traveler." She stripped off her apron. "Has the stage arrived?"

"It's not a stage day, is it? Perhaps a private carriage or wagon, a family passing through?"

A moment later, with a loaf of bread wrapped in a cloth, her aunt led the way out of the house. "Let this not be idle curiosity," Aunt Charlotte worried as she huffed along the edge of the road.

Almyra reassured her, hurrying at her side. "Clearly there's something amiss, Aunt. Oh look, here come the others." They paused as one, looking toward the turn at the end of the village.

Mrs. Sanborn, in a handsome blue cloak that Almyra couldn't help noticing, strode so strongly that her skirt swirled. Something she said to

Susannah sent the Hall girl racing ahead toward the inn. Almyra and her aunt endeavored to match Mrs. Sanborn's pace.

"What can we do?" Aunt Charlotte thrust the wrapped loaf into Almyra's hands, her eyes fixed on Mrs. Sanborn's grim face.

"Nothing until I see what's underway," the neighbor replied. "Although perhaps your niece could run to my house and fetch my basket? It's the one with red cloth wrapping the contents, in the pantry."

Passing the bread back to her aunt, Almyra sped away toward the long drive leading into the Sanborn farm. "Where do I bring it?" she called over her shoulder.

"To the inn, of course," Mrs. Sanborn snapped.

It took two hands to hold up her petticoats from the patches of mud, as she hastened to the farmhouse, knocked on the kitchen door, and burst inside. She saw no one else, and dove for the ample pantry she recalled, from when she used to visit her friend Alice here. "Soup," she muttered, remembering the jest she and Alice shared in the past. Her lips twitched in merriment, despite her haste and concern.

Dashing back out the door, she realized Mr. Sanborn watched her from a fenced yard with some of his sheep. She waved one arm toward him, hoping he'd spot the basket on her other one and guess the urgency. "Back later," she called, just in case, and kept up her pace toward Matthew Clark's inn and whatever emergency it was that summoned the Halls, Mrs. Sanborn, and Aunt Charlotte.

Bursting into the inn, barely stopping to scrape the mud from her own shoes, she met a damp dark silence in the tavern. "Mrs. Clark?"

The door to the right must lead toward the livery stables, so the door to the left would be the house. She eased it open cautiously and was reassured to hear women's low voices ahead.

In the working kitchen, kettles steamed on the stove, and a heap of fresh greens, spring's first roadside growth it seemed, lay on the big table. The little Hall girl sat curled into a corner seat beyond the table, eyes large in her grubby face.

"Hello, Polly," Almyra ventured. "How are you?"

The child stared at her, then lifted a hand with one finger extended. "I stirred it all," she reported defensively, "but I can't get the box open.

For the wood." She pointed to a chunk of split wood on the floor next to the stove. "I hurt my finger."

Almyra winced. "I'll be right there to help you," she said. "Let me give this basket to the ladies first."

The girl gestured toward what had been the Clarks' front parlor, when they all lived at this house. Almyra stepped quietly into the room.

It was still a parlor, of sorts, with shabby furnishings and much-scuffed floor. Her aunt and Mrs. Sanborn crouched over an improvised bed, where someone whimpered, a crescendo of pain and fear. Mrs. Hall stood next to them, twisting her apron in her hands.

"I gave it to her months ago," Mrs. Hall protested. "How was I to know she'd waited to use it? She'd have had no trouble at all back then."

Mrs. Sanborn's, low-voiced and reassuring, took charge. "It's only a blockage, Ruthie," she crooned. "Now my basket's here," she beckoned to Almyra, "we'll have you feeling better in a trice. Harriet," she said more crisply, "boiled water if you please, at least a kettle's worth. And Charlotte, if you'll find some clean bedding, we'll place it underneath so as to keep from soiling Mrs. Hall's settee, shall we?"

Almyra pressed the basket forward, then stepped back. The odor from the whimpering girl on the settee, who looked a few years younger than Almyra herself and must be named Ruth, shocked her. It was worse than uncleanliness, and had nothing to do with horses either, but with something rotten. Spoiled meat. Her stomach lurched and she bolted back to the kitchen.

Mrs. Hall already had a wet compress on her little girl's hand, kettles nudged to new positions on the stove, and had swept the greens into a crock at the far end of the table. "I'll have the boiling water shortly," she said over her shoulder, then turned to look more closely at Almyra.

"First time? Take a chair, girl, before you tumble. I'll have some mint tea for you in a moment."

"A blockage?" Almyra struggled to understand. "Her bowels?"

"No, her womb," the worried woman replied. "You know her, do you?"

Almyra sat down. "I couldn't really see. Who is she?"

"Ruthie Cook. Old Mo's granddaughter, who should have known better than to let him touch her. And now what's to do? Abigail

Sanborn's no miracle worker, and there's no time to send for a doctor. Even my Susannah can't fly to St. Johnsbury."

This startling speech overwhelmed Almyra. Old Mo? That disgusting drunkard who spent many evenings in the tavern? The man who proved by his very being the evils of strong drink and the desperate need for temperance. Had his ever-unwashed state somehow infected his granddaughter, given her some disease? But what was that foul essence rising from her body?

Her aunt's wrapped loaf of bread sat on a sideboard, ignored. Almyra focused on the familiar fabric and demanded of herself that her head stop spinning. She must understand. Mrs. Hall pressed a cup of something steaming into her hand, and she sat up straighter, to be polite.

In pulling herself upright, she recalled the dignity she'd lectured herself about, such a short time earlier. Straighten those shoulders. Lift your chin. Manners.

"Thank you," she managed, and lifted the cup to her lips. The fragrances of peppermint and spearmint reassured her and she sipped, careful not to burn her mouth. "What can I do to help?"

Mrs. Hall looked at her more directly. "I guess you can manage a stove and serve up the tavern meal at noon if I'm in the other room, can't you?" With a swift appraisal of Alymra's shirtwaist and skirt, well enough suited to helping Aunt Charlotte clean, she added, "You'll find an apron on the hooks behind the door. And slice the bread thin. Mind now," she bent to talk to her child, who'd moved from the seat, curling up instead under the table. "Mama's very busy, Polly, so you must do what Miss Alexander tells you, and help her find the bowls and such for Matthew and Susannah and whoever else is there. Take your thumb out of your mouth, I'm not angry with you. Stay away from the stove, though, you're not tall enough."

Carrying boiled water in a pair of ewers, Mrs. Hall returned to the front room. Almyra resolutely refused to watch, hoping the odor wouldn't strike her again. She forced down the rest of the mint tea and rose to assume her assigned duties at the stove.

As she lifted lids, stirred and scraped, adjusted placement of kettles, and eased the air slots a bit wider at the side of the firebox, she sorted through the details. A blockage of the womb. From courses that had failed to flow? Or, heaven forbid, something that had passed into the childbirth passage from elsewhere in the young woman's body? Wait, what had Mrs. Hall said about Old Mo touching the girl?

Suddenly she thought she understood. Mrs. Hall meant Old Mo bore responsibility for his granddaughter's blockage. Could this Ruthie be—the notion stunned her—with child? Surely women who were "no better than they should be" fell into wicked ways and fell prey to unscrupulous men. But could this happen to a girl Ruthie's age, perhaps twelve or thirteen, and, heaven forbid, an old man? A grandfather who should protect her, not assault her.

For a moment she longed to converse with her uncle. As a man of the cloth, he must recognize the presence of evil, perhaps have confronted it before. If a grandfather ensured that his granddaughter was "enceinte," pregnant, with his own child, was that not evil beyond the usual of ordinary men?

She shuddered.

She enlisted Polly briefly to help find the bowls and count out the number needed—the child indicated four, so there couldn't be many taking their noon meal at the inn today. Slicing her aunt's bread with care, she stacked pieces on a plate, gathered up forks, and toted her offerings to the tavern. With its door propped open and a window as well, there was ample light.

Matthew's eyebrows rose when he saw who brought the fixings into the room, but he made no comment, other than to call out the window, "Sukey! Dinner's on."

Almyra didn't recognize either of the men sitting with Matthew. They must be from outside the village. She forced a modest smile, as she presumed one did, in serving paying guests, and set the dishes out. Polly tugged at her skirt and held up a fistful of spoons.

The three men settled around the table. Matthew looked up at Almyra and asked, "Could you fetch those molasses cookies with you when you bring the pot of tea?"

Almyra nodded. She glanced at Polly, who seemed to grasp the request and headed back to the kitchen. "A few minutes for the tea," Almyra said, and followed the child.

Was this what it meant to minister to others? Surely it fit with the Biblical story of Mary and Martha, sisters who met the Lord and took different roles. Mary as perhaps a disciple, certainly a student of the Christ, and Martha laboring to feed some sort of gathering of those doing the ministering. Almyra felt this moment was Martha's doing.

How would Uncle Eliphalet respond if she aired this with him? Was this why women so rarely entered the ministry—because they were better suited to Martha's work than to Mary's?

Caught up in her thoughts, she neglected to add tea leaves to the pot, and only the child's impatient gestures reminded her. She must concentrate. And above all, not inhale the odors of the adjoining room or listen to the cries and murmured assurances.

With Polly's assistance, she located a pan of enormous molasses cookies and placed half a dozen on a plate to carry back to the tavern with the tea. Such a relief to breathe air that only smelled of working men and horses. Susannah perched near the men now, although at her own table. That seemed prudent. Turkish pantaloons or not, a lady must protect herself.

What was this strange set of mind today? Every observation she made seemed the start of a sermon.

Though she'd rather have retreated to her desk and the relative comfort of study and discussion with her uncle, Almyra returned to the kitchen. She set a slice of bread into a bowl, dipped a ladle of thick soup over it, and set in front of Polly with a spoon. The child began to eat as if she noticed no intrusive voices or scents. After a moment's thought, Almyra began to clean dishes.

If the women wanted her in the sickroom, they'd call her, she was sure.

A few minutes later, Mrs. Hall darted through the kitchen, and a door out of the house slammed behind her. When she came back, she carried a lidded milk pail that rattled as though empty. The sounds from the other room seemed more muted. Still, Almyra did her best to not listen, as something wet was added to the pail. Determinedly, she wiped and stacked crockery, spoons, and tinware.

Mrs. Sanborn, her hands grimed and discolored, asked silently for space at the dry sink where she wielded a chunk of lye soap, then quietly asked Almyra to pour clean water as a rinse. Behind them, slower footsteps suggested Mrs. Hall retracing her steps with a laden pail. The disgusting odor threatened again to overwhelm Almyra, and she fumbled for her handkerchief to press to her face.

She felt a tug at her skirt. Polly. She wiped her own eyes and cheeks, then asked the little one, "Would you like your cookie now?"

Mrs. Sanborn patted Almyra's shoulder. "I've asked the child to take you for a walk outside, my dear. It will suit both of you. Mind that you breathe that fresh air for a good bit. Your aunt will want you to walk her home, and she'll call you when it's time."

Outdoors, the soft thickness in the breeze suggested more rain on the way. Almyra followed Polly toward the stables and then around the back of the structure to the brown, barren rows of a garden not yet planted. Or so she thought. Maneuvered by Polly's insistence, she found several rows where buds swelled on short shrubs, and small green triangles pressed upward from the soil. "Mama's," the child said briefly.

So the Halls must have been here since at least the previous summer, Almyra realized. At least some of them, especially Mrs. Hall. She felt foolish, for not observing this before, and promised herself to pay better attention.

She let the child steer her, telling herself it was for Polly's sake, while feeling her own sensibility return with the fresher air. Horse manure seemed mild compared to that sickroom!

A woman's voice called from the front of the house, and Polly, looking up at once, lifted her skirt and ran. Almyra followed with more refinement, and, as expected, found her aunt waiting for her, alongside Mrs. Hall.

"I'll make up a bed for Mrs. Sanborn," Polly's mother was saying, "and we'll see whether the two of us can bring the girl through the night. If the fever breaks, there'll be some hope." She paused, then added in a lower voice, "I'll send for the minister if he's needed. But I daresay there's time still to work with what we have."

Aunt Charlotte nodded, and tucked Almyra's hand into the crook of her own elbow. "You know where to find us, and I'll be sure he's well rested, just in case."

They walked slowly back through the village. Each time Almyra thought she could begin to ask a question, she swallowed the words. The cleanliness and peace of the afternoon seemed more vital than mere information.

But when they'd hung up their cloaks in their own clean, settled kitchen again, and a pot of tea sat in front of them at the well-scrubbed wooden table, Almyra said at last, "I would like to understand."

Aunt Charlotte closed her eyes a moment. Then, slowly, she began an explanation, beginning with a vague description of how a married man and woman would lie together to "go forth and multiply," as Scripture commended. This soon confirmed what Almyra suspected, that Old Mo, in his drunken state, indeed embodied evil, and the state of a girl in such a household was perilous indeed.

Just as the explanation began to grow more detail concerning the contents of the milk pail and its terrible stench, the kitchen door opened with a snap.

Uncle Eliphalet said cheerfully, "Word has it that John Sanborn's on tomorrow's train to St. Johnsbury. I daresay Mrs. Sanborn will spread a meal for company tomorrow evening, my dears."

Aunt Charlotte looked up at her husband in silence a moment, then shook her head. "I daresay she may not have the time to prepare," was the quiet reply. "I believe Almyra and I will make a ham pie for them tomorrow." She turned back to Almyra. "We'd best set more bread to rising, too. Perhaps you'd start the yeast proofing while I talk with your uncle in his study."

For a moment, Almyra wanted to protest, to take part in that conversation. Then a wave of exhaustion struck her, and she realized a quiet kitchen with a small task would suit her perfectly. Nodding her understanding, she rose and donned an apron.

Mary or Martha, she asked herself as she measured out water and flour and stirred them into yesterday's yeasty sponge.

~ 12 ~

Almyra sat on a sun-struck bench behind the livery stables of Matthew Clark's inn. Susannah perched beside her—not exactly sitting, but poised as if ready to leap off,any minute, whether to welcome a horse or to carry a message. Almyra felt just as urgent, especially since she shouldn't be out here in conversation. With John Sanborn due to arrive, she should be helping her aunt with baking, or at least filling the enormous wash boiler and tending the stove.

But she needed to know more about the previous day's efforts, details that Aunt Charlotte wouldn't divulge. Besides, Aunt Charlotte specifically wished to know whether Ruthie Cook's condition had improved. How could she bring home a proper report if she didn't grasp what that condition was?

Susannah sighed with impatience. "You've never seen a birth at all? Not even lambing?"

"I don't go inside the barns during lambing," Almyra protested. "Everyone's too busy for guests, and I'd be useless. Plus all that mud and muck—I don't dare spoil the dresses I have here, now that I can't dash off to Boston."

"No, you can't, can you," Susannah said wryly. "Poor little city girl stuck in the country. Why did you come here, anyway? Didn't you want to stay in Boston?"

Was that an honest question or a taunt? Almyra paused to consider, then gave the simplest explanation. "My mother died. My father's very busy and often not home. And my sisters have both left home for marriage. My aunt and uncle asked me to stay here, and my uncle can help me with my future path." She watched the changes in Susannah's expression, first a hint of shock, then pity, then frank curiosity.

"You mean he'll help you find a husband? Here, in Vermont?"

"No, no, that's not what I mean at all. I'm going to become a minister of the Gospel. To lead a congregation. A church."

Now Susannah looked baffled. "A woman can do that? Be a minister?"

"Yes." The reply called for firmness. She would accomplish this, she knew it. "There haven't been many yet, but I will be one of them. A woman who knows her way can't let her skirts deter her."

After a quick look down at her own Turkish pantaloons, and a half smile, Susannah answered, "I agree. There's no sense in wearing skirts, petticoats, all that foolery, when you're taking care of horses, and riding. But I imagine when I'm married, I'll have to wear my skirts again."

Almyra's sympathies were aroused. "Perhaps you'll marry into a livery business and still have days when you indulge in a more free attire."

"Tchaw. I don't suppose I would, here in North Upton. I can't marry Matthew, can I? He's too old. And the livery fellows in Upton Center and even South Upton are married already." Susannah shook off the notion. "Anyway, you asked about Ruthie. You see, her grandfather, that's Old Mo, he put her in a family way, and she came to my mother for the usual remedy to get rid of it. Except she waited too long, and things got complicated. Then the baby inside her died and started to spoil and made her infected. It smelled terrible. You smelled it, didn't you? I saw your face. I know you did."

This made sense of the previous day but spoiled almost everything else. A grandfather who did that, whatever it was, to a granddaughter. Without anyone stopping it. And a remedy that would—no, Almyra didn't want to think about it further. No wonder Aunt Charlotte kept avoiding the conversation.

Other considerations spilled into her thoughts. Was it wrong or right to provide such a remedy, knowing the consequences? Was it womanly, full of care, or did it come from foreign ways like those of the gypsies that sometimes rode through, or the families visiting with patent medicine wagons? In Boston, of course, there would be dispensaries, perhaps even doctors to assist.

A bell rang from the front of the inn, and Susannah jumped up. "That's the stage arriving. I've got to tend the horses."

The stage! Almyra leapt to her feet also. Her shirtwaist, the working one worn for the morning's kitchen labors, did not suit the impression she wanted to give to John Sanborn if he'd just arrived. Instead of following Susannah toward the front of the inn, she strode as rapidly as she dared around the back of the structure, circling to the road where she'd be more or less out of sight of the stage arriving from the other direction. She must go home and refresh her attire and adjust her hairpins.

As she hurried back to the parsonage, she pictured John Sanborn as she'd last seen him, dressed for the long journey westward. Most likely he'd go home first to see his mother and father before heading to the store to talk with the rest of the neighbors.

So, she had plenty of time to prepare.

Aunt Charlotte wasn't in the kitchen, nor the rest of the house. Uncle Eliphalet, writing in his notebook as he regarded a passage in the Holy Bible, looked up when Almyra paused at the doorway into the study. "Does your aunt need me? No, no, I was to tell you something for her. Ah, she's taking something to the Sanborn house, and would you watch the bread — I think it was bread she mentioned? Oh dear."

Almyra bobbed her head and returned to the kitchen. Yes, the loaves were in the oven; she closed down the draft to the firebox a bit, to slow the heat, then scurried to her chamber to brush her skirt and exchange her waist for something at least a little less worn. Indeed, she scarcely looked like a Boston girl these days, but she could present her most womanly appearance. And she must pin her hair all over again. *How had it come so loose, so quickly?*

As she combed and tucked, she thought further about Susannah's information and perspective. Surely understanding birth mattered when she herself expected to nurture a congregation, leading people along the paths of righteousness "for His Name's sake." Perhaps she might have learned more from her own mother by now, had illness and death not intervened.

Enough. One must not live in the past, or in "perhaps." She rehearsed the most important things she wanted to ask Alice's brother John, about Alice and Caroline, and the West, the railroad business that John and his brother Charles were conducting, and the cause of abolition in the territories. So much to discover!

Her aunt's return brought scant news. Indeed, John Sanborn and another man, an African, had arrived on the stage and had walked into the Sanborn kitchen while Aunt Charlotte provided Mrs. Sanborn with a ham pie and a pan of biscuits.

"She looked exhausted, poor thing, up all night nursing the Cook girl, and still not sure whether the girl will pull through. There's no money for a doctor, but Abigail Sanborn's the best around with childbed fever, surely, so perhaps ...." Aunt Charlotte stopped, looking somewhat worn herself.

Almyra patted her arm. "I talked with Susannah Hall also, and she said her mother will mind the nursing today so Mrs. Sanborn can visit with her son and take some rest, too. With that kitchen full of herbs, I'm sure the Halls can prepare a tisane readily, or whatever else the poor girl needs."

Her aunt sniffed, then turned to check the stove. "We'll have soup for our own noon meal with the remainder of that ham in it. And biscuits, your uncle will appreciate those. Fetch the last jar of strawberry preserves, child, and we'll keep his spirits up. There's no sense burdening him with more, today. And besides," her voice became more brisk, "with two extra men in the village for a few days, we must prepare for guests here as well."

"Only a few days?" What a long journey, from the frontier lands of Illinois, to visit his mother for such a short time. "Why won't John Sanborn stay longer? And who is the African with him? Another settler? Or someone from Boston?"

"Curiosity killed the cat," Aunt Charlotte smiled. "Fetch the preserves first, and a few more splits for the woodbox, if you please."

Smiling, Almyra added the other half of the cat's tale. "But satisfaction cured it. Tell me all, Aunt."

By the end of the noon meal, between Almyra's questions and her uncle's, any cat lingering nearby would have been restored to good health. All went well with Alice and Caroline, Almyra's friends who'd gone West to teach and to forward the cause of another free state for the Union. Alice and John's father's brother, Martin, who'd hauled a printing press to Kansas, now published a weekly broadsheet there. Aunt Charlotte knew nothing of any business that John and Charles were pursuing in Illinois or further west. Of course, one exchange in the Sanborn kitchen did not address everything Almyra wished to know.

"What about the African who came along?"

Uncle Eliphalet looked up from his dish of stewed apples with interest. "African? Is it another freedman, looking for a position on a farm or in a stable?"

Aunt Charlotte shook her head. "I don't believe so. I didn't catch his surname, but John called him Isaiah. I believe he's employed in the central part of the state. There wasn't time to discover his reason for coming here."

"Then I must go discover this myself." Uncle Eliphalet pushed his chair back from the table. "My sermon's done, and I daresay I can spare an hour or so."

"May I accompany you, Uncle?" Almyra couldn't keep from asking.

"Not this time, child. I'm sure there will be a gathering of men forming, whether at the Sanborn farm or the store. That's no place for you." He smiled gently. "Assist your aunt, and I'll deliver an invitation for the visitors to join us for tomorrow's noon meal. Besides, though my sermon is written, I daresay yours is not yet so. Have you chosen your approach to the passage?"

Almyra nodded. "Mine will be complete before supper," she announced. "But there are more things I wish to discuss with you."

"Of course. Later, we will make time to study together." In a trice, he was out the door, and once again the kitchen held only two women, dishes to be cleaned, food to be prepared, and the steamy simmer of the wash boiler at the back of the stove.

I definitely do not wish to follow Martha's example, Almyra told herself, with gritted teeth. She hastened into the tasks, determined to get to her own writing in good time, and trying her best not to wonder more about John Sanborn and his African friend. Or whether they'd come with Uncle Eliphalet for tea and cookies, or perhaps the evening meal.

Just as Aunt Charlotte released her from household necessities to spend time with her effort to write from the Bible text she and her uncle both considered for the week, a boy from the store arrived with a pair of letters. Oh, the stage. Of course there would be a bag of postal items.

One went directly to Uncle Eliphalet's desk. The other, her aunt held for a long moment, smiling, before reading aloud the sender's name. "A. Sanborn. Sent from Springfield, I see. Of course you'll wish me to hold this for you, Almyra, so you can pursue your study in peace." Aunt Charlotte pretended to slip the missive under her own apron, while Almyra laughed and delivered a quick hug, sliding her own hand onto the missive and darting away with it.

She sat at the kitchen table so that her aunt could lean over her shoulder and enjoy the letter at the same time.

*Dearest Almyra,*

*We speak of you daily, missing your companionship and merriment. And soup, of course.* Almyra smiled and hoped Aunt Charlotte would not recognize the enduring humor of "soup" among the friends. *Have you studied the newest fashions? Does the Boston news reach you? We count ourselves grateful for such scraps of muslin or calico as may come our way, and dream of the ample fabric of your green and gold silk skirt. Thus you see how we become frivolous in our desperate straits.*

*You must feel poorly treated, so few letters in an entire three months. So I hasten to announce that Caroline is now an assistant teacher at the Illinois Asylum for the Education of the Deaf and Dumb. Lest you think she has become very grand, know that she is the only assistant teacher here, for the building's first wing has been completed in the past year, the sounds of bricklaying surround us as the second wing rises, and there are ELEVEN students in our portion. However, several dozen more are expected soon.*

*Sharp as you are, I am sure you noted the word "us" and wonder what I am doing here at the school with Caroline. I have leased a small room for an office, around the back, with a sign that says "Territorial Weekly Champion. Subscriptions." Uncle Martin of course is printing his paper at the edge of what is intended to be a town called Lawrence, when the Kansas Territory is properly formed. But he requires that readers in such influential cities as Springfield Illinois subscribe. And likewise in Boston and New York, for which, see the following. At any rate, I am the clerk of subscriptions here! When I can, I also sit with the smallest children from the school, teaching a bit of arithmetic and keeping my hand in for my own profession.*

The writing crossed to the side of the paper, and Almyra rotated the page.

*We have shockingly found many wealthy women here with enslaved girls and women in their kitchens. Like myself, you may have seen slavery as driven by men who demand field workers. I assure you, the demands of women in fine attire appear to be at least as fierce. We try to speak with the workers when we can, at the market and such, but they are often afraid of us. We weep at night. Almyra, they are so shackled by this Evil Power of Darkness. Our hope is in Congress and the Vote. For which the following: Kindly scour your memory for persons in Boston that Uncle Martin may write to. Or those in the weekly papers of New England. This we can do and prepare a list of potent possible subscribers. Send me as many names and their locations as you can, and many who require the breath of freedom will someday benefit. Yours in haste, and always your own in friendship and honor, Alice Sanborn.*

Almyra saw Caroline's scribbled signature wedged under Alice's. Her heart pounded with fury on behalf the women and girls who found themselves without escape or remedy. A sharp intake of breath told her Aunt Charlotte, too, had finished reading the letter.

"We will share this with your uncle," her aunt said firmly, "and then set to work. I believe we might recruit a few others to assist us. And we must discover when Alice's brother John leaves for the frontier lands again, as it may be quicker to send our first list with him, if he goes to Springfield."

Thoughts spinning, Almyra nodded and set the letter on the sideboard. She walked slowly toward her own table, her pages, her notes for a sermon like her uncle's. For a moment she stared at what she'd already written. Then she turned her page and began a new approach to the text. One that established protecting the dignity of human liberty, as a necessary charge for all good people.

She wrote determinedly, though her thoughts often drifted to the very real face and life of Ruthie Cook. Had the fever broken? Would Ruthie survive the attack? How should a person—a woman—best stand for Godliness and human liberty?

The aroma of fried pork and baked beans with molasses reached Almyra at last, as she realized she'd scraped out three more inked pages, and that the low sun indicated she'd written past teatime, nearly to supper. And that the scrape of boots and mingling of voices at the kitchen door indicated that her uncle had returned home and not alone.

~ 13 ~

It might be May by the calendar, but with the sun's setting came a sharp chill. A gust of outdoor air swept in with the men in the kitchen. Almyra caught a whiff of the cold from nearby mountaintops, settling into the village for the evening, underneath a mingling of tobacco, damp wool, and muddy boots.

Her aunt's polite bob toward the huddle of men signaled that this was not only Uncle Eliphalet and Matthew, but it took a moment to focus on the other three men cuffing their feet by the door. By the light of the one kerosene lamp on the table, Almyra picked out narrow shoulders and a military closeness of attire, and realized Captain Young was nodding toward her across the kitchen. She bobbed her own half curtsey but did not move forward.

As the next man turned toward the lamplight, she saw he carried his left arm in a sling. A short bristling beard and untrimmed moustache kept her from recognizing her friend's brother at first. John Sanborn, blue eyes sparkling at her, and a grin that boasted a bright gold tooth to one side. Then the fifth man must be—yes, he came the rest of the way into the kitchen, and it was indeed an African. Isaiah.

Uncle Eliphalet made the introductions, in some haste. When he finally gestured toward Isaiah, he explained, "You won't have met Mr. Hutchinson before, Charlotte. Nor you, Almyra. But he's one of the men who traveled East last season with Charles and John, to bring his expertise from the gold fields to the copper explorations northwest of Hartland."

Ah. Now some pieces came together. Almyra had heard of Isaiah and another African who had come to Vermont with Alice's brothers. She knew that Alice and Caroline had taken part in the men's railroad travel north from Boston, as the dastardly Fugitive Slave Act made all such travel perilous for people with dark skins, even here in northern New England.

But were there any mines in North Upton? If not, what was Isaiah doing here? Exploring the state, with John Sanborn? She doubted it. Instead, Captain Young's presence made her wonder whether this visit involved the politics of abolition.

Introductions complete, her uncle ushered the group toward his study, gathering two chairs from the big table on his way. He told Aunt Charlotte, "We'll conduct our business first, my dear, and perhaps you'll be so kind as to lay out a light supper for us afterward."

Did she dare to follow the men into the study, as if she were part of their gathering? No, she wasn't yet a minister, or even fully an adult. Besides, Aunt Charlotte's faint glaze of panic wasn't lost on her.

"Cornbread," her aunt murmured. "The oven needs to be hotter, so it will be quickly baked. That will go well with the beans. What else, Almyra? What can be prepared in haste?"

"Stewed apple rings? If we place them at the back of the stove, they should be soft for a second course. We can add some dried cherries to give them color. And those salted pecans from Eastertide, they can be set in small dishes." With her aunt's eager nod of approval, Almyra turned out the materials from the pantry shelves, then took over mixing cornbread batter,with drippings from the fried pork added, while her aunt set out bowls and spoons. Considering what she'd heard military men confronted for meals, not to mention her imaginings of miners' fare, the supper should seem ample and tasty. She smiled reassurance toward her aunt. She endeavored to work quietly, so as to overhear as much as possible from the other room.

The clinking of coins in the study startled her. Someone swore, then apologized and dropped his voice. She heard paper rustling, and wondered whether that meant bills of tender, accompanying the coins. Was someone being paid? Or exchanging currency for some goods or favors? She edged closer to the half-open door.

"Drifting here from both Peacham and St. Johnsbury," Matthew declared to the others. "We see more of them daily. But I can't think the forgeries begin here. Boston was my guess."

Other voices overlapped. Then Uncle Eliphalet added clearly, "My niece suggested these are coming across from Canada. She suggested that landowners with trade on both sides of the line could readily move the currency."

Someone else spoke, muffled, and her uncle replied, "Yes, well, she's a good thinker, and quick to notice things. She's studying for the ministry, you know."

Almyra blushed. Her uncle would never have said such a compliment directly to her, for fear of encouraging sinful pride.

She shouldn't be trying to overhear them. Her face now flaming with embarrassment, she spooned the cornmeal batter into a sizzling-hot cast iron pan and slid it into the oven, bending close enough to excuse the flush on her cheeks. All the dishes on top of the stove needed stirring and moving around, too, set to lower heat on the surface, now that the firebox worked fiercely to start the baking.

A knock at the outer door spun Aunt Charlotte in a panicked hurry to open it as she muttered, "Oh no, not more."

Almyra moved to see. Susannah's older sister stood in the doorway, in a dark cloak and head scarf, wet with rain. She leaned close to Aunt Charlotte and murmured something.

"Oh. Oh my dear, that is terrible. Do you need the minister? Yes? You don't need to wait; I'll send him after you. Oh dear, oh dear."

The sister, what was her name? Ah, Jane. She turned and was gone, as Almyra's aunt shut the door slowly. Her pursed lips and lowered gaze told the news.

Almyra spoke anyway. "The Cook girl? Ruthie?"

Aunt Charlotte nodded heavily. "Gone." She looked anxiously at the stove. "I don't see how to do this."

Reaching to ease the air slots on the firebox smaller, to damp the flame, Almyra suggested, "We'll slow it all down. There won't be much for Uncle to do, other than to comfort Mrs. Hall should she need it."

"Then I should go with him," her aunt said abruptly. "Mrs. Sanborn is likely to be there also. And that's the end of serving a proper supper."

Crisply, Almyra disagreed. "You may stay with the women, Aunt, if needed. There's sure to be something hot and waiting there, with Mrs. Hall cooking for the inn all the time. I shall dish up the meal here in half an hour, and at least the men will be fed. Who knows, you may be here again yourself by then."

So it indeed proved to be. Given the news, Uncle Eliphalet hurried from the house with Aunt Charlotte at his heels. Captain Young nodded toward Almyra in a friendly fashion but closed the door to the study firmly so she could overhear nothing more. And just as her crisply browned cornbread came out of the oven, both her uncle and aunt retuned, shaking off wet outer garments. The commotion brought the others from the study, and the six of them sat down to a meal that, in Almyra's opinion, at the least would rival a good inn's provisioning.

She waited until the men's bowls were half empty, then asked quietly, "Has your work in Hartland gone well, sir?"

Isaiah looked startled for a moment, to be addressed at the table and perhaps also to be called "sir." But Almyra didn't know his surname, to her own embarrassment.

His voice was deep and slow, and she didn't know whether he spoke as a Southerner would, or a Westerner. But he clearly knew her name and wasn't shy. "That's very kind of you to ask, Miss Almyra. We've almost finished the assay work for the three copper mines near Thetford. I expect Walter and I will work ourselves out of a job there for the time being." He smiled. "Which makes it quite fortunate that we're needed in Brome County for perhaps four more mines."

"Brome County? I don't know the name. It's not in Vermont, is it?"

Captain Young's eyes sparkled, as if he realized how Almyra was excavating for information. "It's across the border in Lower Canada — that is to say, in Canada, as we must now call the united provinces of Upper and Lower. And we understand you're already acquainted with one of the leading families farming wheat and milling it, on both sides of the line."

Almyra gasped. "The Blake family? Oh, but I've only met an African who works there and has taken the name. That's not the same as knowing the family."

Her uncle lifted an eyebrow but allowed Captain Young to reply. "No, of course it's not. Yet it's a start, and we'd value your assistance in helping Mr. Sanborn and Mr. Hutchinson to meet the Blakes and begin their investigation. That is, their assay work for the mining companies."

"Investigation?" It was Almyra's turn to aim an inquisitive look at the captain. "This wouldn't have to do with a certain Mr. Pinkerton, would it? And, if I recall correctly, Foster Pierce?"

Her aunt interjected, "This hardly sounds like a fitting conversation for the supper table, my dear. Or," she looked meaningfully at Uncle Eliphalet, "for an evening when there's loss to be addressed in the village."

Matthew finally spoke up. "Your pardon, ma'am, but I believe Mrs. Sanborn and her husband are best suited to sitting with the Cook family tonight, all things considered. No doubt we'll know their wishes by morning. And though I'm sorry to weight your supper table with such topics, I'm afraid we're short of time."

Uncle Eliphalet nodded. "Though Mo Cook was never a godly man, it will still take time for the family members to hear of his death. I'll provide only a short graveside service on the morrow. Meanwhile, I'm afraid there's a pressing need for Almyra to ride to Peacham in the morning, weather permitting, of course with Susannah to accompany her. We've also sent word to Miss Farrow and Doctor Jewett in St. Johnsbury. If we're to stop those ruffians from dragging down the region and the movement, with their forged currency, we've no time to lose."

"But she's too young to go gallivanting around the countryside, no matter the vital mission," Aunt Charlotte objected.

Captain Young said quietly, "You've a fine young woman here, ma'am, and we won't place her in danger. But if she can open the doors for the others to move forward on this, she'll be doing a great favor to the cause. A cause I know you favor yourself, ma'am, for you've told me so in the past."

Almyra held her breath. She dreaded spending hours on the miserable sidesaddle again, and she wasn't clear what these men expected her to do in Peacham. But if it meant something to the battle against the Slave Power, she wanted to take part.

Her aunt seemed to follow the same line of reasoning. After a moment, she sighed. "Very well. But only to Peacham, only with a companion, and the rest of the details shall follow our meal, if you please. The guidelines of both manners and digestion recommend a more fitting topic for the table."

When all manner of supper items had been removed from the table, Almyra looked hopefully at her aunt, who nodded. The details of her mission for the next day, however, seemed vague and awkward. Her uncle and the other gentlemen wished her to make the acquaintance of whichever members of the Blake household might be at the Peacham house now—and establish a reason to visit their farm north of the border.

"But that is a social call," Almyra objected. "That is, I wished—I thought you meant me to actually do something. An action toward ...." Her voice faltered. The faces around her displayed amusement, although kindly.

Aunt Charlotte explained, "You are opening a door for action that reaches far beyond this moment. If your uncle can approach the Blake residence near Memphremagog as a neighbor of sorts, he in turn can open a path for Mr. Hutchinson to be present. Then even for Mr. McBride, should he reach here in a timely fashion."

The mention of Simon McBride, newly married to her own Boston sister and known to be a political assistant to the mighty Abolitionist William Seward himself, convinced her at last. She asked, "Has Susannah consented already? About tomorrow?"

"Yes," Matthew assured her. "Not that we took it for granted that you would go, but we surely did hope you might agree. We thank you, Almyra."

And with that, her uncle rose from his chair and the other men joined him to stroll toward the inn together in the deepening twilight. A whiff of newly lit tobacco drifted back to Almyra as she closed the kitchen door and turned to meet her aunt's assessing gaze.

"Afraid?"

"No. That is, I don't know how to do this. But it doesn't frighten me."

"Fair enough," Aunt Charlotte said firmly. "Come, let us restore order to the house, and rehearse some lines of gentle sociality as we do so."

$$\sim 14 \sim$$

This time everything went more quickly and more quietly. Partly, Almyra realized, this impression came from the time they departed—before the sun came fully above the hills, while most in North Upton tended animals in barns, or stoves in kitchens. She and Susannah mounted on the same horses as before, although it salved Almyra's pride that Susannah didn't hitch a tether between the two animals this time.

Riding was less painful, too, even though the rubbed area on her thigh still chafed. This time, Almyra had padded the region discreetly with her aunt's assistance, before walking to the inn's stable. The added fabric bunched up some under her petticoats, but oh, such a relief it provided, up on the horn of the saddle.

Without needing to discuss it, they took the circular road around Upton Center, crossing paths with only one wagon and a lone rider headed the other way. At midmorning they reached South Upton and stopped briefly to water and feed their horses, while Susannah delivered a paper-wrapped parcel to someone within.

Then they rode directly to the Johnson farm. Mr. Johnson came out of his barn as they let the horses walk toward the farmhouse. Almyra noticed that he held a heavy-headed hammer, as if he'd been mending fence or a stanchion. It hung alongside his leg, ready to swing. When he recognized them, however, he set it down next to the barn door and stepped up to greet them.

"I confess, I'm surprised to see you again so soon. There's no packet ready to carry yet. Or are you bringing something here from St. Johnsbury?" Almyra appreciated the mild tone of inquiry, even as his sharp eyes never left their faces.

She leaned forward to speak quietly. "Sir, I regret the lack of notice. But might your wife be at home? I'm in need of her assistance, to be able to talk with one of your neighbors."

Minutes later, with Susannah leaning against the barn and the horses tied, Almyra followed Mr. Johnson around to the side of the house as he called out to anyone who might hear, "I have a guest for a cup of tea, from out of town."

A flicker at an upstairs window suggested someone moving out of sight, while Mrs. Johnson came to the kitchen door and stiffly invited them to enter. Almyra could witness their interaction—his nod of reassurance, before he stepped across to fill the kettle with water from a pump next to the dry sink, and her initial alarm quieted as she waved toward the wooden chairs at a well-scrubbed table.

"Word from Miss Farrow, or the doctor?"

"No, ma'am, and I do apologize for calling on you without invitation. But if you'll allow me to go straight to the point, I'm in urgent need of an introduction to the Blake family in order to forward a connection for some gentlemen riding north later in the week. I hoped perhaps you could help."

The elderly woman asked sharply, "You're not moving someone across the border, are you? There's no need for that here. There's the horse farm in West Upton, for one thing, or rooms in Hardwick if there's more immediate danger."

Almyra shook her head. Mrs. Johnson of course meant providing sanctuary for a fugitive, whether dark-skinned or otherwise. "That's not the case this time," she said carefully. She would have liked to explain at length, about the forgeries, the weakening of funding, even the copper mining although she wasn't quite sure how this fit in, but her aunt had been firm. Say only what's needed. "Least said, soonest mended," as the expression went.

So Almyra gave the explanation she'd rehearsed the previous evening. "It's a matter of establishing some trusted persons for messages only," she said. "I've to make the acquaintance of some of the Blake family because the brothers own so much property along the borderline. I'm sorry to hold back other explanations, ma'am, but I know you're aware that it's best to keep some things quiet."

"Hmm." Mrs. Johnson clearly wasn't convinced. "I wouldn't necessarily trust the Blakes."

Aunt Charlotte had prepared Almyra with a second approach for such a case. As Mr. Johnson set a steaming teapot on the table and stepped back next to his wife, who'd remained standing, Almyra continued: "May I add that the intention is to reunite a family that's been separated, as members of the household strive to locate each other? I'm sure you're aware that Mr. Blake's grandfather was a slave owner in his time."

Mr. Johnson cut in, "He emancipated them all upon his death. Which was almost twenty years ago now, just before the British Empire's abolition of slavery. There hasn't been a single accusation against the Blakes since then."

"No, of course not," Almyra assured him. "But we have word through a certain Pennsylvanian Vermonter that there are other family members who've found Philadelphia too risky, and we'd like to make sure their communications go to the correct persons. So they'll be hand carried for the time being."

This indirect reference to Senator Thaddeus Stevens, of whom all Peacham residents were inordinately proud for his abolitionist stance and labors in Congress, seemed to melt the frost in the room. Mr. Johnson nodded to Mrs. Johnson, who said in turn, "I can direct you on an errand to Mrs. Blake, if you ride well enough not to break a few dozen eggs."

Almyra blushed. "I might not be a skilled rider yet," she admitted, "but Susannah Hall, who accompanies me, could surely do this with success."

At this, Mrs. Johnson unbent far enough to pour tea into two cups on the table and left the room to fetch pen and ink and a bit of paper. Her husband remained near the stove, adjusting the firebox while also clearly keeping an eye on Almyra and glancing out the open door to where Susannah now stood talking with a young man half shaded by the barn door.

Almyra sipped gratefully at her tea, mindful to raise and lower the cup in a polite fashion. The tension in the room still felt thick and edged, but she'd made progress toward what she and Aunt Charlotte had planned. *Please let Susannah be adept with packing the eggs,* she thought. *How do you carry eggs on a moving horse and not break them?*

Soon enough, though, their horses carried them half a mile closer to Peacham village, and across a short wooden bridge into the yard of a clearly prosperous farm. Wooden fencing stood whitewashed, the track's ruts cut deep with steady use, and several wagons and more comfortable conveyances stood visible in a long carriage shed. At the kitchen door, a short woman in an apron and bonnet greeted them—though Almyra could barely parse the words spoken, since the woman's accent marked her as not long since arrived from Ireland.

Handing over the case of eggs that she'd transported, Susannah seemed able to understand the cook, and replied, "If it's not too much trouble, we've a message for Mrs. Blake herself. Is she home?"

A clearly apologetic reply followed. Apparently Mrs. Blake must be out making calls. How unusual, a farmhouse with a servant, and the lady of the house free from the kitchen. Almyra admired Susannah's continued negotiations, which led to a young man greeting them in an interior chamber, part library, part accounting room.

"Adam Blake at your service, ladies." The tall youth's sparkling eyes fastened with appreciation on Almyra, and he gave a half bow. She returned a modest curtsey, careful not to dislodge her padding. He continued, "Lucy tells me you've called to see my mother? I regret she is not expected to return until mid- afternoon. May I provide her with some message?"

Though her riding glove scarcely fitted the usual manner, Almyra extended her hand with an arched arm, fluttering her eyelids slightly as if impressed. "Master Blake, such a pleasure to make your acquaintance. I'm Almyra Alexander from North Upton. We were asked simply to let your mother know that Mrs. Johnson has her woolens ready for her, as we pass through."

Curiosity flickered in the young man's face. "Pass through? And where are you headed? Do you require an escort?"

Almyra gave a girlish titter. "Why, I don't know what my aunt would say to an escort I've only just met. After all, I have Susannah here with me, and it's broad daylight. Are you telling me there are brigands along Peacham's main street, in this season?"

Adam Blake barely spared a glance for Susannah, moving closer instead to Almyra. "Not at all, but how shall I make your better acquaintance if I don't keep you company on your ride? Won't you permit me?"

"I couldn't possibly detach you from your home on such a feeble excuse," Almyra flirted back. "But I do trust you'll let your mama know her message from Mrs. Johnson, and perhaps you and I shall meet again. Perhaps you'd care to visit my uncle's church in North Upton—he is an accomplished preacher, you know."

This seemed to induce mixed feelings in the Blake youth, who swallowed hard, then persisted. "I shall certainly inquire about a visit to North Upton," he responded. "Though I'm not always in Peacham, which challenges my time for travel nearby."

Almyra dared push this just a bit farther. "Oh yes," she said, with a quick smile, "isn't your farm connected to the mills in Lower Quebec? I do believe I've heard of them. You must be very much engaged in travel north, and back again."

A small snort from Susannah indicated her companion was losing patience with this dance of words. So Almyra added, "Oh, Sukey, don't you think it's marvelous that a family's milling spans such a distance? I could never ride so far."

Her blush, which really reflected her own rising embarrassment at saying such nonsense, clearly indicated something different to Adam Blake. "There's a stage route," he urged, "and if you came to visit our Canada lands, of course we'd make you welcome." His nod included Susannah, in a dismissive sort of way, as he continued to focus on Almyra.

She was starting to feel like a Boston market display and opted to end the discussion before some version of pricing emerged from the conversation. "Well then, who can tell? I will certainly ask my uncle to call at your Canada lands, should he cross the border this summer." She bobbed a half curtsey, again fluttering her eyelids, then turned to Susannah. "Sukey, we should be on our way."

Somehow they made it back out to the yard, where a man in work clothes gestured toward a mounting block. Susannah of course swung up into her saddle without need of such a device, but Almyra, attempting the same sweet-and-grateful smile she'd used inside, led her horse to the block, to make things easier and allow her to adjust all her fittings.

Susannah led the way back to the main road, but to Almyra's surprise turned her mount to the left, toward the main village. Almyra hurried to catch up. "Aren't we headed home? We've done what they asked for."

"Not the way we came," Susannah called over one shoulder. "Mind now, single file on this road, there'll be wagons for sure. No, we'll circle through Peacham Hollow. I've another parcel to deliver, and then we'll take the Daniels farm road homeward."

Grimly, Almyra hitched her skirt and petticoats into the best positions she could. It seemed clear that she wouldn't be off the horse for some time yet. However, she'd accomplished more than her assignment. For young Master Blake would urge his parents to welcome Uncle Eliphalet across the Canada border.

Despite this satisfaction, she scolded herself. What a dreadful flirtation she'd just portrayed, and none of it truthful. Was this any fit preparation for a serious role in the ministry?

For once, she failed to see a sermon's theme emerge from the moment. She pressed forward in her contemplation, seeking some benefit from the experience. But what she saw instead, very clearly, was another of Susannah's deliveries of bottles that clinked gently. Surely those were not liquor. And if not liquor—were these more of Mrs. Hall's kitchen-brewed remedies?

Almyra shivered. Would another woman find herself bleeding or infected from such treatment? What else could the bottles contain, and how dangerous were their contents?

~ 15 ~

Inside the cool, damp stables, Almyra held the bridle of her unsaddled horse and leaned against an upright beam, to steady herself. There'd been no nice long break on this ride—only the hurry to make the precious connection with the Blake family, then see Susannah provide a second parcel, and what felt like an endless ride back to North Upton. Yes, they had paused after crossing Joe's Brook on yet another wooden bridge. But that wasn't the length of rest her body now craved.

Almyra had tried to begin a conversation then by the bridge asking about the parcels. After an exasperated huff, Susannah had only snapped, "I can't get over to Peacham all that often, you know. My mother's been worried all week about things getting here."

Then she refused to say more, nimbly mounting her own horse and starting across the rattling bridge, the rushing waters thick and brown. Almyra didn't dare let Susannah get too far ahead; her own horse might indeed know how to return to the stables, but what route through thick woods or across too-deep rivers might it select?

At last, waiting behind the Clark inn for Susannah to finish taking the saddle and other gear off the first horse, Almyra mused aloud. "There must be women who are left to manage childbirth and illness on their own. Without Mrs. Sanborn or others like her, and without the various tinctures and such that your mother provides. Even without a sister or mother to assist them. What happens to them?"

Susannah made a rude sound and switched to the other side of her horse, with a wide brush in hand. "Either they die, or they don't. And it's not always the result you'd expect. We've seen strong women fail, and fragile ones somehow keep going."

"Perhaps their prayers comfort them. Do you think so?"

Susannah glared across the horse's neck. "I've never known a prayer to give as much comfort as a well-managed cookstove and a kettle of hot supper."

Despite this disrespect for prayer, Almyra choked back a chuckle. "I'm ready for both of those," she admitted. "I suppose I can't just leave this horse with you and go home to my aunt?"

"Not if you want to ever travel again with me," came the sharp response.

"Then you should be teaching me to do some of this work so we can be done with it more quickly."

After a quick surprised glance, Susannah placed her own horse in its stable, leaning back so that Almyra could see the fastenings and giving a slow demonstration of how much grain to place in a pail. Then, eyebrows lifted in evaluation, she approached Almyra and began to give directions.

My skirt can be brushed clean later, Almyra told herself as she reached for Susannah's clumsy wood-backed tool and began to clean the animal's sides. She hoped the restless horse's hoofs would not land on her own thin-shod feet. Where did one commission riding boots for a woman so far from the Boston shops? Could the local cobbler craft a pair for her? How could she pay the cost?

Susannah leaned close to help her figure how to clean the horse's face.

"What about this part, the long hair here, the mane?"

"Don't bother, it's all matted. If I have time later, I'll pick at it a bit. But it doesn't really matter, as long as the bridle goes on and off properly."

That couldn't really be true. Almyra guessed the mane could matter for the animal's health, as well as its appearance. But she had other things to ask. "The remedies you carried today. Were they all the same?'

"Naw." Susannah ran her hands down each leg of the horse in turn, feeling for something. "The bottles at Greenbank's Hollow, those were for the mill owner. Strengthening, like. For vitality. His wife asked for those."

Avoiding the subject of the mill owner's "vitality," Almyra pressed instead, "And outside East Peacham?"

"Tansy, rue, wormwood, yarrow," came the quick recitation. "And oil of pennyroyal. Mother adds oil of peppermint as well, for digestion."

Almyra waited for Susannah to add more.

"You must be careful when and how it's taken," the girl added. "Mother always tells them. What happened to Ruthie Cook, that wasn't my mother's doing. She said how to do it right. And Ruthie must have done                    it                    wrong."

Almyra nodded, made a reassuring hum of agreement. Best to avoid this part. "How far away are the women who ask for remedies? Do you carry all of them yourself?"

But this seemed more than Susannah could answer, or perhaps she didn't want to. A shake of her head and fresh attention to correcting Almyra's effort to close the stable gate made it clear there'd been enough on the subject.

Almyra straightened, shook hay out of her skirt, and declared, "There's supper waiting. My aunt will want to know all we've seen and done today."

"Don't be telling her Mother's recipes in remedies," Susannah cautioned. "She's not for sharing in that way."

"You could come with me for supper," Almyra said tentatively. She felt polite, but a bit awkward.

"Some other time." A glance toward the animals and a half smile made Almyra glad she'd asked to learn some horse care. There weren't many young and unattached women in North Upton; she'd best find friendship where she could.

If indeed Susannah had come to supper with her, Almyra suddenly realized that the same manners would require taking a meal with the Halls. Well, she already knew Mrs. Hall to be a good cook.

Matthew met them at the barn door and gestured toward the house. "Best get inside, Sukey. Your mother says she needs you in the kitchen." He nodded to Almyra. "Heard the two of you made a quick journey today. Tell your uncle from me, four more bad pennies here, all headed south."

Almyra repeated the message, then bolted toward the parsonage. Supper called to her, but even more importantly, she wanted to unburden her garments of the extra padding and place her latest discoveries into perspective with her uncle and aunt.

Aunt Charlotte met her at the kitchen door and urged her away from the front rooms of the house where men's voices rose in merriment.

"Captain Young," her aunt hissed, and pressed her toward her chamber. "Be quick."

The presence of Captain Young at the parsonage meant she must swiftly remove her extra layers and change to more appropriate attire. A ewer of warm water for washing awaited her in her chamber, a thoughtful and timely gift from her aunt. Indeed, the aromas in the house suggested Aunt Charlotte had prepared well beyond a casual supper—a proper evening dinner instead. Almyra fumbled with her petticoat's strings and the tiny buttons of her cuffs. This was no time to be fatigued. And her hair must be re-pinned.

A few minutes later she stepped back into the kitchen, feeling "put together" again, just in time to help carry the first course, a golden broth, to the gentlemen. This time Captain Young was the only guest, and he and Uncle Eliphalet seemed on warm terms, discussing the condition of the Bayley–Hazen military road, now simply a route for trade. "The blockhouse in Greensboro collapsed some years ago," said Captain Young, who then ceased speaking in order to draw out Aunt Charlotte's chair for her.

After several other topics considered suitable for a mixed table engaging ladies, Aunt Charlotte took the leap into the exchange of information that Almyra longed for, asking first of Uncle Eliphalet, "Do you have news from Judge Paddock, regarding those deceitful printed bills that so concerned you last week?"

Uncle Eliphalet gestured toward Captain Young who admitted, "We know a great deal more than we did, but much of this concerns larger towns and the contributions toward political efforts. There seems widespread agreement that many of the forgeries do come from just north of the border of Canada proper, where a dozen or more miscreants have taken up residence as a group in the small farming towns."

Almyra leaned forward. "How is it accomplished? I know so little of printing. Do they steal the blocks from banks, and ink them there?"

The captain smiled. "Strange though it seems, they number gifted artists among them, who draw and sign the designs themselves, then form their own printing plates. I believe you saw the pages that

Matthew Clark uses to discern which bills are good and which are fraudulent?"

"Yes, of course."

"Week by week the pages must be adjusted, as the villains craft new artwork that can be entirely convincing. Look here." From a folded leather pocketbook, he withdrew two printed bills. "If I were to tell you that one is fraudulent and the other is valid, how would you choose?"

The two slips of paper looked similar to Almyra, the signatures of bank officers florid and clear, the images—on one, Lady Liberty, and on the other, Justice holding her scales, blindfolded—seemed elegant and formal, and even the colors of the ink and paper seemed similar. At last she guessed, "I would hazard that the more worn one is more likely to be valid, for it's clearly been honored in many hands already."

Aunt Charlotte nodded her agreement. But the captain gave a wry smile and said, "You'd be in good company. But it's a clever forgery that's been deliberately aged. The womenfolk among the criminals are expert in this process, as well as in what is called shoving, providing the forged bills as payment for smaller amounts so that they receive good money in exchange. There's little hope of sorting the issue without an expert, and the villains take full advantage of this."

Uncle Eliphalet added, "Judge Paddock reports that as much as one quarter of the funds donated toward Congressional campaigns to oppose Senator Douglas's latest bill have failed to pass bank scrutiny. And reports from Congress indicate the bill may come perilously close to passage by the end of the month of May."

A shiver of apprehension coursed down Almyra's back. She turned to her aunt to ask, "What about Alice and Caroline? In Illinois, they must be outspoken about this injustice. Alice's uncle and his printing press on the Kansas frontier, is there danger for him?"

Captain Young gestured reassuringly before Aunt Charlotte could reply. "This is a democratic republic. There's no cause to fear harm on account of political expression. Look at the law against dueling, some fifteen years ago. Since then, most opponents have been persuaded to settle their issues in other ways. You may lay your concern in other areas, instead. Which brings me to my request."

All around the table froze in anticipation. Almyra felt her heart pounding. Her older friend Alice, she knew, had once ridden north toward the border in a March snowstorm. This was May, a far easier season, but still—would she ride, like Alice, northward, to do something important for the pressing needs of the abolitionists? She could see herself clinging to a horse's neck, urging it forward, while a somewhat younger version of Captain Young—an elegant version perhaps of his nephew Sam, the stage driver—rode dashingly at her side.

Aunt Charlotte leaned forward, meeting the captain's gaze steadily. "We will of course do whatever morally can be done to assist you," she said quietly.

Her husband cleared his throat. "The captain would like me to accompany John Sanborn and the African on their mission to the Canadian copper mines. To Stanstead Plain first. Perhaps Potton also, to meet the Blake family there. And then to stop in the village of Upton, Canada where there is word of a cabal of the counterfeiters, and assess what can be done to halt their efforts. Only assess," he emphasized, grasping Aunt Charlotte's wrist. "Only assess."

Almyra realized that Captain Young was watching her, not her relatives. As she attempted to dismiss any disappointment from her own face, as well as an uncomfortable tightness in her chest, she noted his sympathetic expression. "We have no role corresponding to that of the counterfeiters' wives," he admitted with a regretful half smile. "Still, Mr. Alexander can't undertake this journey without a great deal of support from his family. And I understand that his position in the church will need attention, and that there is someone here at the table capable of filling that gap while he pursues his task. Is that not so, Miss Alexander?"

Under Aunt Charlotte's sharp gaze, Almyra could only swallow hard, force her face to an accepting and, if possible, courageous expression, and reply, "I shall be honored to do my part."

## ~ 16 ~

Heavy rain slid in overnight, and at breakfast, Uncle Eliphalet announced that the men's journey north would not begin til the next morning. "Which," he added cheerfully, "will allow time to review a Scripture passage together and adapt one of my sermons to your use."

Almyra looked up from her porridge, startled. "Why, Uncle, I planned to write a fresh sermon on my own. Tis only Wednesday, so if I begin now …" She faltered at the grave look he gave her, with a negative shake of his head.

"Dear girl, four days may be adequate for one who has already studied the material in depth and has few distractions. But we cannot describe you yet in such a manner, I fear. No, this is why I pen my sermons into my notebooks—for just such an occasion. Let us look back, say, five years, and find something that is both fitting for the moment and adaptable to your presentation."

Aunt Charlotte shooed them off to study together, and Almyra discovered without surprise that her uncle wished her to use a sermon based on chapter 13 of the book of Matthew. After all, the passage was all about planting seeds, timed well for the farm families and all those who depended on such efforts. "Which of course is all of us," Almyra pointed out, "for how should any of us be fed without seeds sown first?"

"Indeed. And here is one of my sermons that makes that very point. Now, let us refine it to a shorter address, one that you may deliver within an hour or so of the morning. We mustn't presume the congregation will wish to listen for longer than that, to a substitute in the pulpit. I believe we might then add some additional hymns to sing, and an extra psalm to line out." Glumly, Almyra agreed. This did not sound like an opportunity to stretch her own thinking. Surely Miss Clarissa Danforth would have made the most of such work—though she'd preached so many years ago that it was hard to say now whether her sermons had been wise ones. The only sample Almyra had ever found was old-fashioned in diction, printed as a circular, and dull in thought. Why did women not assist each other to advance into the ministry, and any other direction beyond simply teaching in village schools? How dim the future of women would be if they did not band together. Marriage, however, could undo such weaving of support. Almyra sighed. Struggling to find a silver lining to her own dark cloud, she reminded herself that her labor in this way would make her uncle's own efforts possible, and what took place across the border would be significant.

She spent the rest of the morning copying out the selected portion of her uncle's sermon into her own pages, occasionally altering a phrase here and there—to reflect her own city upbringing, and of course her gender.

The aromas of the noon meal encouraged her to work more speedily so that she would not have to face such dull effort again after eating. She inked a note to the side about the enemy who planted bad seeds among the good wheat, reflecting on the Slave Power as she did so. Perhaps she'd craft her own homily later for use in a future class or pulpit. This cheered her a bit, just in time to join her aunt over an excellent lamb stew.

"Where is Uncle Eliphalet?"

"Oh, you know how men are, they all gathered at the store this morning and are probably still parsing the news in the Boston papers." Aunt Charlotte pursed her lips in frustration. "Who would have guessed, two years after Miss Stowe's eloquent revelations in *Uncle Tom's Cabin* that abolition would not have come to pass? Perhaps we ladies must become more forceful, ensuring that the men grasp the moral points with urgency."

Almyra agreed, wishing she could turn Uncle Eliphalet's sermon into something that made exactly that point. Or, alternatively, that she could ride to Canada and have some effect, though she could not see clearly how the expedition might change things. She drifted back to her desk, hoping to finish her task soon.

A rap at the kitchen door interrupted at mid-afternoon. Susannah! Almyra hurried to let her into the kitchen.

"Can you sit down for tea?" Turning toward her aunt, she asked, "Perhaps we could all sit down together?"

But Susannah shook her head impatiently. "I can't be visiting, not today, there's too much to do this afternoon and I have to get back to help. But Matthew asked me to convey word to your uncle. Is he here?"

Aunt Charlotte replied, "He'll be back shortly, Susannah. I believe he went to call on Mr. Sanborn."

Susannah blinked, nodded, then said, "Might I ask you to tell him for me, ma'am? I really don't have time to go to the Sanborn place just now. It's just, Matthew wanted to tell him there's no conveyance on hand, but he has four horses for the morning."

"Matthew's not going with them?" The minute she asked, Almyra felt foolish. Surely her uncle, Captain Young, and John Sanborn were sufficient to escort Isaiah safely across the border into Canada, and once there, who would harm them?

A scornful glance from Susannah confirmed it had been a foolish question. "Matthew can't leave the inn to itself," came the sharp response. "And Mother's in the midst of bottling a large batch, so I need to help her."

"Wait," Almyra said impulsively. "Would it help if I came to assist for an hour or two?" She turned to her aunt. "My sermon's nearly complete."

"Complete it first, then," her aunt said. "And it would be a kindness if you'd bring in a bit more wood from the shed before you go out."

Almyra nodded. She turned to Susannah. "I'll be there in half an hour."

It wouldn't do to have Uncle Eliphalet think she'd hurried and left details incomplete. First, be the minister in training, she reminded herself. But it truly didn't take long. Aunt Charlotte reminded her to carry an apron with her, and after two quick armfuls of split wood moved from the shed to the kitchen wood box, she dashed outside into an almost warm May afternoon.

Several older men sat outside the store, and Almyra gave a polite nod and smile as she passed. Her uncle was not among them, so she presumed he must have gone with another man for the noon meal and be paying a call on a family. Though it seemed unduly thoughtless of him not to have told Aunt Charlotte.

Clean sheets hung outside the Carr home. Raw soil alongside Mr. Morse's house showed an early start to a vegetable bed. Was this what it felt like to tend a flock, examining each home for the activities of the family living there? Or was it simply a womanly activity? She watched for young Polly Hall, who seemed to scurry so often along the roadsides in the evenings. Perhaps it was still too early in the day for whatever the child did then.

All the Hall girls were in their steamy kitchen with their mother. A clatter of pans and glass bottles and instructions filled the air as thickly as the steam. Sniffing curiously, Almyra said, "Wintergreen? Spearmint?"

"Some of each, in different tonics," Mrs. Hall confirmed with an approving nod. "And our Polly's been out on the hill and gathered a good mess of dandelion greens. Sukey, mind now, don't let the molasses come to a boil. Quick, move it off the stove."

Jane, Susannah's older sister, hissed like an angry hen from the other side of the room where she flourished a small iron ladle. "Place Sukey over here, Mother, and I'll return to the stove. If it doesn't look or smell like a horse, she can't pay enough mind to it."

"And if it can't reflect your face, you don't want to clean it," Susannah retorted. Her face glowed red with the stove's heat and with emotion. Mrs. Hall gestured for her daughters to exchange places, and Almyra joined Susannah at a table cluttered with short glass bottles, some full and corked, some still empty.

Recalling what she'd learned before, Almyra asked, "Should I tie some sort of string around the necks?"

"No need." Susannah pointed to the filled bottles. "The green shows well enough, and they'll be empty in just a few days. These are all spring tonic, and Mother says we need close to fifty of them. If you'll hold the bottle and funnel, I'll dip from the kettle."

They worked steadily, with an occasional pause to set filled bottles into large baskets on the floor. Polly, positioned as usual under the table, seized each basket in turn to tighten the fit of the contents by stuffing handfuls of musty-looking wool around and between the bottled portions.

"One teacup molasses, three tablespoons sulfur." Mrs. Hall counted aloud as she measured other ingredients. Jane pushed up close to her, and Almyra noticed how similar the two of them looked.

Susannah elbowed her. "Pay attention over here. You've got to move those full ones and set a row of empty ones in place."

"Do all of these go out to other places?"

"More than half of them do. More, really, if you count Upton Center. Mother sends a dozen of them there."

"Twenty this time," Mrs. Hall corrected, seeming able to hear all her daughters at once while measuring and stirring. "And I wouldn't be surprised if there's call for a second batch after that. You'll need to mind carefully who asks for more, Sukey. And mind the pence you accept, for I'm sure there were two leaden ones in the last batch of payment you brought in."

"As if I could help that, when they're all rushing at me at once," Susannah retorted. "Send Jane if you want someone who'll stand there and check every coin."

"For Upton Center, I may do just that," her mother said, still measuring and stirring.

The sulfur odor permeated the room. Almyra felt it burn her throat, and she tugged out her handkerchief to dab at her nose. In a low voice, Susannah offered reassurance. "Just a few more. We'll finish putting up the green tonic and then go out to the horses. Mother won't want us handling the sulfur anyway."

Under the table, Polly wore a length of fabric across her face like some sort of mask, and danced a dolly up and down, humming. Jane's steady litany of minor complaints continued. Almyra wondered how anyone could think, let alone contemplate ethics or morality amid such chaos.

Aha, she realized. That's another sermon in the making. Knowing her mind had settled back to such habits comforted her, and she set the last few bottles down into a basket. With Polly ignoring the task, Almyra tucked in some loose wool from the pile, then wiped the sheep grease off her hands. Thank goodness for this apron.

Susannah carried the kettle and ladle across to the dry sink, rubbed them with a cloth, and stripped off her own apron, revealing the incongruous billow of her Turkish pantaloons. "Mother, we'll go gather the bowls from the inn and maybe see if Matthew needs a hand."

"Mind you bring in the tankards, too," Mrs. Hall called out as Almyra followed Susannah into the connecting hallway. Ahead of her, Susannah nodded without comment, pushing forward into the tavern.

The aroma of men and their tobacco lingered in the tavern's large room, and half a dozen bowls, rimmed with the remains of bread and gravy, waited at the long table. Without discussion, Almyra began to stack the dishes and spoons, while Susannah seized a broom and attacked the clumps of dirt and manure scattered across the floor. When the room seemed presentable, the two of them exchanged glances, and Almyra hung her own apron near the door.

From the stables, several men's voices echoed. One was definitely Uncle Eliphalet, and another must be Matthew.

Captain Young's voice rose above both. "There can be no question. Isaiah's visit to the mines must appear the only reason for any of us to be there. If any suspicion should arise …." He cut off, having noticed the girls approaching.

"Miss Alexander." A tip of his cap and a partial bow recognized Almyra as a young woman, not a child, and she felt an unexpected pleasure at his smile.

Into the slight awkwardness of his noticing Susannah, younger and attired so strangely, Almyra moved forward with a slight curtsey and a drew her friend forward. "This is Miss Hall, who assists Matthew and has been equally helpful to me of late."

Matthew quenched a half snort of amusement. Almyra ignored him and looked the other way. "Uncle, I believe I'm prepared for Sunday. How else can we ladies ensure the best results from your journey?" There, that would show Matthew that she and Susannah counted for something.

Her uncle nodded to acknowledge the question, then turned to the others. "Mrs. Sanborn is packing the saddlebags this evening with extra clothing in case of rain, and provisions of course. I need hardly add that each should be prepared for defense, whether from man or beast. But on the main stage roads, I think we need not fear."

"No word from Miss Farrow or Doctor Jewett?" Almyra asked, without being quite sure why, and noted Captain Young's surprised glance.

Uncle Eliphalet said, "They have other tasks of their own. We'll only hear from them if something goes awry. No, Almyra, I believe we're prepared, and if you'll hold the pulpit and keep village attention on that unusual event, it should be of some benefit to us in both the short and long run. Gentlemen, I shall walk my niece home, and will see you at five tomorrow morning."

Almyra winced, but had little choice, and raised an apologetic hand in farewell to Susannah.

"Oh, your apron," Susannah said. "I'll fetch it for you and meet you at the other door."

In front of the tavern Almyra waited for Susannah as her uncle continued to walk toward home. Susannah came out with the apron rolled into a bundle, cushioning a small bottle of the spring tonic.

"Give it to your aunt, from my mother." She leaned closer, in a whiff of horse and sheep. "I'll send Polly to you once a day while they're gone," Susannah whispered. "If I can't get away from the tavern often myself. You can always send a message with her if you need me."

Almyra nodded. Need her? What on earth did Susannah have in mind?

~ 17 ~

Though Almyra rose early to see the small expedition off, Uncle Eliphalet insisted that she stay indoors in the sharp chill of dawn. The last remains of winter clung in the frosty air. Though May sunshine would warm the village in a few hours, the men wore bulky winter coats to start their journey.

Uncle Eliphalet carried a satchel that seemed curiously empty. He strode toward the inn, and from this end of the village road as she stood outside the kitchen door, Almyra caught a glimpse of the other men, John Sanborn and his friend Isaiah, crossing from the Sanborn farm lane toward the tavern. She pulled out her handkerchief to wave, but they didn't look her way.

How disappointing that Alice's brother John seemed never to have time to linger. Almyra determined to ask him, next time to tell her in more detail about his adventures in the West. She'd barely had enough time to draw from him some reassurance about her friends: Yes, Alice and Caroline both were teaching at the new School for the Deaf not far from Springfield, Illinois, and yes, they were staying in a boarding house but should soon locate something more appropriate to single females. From John's expression, Almyra confirmed that even on the frontier, a boardinghouse verged on impropriety. She would like to witness the mingling of settlers, political operatives, railroad crews, and men opening shops and manufacturing for the taming of the wild lands.

But that could not happen until she'd completed her studies, which were sadly lagging just now. If she wished to apply to Vermont's seminary in Springfield, she must be fully as prepared as any young man entering the ministry. When she went to the kitchen to move water and wood for her aunt, she resolved to spend more time at her desk and less on horseback with Susannah. A stiffness in her own gait suggested a bit of healing time might be wise.

Released sooner than she'd expected from the household tasks, Almyra opened her Bible and Concordance with relief. Her insight from the Hall kitchen—about the need for some peace in order to think about the moral basis of life—drove her into the Book of Proverbs, and then with eagerness, to a passage her uncle had bookmarked in chapter four of Ephesians. "That we henceforth be no more children, tossed to and fro, and carried about with every wind of doctrine." It moved her. With abolitionist leaders in mind and their strong force of moral imperative, she wrote steadily across her own bound pages.

Letters that afternoon included several for her uncle, one for her aunt, and one for her, an unusual abundance. She sat with Aunt Charlotte over her aunt's own spring tea, which seemed mostly mint, and took a deep breath. She noted that the thin folded sheet was franked with Solomon McBride's scrawl, a surprise. Within, a short note caused Aunt Charlotte's eyebrows to rise before she passed it across to Almyra.

How strange. Just a sentence from her sister's husband, who was also working throughout the nation for William Seward, saying he'd be in Vermont the next week, and to please let the Sanborns and Matthew Clark know. Why would Solomon McBride write to Aunt Charlotte, instead of directly to the others? "Does he have an arrangement with you about this?"

Aunt Charlotte shook her head. "It baffles me. I see no sense to it. Unless," she added slowly, "somehow he too has received the rumor that some postmasters are interfering with abolitionist communication."

Almyra shivered. "Uncle Eliphalet said to trust Mr. Weeks here in North Upton."

"Ye-es," even more slowly, "but there are other hands and eyes in between. Including in the Capitol. Perhaps a note to a minister's wife seemed more secure. Well, I shall do as asked, I suppose, but it is quite odd." Aunt Charlotte tapped Almyra's letter. "Aren't you going to open this one?"

"Oh, of course. But it is from my father, you know, and I'm sure he is simply inquiring after my health and studies." She smiled at her aunt as she carefully slit open the fastening. "And where do you suppose he's needed next? I see this has come from Boston, but he's rarely in the city all that long, especially now the snow's retreating."

The familiar greeting of "Dear Daughter" made her smile, and she followed the lines eagerly. Choosing to stay with her aunt and uncle after her mother's death felt right in so many ways—her father traveled a great deal and she had no desire to manage his empty house in Boston, worrying about draperies and rugs and the next season's styles.

She slowed, and read a line again, then aloud to her aunt. "'When this letter reaches you, I shall be fairly settled into my new marriage. Lydia, on whom the mantel of widowhood has rested for some six months, after the passing of Captain Jonathan Perkins, consented to be my wife and we married in February, followed at once by a summons from the Secretary of State, so I beg your forgiveness for being thus late in advising you of this happy change. I am sure you will welcome her, and value her care for both your father and his home. Her own two daughters and several sons are of course already married on their own. She asks me to notify you that she is, of course eager, to welcome you, in turn, and to offer you such care as a step-mother may provide.' A step-mother. I always knew Papa would be snatched up as quickly as he wished, but I've no use for any step-mama myself. What on earth was he thinking?"

Aunt Charlotte pressed her hands to her own face. "Oh my dear, must you go directly to Boston?"

"Not at all," Almyra said firmly. "He didn't tell me in advance, it's nearly three months since he wedded this widow, and he is clearly absorbed in his own labors. I'll write a letter of course, and perhaps, Aunt, you will want to add your own message? Or Uncle Eliphalet, to his brother?" The look of relief on Aunt Charlotte's face made her giggle. "You'll not send me off to Boston so lightly, will you, now? I thought you and I were dedicated to managing this anchor for the great expedition to Canada?"

Together they laughed, and the room seemed golden with acceptance. If her mother had lived longer, might this have been the case, even in Boston? Almyra doubted it. Aunt Charlotte's clear delight in having a young woman in the household felt entirely different from Almyra's mother's endless complaints and illnesses. She felt a short pang of regret, eclipsed by gratitude.

To distract herself from this confusing muddle of emotions, Almyra reached to examine the letters addressed to her uncle. Two were in envelopes with engraved identification, probably from others in the denomination. The third, however, was a simple folded sheet of paper, not unlike the brief missive from Solomon McBride.

She hesitated. Letters were private vehicles of information and expression. Within marriage, it was always the husband who might open mail addressed to his wife, never the reverse. Yet after a moment, she lifted it and handed it to her aunt.

"This one looks more urgent. Might Uncle Eliphalet wish you to inspect it for him, since he will not return for several days at least?"

Aunt Charlotte looked, first at the letter, then at Almyra. "But this is also from your father. I should think he's writing with the same news for your uncle and me, though it seems odd he'd post two letters when one will do."

Almyra ran a finger across the sealed page. "It's not the same paper," she said slowly. "Perhaps it was placed in the post at a different date entirely. Perhaps it concerns something else."

For a moment longer, Aunt Charlotte hesitated to open the letter addressed only to her husband. Then she lifted it, slid the fastening open, and scanned the scrawl within.

"What is it?" Almyra wondered whether her father could demand that she return to Boston. But of course he could. Could she decline a direct request?

Aunt Charlotte shook her head from side to side, as if arguing with the letter. She said, "I don't know what to do. I truly don't know how to reply. How can I reply, when it's a letter from your uncle that he requires?"

Baffled, Almyra reached to take the page. Her aunt released it, and began to pace in the kitchen, still speaking aloud, some confusion of intent persisting.

*My dear brother Eliphalet, I write with haste and urgency, to request your immediate assistance. You may not yet know of the arrest of Anthony Burns, a Negro fugitive, here in Boston. It is essential that this man receive the best legal defense, and those of us concerned for his welfare are convinced the best defense must come from the lawyer Richard H'ry Dana Jr, of whom we have spoken in the past. Dana has, on first approach, declined, so I beseech you to write directly to him with a reminder of what he pledged to you, that we may obtain what is owed. I need hardly say that more depends on this than the free life of one man, but that must be our first and only goal in this moment. Begging your instant and persuasive action, Yr brother in this and more, Charles.*

Aunt Charlotte stepped to the table and gripped it. "This, Almyra, is what comes of doing something improper. I should never have opened a letter addressed to your uncle, and then I would not be in this terrible quandary."

"Oh no, Aunt, then you would not have the opportunity to assist justice being done. We must take the letter to Uncle Eliphalet at once."

"We cannot," Aunt Charlotte complained, "as he is halfway to Canada by now."

Almyra quickly proposed an alternative. "There is a stage that goes north. We can send a letter to intercept him."

"But that stage goes from St. Johnsbury, not North Upton."

"We can have Sam Young take the letter on the stage from here to St. Johnsbury and send it north on the second stage." This, however, Almyra said more hesitantly. "That is, if the North Upton stage is headed east today, not west."

At once, the two of them shared a dismayed realization. The stage, regardless of direction, must already have passed through the village, for the mail to have arrived.

Almyra said firmly, "I shall ask Susannah to carry the letter to St. Johnsbury. She can place it on the stage headed north."

"And if that stage, too. has already departed?"

There was only one way to end this chain of half certainties, and a moment later, Almyra half flew through the kitchen door, determined to fetch Susannah to her aunt for all proper decisions to be made. Her aunt's voice followed her, "Your skirts, Almyra. Moderate your pace, or they'll be all over mud and worse."

Dodging along the edge of the village road to avoid the soup of "worse" down its soft and puddled middle, Almyra gripped her skirts and petticoats on both sides to hold them just above her ankles as she sped toward the Clark tavern at the far end of the village. She raced past the house door and the tavern door, circling the structure to the stables, calling Susannah's name aloud.

Minutes later, with Susannah at her side and asking more questions than she had breath to answer, Almyra burst back into the parsonage kitchen. The scent of fresh bread pulled from the oven made her stomach beg for sustenance, but that would have to wait.

Aunt Charlotte began to speak before Almyra could catch her breath. "Miss Farrow," she announced firmly. "I need to go to her, right away. She will know how to get word to Canada, faster than any of us might otherwise for she must relay messages regularly. Susannah, is there a carriage available at the tavern for me to use?"

Almyra cut in, knowing she shouldn't, but unable to stop. "We could ride. Susannah and I could ride to town immediately and carry your message."

"No," her aunt said firmly. "The proper way to convey both the message and its urgency is to go in person. I shall ....." she faltered a moment, then turned back to Susannah. "I am not accustomed to travel in mud and other spring conditions," she admitted. "Might Matthew be able to drive me?"

But Matthew, of course, could not leave the inn, and the few men one might otherwise call upon for such effort were, it seemed, headed north with Uncle Eliphalet.

At last Aunt Charlotte repeated her earlier question. "Susannah, is there a carriage I might use? Would your mother allow you to drive the horses with me?"

Almyra bit back a protest and waited for Susannah's considered response. "There's a light two-wheel buggy that's built with an extra bench," she said at last. "One horse might draw it with the three of us, it's that light. And Mother might have a delivery for me to make in town if I offer to go." A sideways glance at Almyra resulted in a rather startling second statement. "Mind now, I could be teaching both of you to handle the horses. Just in case you'd maybe wish to make another trip to town one day this summer."

But in fact, Aunt Charlotte had no wish to learn to drive a horse and buggy.

Perhaps the mild afternoon air tilted the decision at last. Almyra might go with Susannah also, and learn both the reins and the management of the conveyance on spring roads with Aunt Charlotte to supervise them both. Provided, of course, that Susannah's mother agreed.

Half an hour later, they jounced out of town, a fresh horse stepping quickly and directly from the stables onto the road toward town. Almyra sat on the front bench beside Susannah. Her aunt sat wedged into a better bench, with a bit of sides to it, each arm steadying a basket of medicinals and packets of dried herbs, trying to keep the bottles from clattering. A small satchel of clothing helped fill the space also, a few necessities just in case.

"My mother says she won't worry if we stay overnight in town and return in the morning," Susannah announced, reins in one hand, the other gripping a long stick that reached toward the horse's haunches. "She says that's to be expected."

Almyra glanced over her shoulder, then tried to appear entirely focused on the driving. Her aunt, faced with the possibility of staying a night in town without a plan to do so, a full change of clothes, or a proper invitation from anyone, held one hand over her eyes and said only, "Eliphalet must surely wish to receive this message, with a man's freedom at stake, and his own influence so important in achieving a proper lawyer for the man."

To herself, Almyra began a scrap of doggerel that kept rhythm with the horse's motion. "A proper lawyer, a proper letter, a proper road to town. Again. A proper lawyer, a proper letter."

She knew better than to say a word aloud, however, until Susannah half turned and asked her, "Are you paying close attention? Here comes a narrow stretch, and a long curve. Two hands on the reins all the time. Watch, I'll show you."

So many more straps and such on the horse pulling the buggy, nothing as simple as the saddle she'd been on. A wave of panic made her stomach churn. She couldn't possibly learn all this. Such folly.

But Susannah kept talking, and only about the reins, the long stick, and the buggy whip. "Because she can't feel your hands or your seat, you know, so you have to talk with her in all these ways. But it's never actually to whip a horse, of course, just to tap on her back and side. The horse is your friend."

Almyra couldn't press back a small whimper of dismay. Susannah frowned and repeated, "The horse is your friend, and you are hers, but more than that, you are her leader from behind. She needs you to know what you're doing. She knows more than you about some things, even how to get home again, but you're the only one who knows where you are going."

Just past the long curve, Susannah abruptly moved the reins to Almyra's hands, though not the buggy whip. Focusing fiercely, Almyra tried to assure the horse that she knew the way forward. Of course, that seemed simpler as a passenger than it did now. She asked, "Do I need to know where to make a turn? Does she always go so fast? What happens if I slide off the bench?"

Behind her, Aunt Charlotte's unladylike snort suggested the questions were ridiculous, but at least Susannah didn't snort also. And although the labored patience in Susannah's voice made Almyra feel a bit like a not-very-smart horse in training, at least, mile by mile, she felt less frightened.

"That's enough for now," Susannah finally said, recapturing the reins. "The four corners are just ahead, and from there, we go downhill. I'll manage the brake and the horse. She's staying in town, at the livery, and we'll drive another one back. But first I'll take you to your friend's house. How long will you need to be there?"

Aunt Charlotte replied from the rear, "I should think an hour will suffice for a cup of tea with Miss Farrow and leaving the letter with her. The house is near the north end of the Plain."

Not quite an hour later, gratefully sitting on a chair that didn't bounce at all, with Miss Farrow pouring tea and Aunt Charlotte's explanations complete, Almyra leaned back at last to take a deep breath and look around her. Little had changed in the kitchen, with its well-scrubbed table and the many shelves of Chinese bowls and platters. Past the half-open door, allowing the kitchen's warmth to permeate the next room, the elegant wall papers in the judge's dining room hung shadowy and mysterious from this vantage.

In the year and a half since she'd last visited here, the bend of Miss Farrow's back and shoulders had deepened, although a gathered cotton cap hid the housekeeper's hair, a few gray strands poking out at the edges. More than a dozen letters must have passed between them in that time, with the first ones carrying Miss Farrow's condolences for Mama's untimely death. Others exchanged discussion topics for the ladies' groups they took part in, and sometimes portions of sermons. Was it sinful to so much appreciate Aunt Charlotte's abundant cheer and strength, compared to Mama's ever-present physical weakness, her demands, and requirements?

That must wait for this evening's prayer, for full consideration. Even so, Almyra treasured her rebirth in her aunt and uncle's home. A minister of the Word. Her heart's desire sang in her. If this was sinful desire—oh, but it couldn't be.

Aunt Charlotte must be almost finished explaining. Such a complex prologue to this moment, full of legal peril and the possibility of enslavement. Miss Farrow's knotted brown fingers tapped restlessly as she listened.

"So," Aunt Charlotte concluded, "you'll see how important it is that this message reach my husband quickly. He may even need to return to North Upton, or proceed direct to Boston, depending on the situation. Are we in good time to send word with the stage?"

Miss Farrow settled her own teacup and cleared her throat. In her deep slow voice, she replied, "In a word, my dear, No. The stage hasn't yet returned from the border. Word arrived yesterday that the horses were stolen. I'm afraid the Canadian border region's turned nearly lawless. So much commerce there keeps failing for lack of verified bank notes, and they say the only tradeable currency is now horseflesh." Her eyebrows lifted. "There's some doubt of whether even our sheriffs can reclaim the animals, as most likely they've been shifted West already. But there is a posse headed north tomorrow."

Almyra held her breath. The next step seemed obvious. Her aunt apparently realized it a moment later, and said, "Then the sheriff perhaps will carry our message?"

Miss Farrow shook her head. "I think the risk's unfortunate. It's Henry Hastings leading the group, and you know he's always been suspected of selling those two small boys across into Quebec. Whether he did so or not, the sting of suspicion's hardened him. I'd not be trusting him with something so crucial and so political."

"But I would seal the envelope," Aunt Charlotte protested.

Miss Farrow held silent, conveying only through her pursed lips that a sealed envelope could not guarantee a safe delivery if the carrier lacked honor.

In Almyra's thoughts, the chant from earlier resumed. "A proper lawyer, a proper letter, a proper road to town. A proper message found. A proper minister in town."

A thought occurred to her. She turned to Miss Farrow and asked, "Tracts. Do you have a few dozen, set aside? Something Biblical, printed on single pages?"

"Of course," the older woman said. "Is this another topic altogether, Almyra?"

"No, not at all." Swiftly, she outlined a plan. Their interaction with Uncle Eliphalet, wherever one could catch up with him, must speak to his position as a man of the cloth. So she, as his student, would profess to having accidentally neglected to pack the tracts he needed to distribute, and could ride north, either ahead of or behind the legal posse, reach her uncle, and deliver both a bundle of tracts and, within it, the crucial letter from Boston.

"Ridiculous," Aunt Charlotte pronounced at once. "You've taken a short ride with Susannah, and you think you can ride north on your own? This is not some Western drama, niece. You are a young lady. And moreover, there is no way to say where your uncle and the others have taken themselves. We must locate the stage driver and determine from him where they left the stage, and what direction they've taken. That is," she hesitated, turning back to Miss Farrow, "the stage horses were stolen after the stage reached a destination, I trust? Not some highwaymen in action along the river roads?"

Miss Farrow agreed. "But Mrs. Alexander, when you say 'we,' surely you are not considering riding north yourself? With your niece? Or—without her?"

"Piffle," Aunt Charlotte declared, her cheeks flushed and eyes bright. "Haven't we a buggy and a driver? And wouldn't I wish to call on my former schoolmate in Newport, Mrs. Adams herself? Who is married to a border officer, I believe." She beamed. "I doubt we'll have to go so far, but we can thus confirm whether our menfolk have crossed, and if they have, their destination."

What a dreadfully outrageous notion. And yet, Almyra admitted, her aunt's proposal could well benefit all, and locate Uncle Eliphalet rapidly, though she hoped it wouldn't mean crossing into the wild lands of Lower Canada. Who knew what runaways from the Revolution still hid among the hills and forests there? Not to mention the counterfeiters. Even Foster Pierce himself. She shuddered at the recalled name of the notorious outlaw.

Would Susannah think the whole plan folly? Oh, it was, truly a mad notion, for how could Susannah gain permission from her mother to drive north, abandoning her tasks for Matthew, and using someone else's horse? Almyra began to explain these issues to the two women now wrapping tracts in a length of worn cotton cloth.

Miss Farrow stopped and looked expectantly at Aunt Charlotte who sat erect with her eyes half shut, a frown over them.

After a moment, Miss Farrow said quietly, "The judge?"

Almyra's aunt shook her head slowly. Then she seemed to change her mind. "A conveyance? Or only a rider?"

"The Youngs," Miss Farrow said cryptically. "One might be amenable."

So when Susannah returned to collect them for the return to North Upton,

and with a heavy bay horse between the shafts of the buggy, only Almyra climbed to the front bench with a pair of folded letters in hand. "The livery stable by the railroad station," Almyra said. "And then the courthouse. I'll explain as you drive. Then we come back to get my aunt." She meant to be calm and mature but couldn't help scowling. "And go back to North Upton."

"Wasn't that always the point, going back after leaving messages here," Susannah probed, as she endeavored to get the ponderous beast to step more quickly toward the downhill Avenue. "Blast this buggy. It's too wide to drive in town."

"I thought we'd find a way to take the message north ourselves," Almyra admitted. "But I wasn't thinking clearly. I'm the supply pastor for the church this weekend. So we're collecting a messenger from the stable, who'll take the letter north and set my uncle into action." She added, "If God wills," feeling less than certain of the success of this plan. But how else could it be accomplished?

A man's life lay in the balance.

~ 18 ~

The next morning, despite aching arms from driving with the second horse for much of the long return to North Upton, Almyra helped turn out the floor coverings from her uncle's study, as Aunt Charlotte saw the opportunity. After the rugs were hung on the clothesline, however, she excused herself from beating them and retreated to her desk. Sunday's sermon must be polished, the hymn selections finalized, and she should read through the sermon aloud at least once more, to smooth her delivery.

"When I arrive at Seminary," she said to the empty room, "I'll be one of the most practiced there." Perhaps that would speed her years of education and set her out into independence sooner rather than later.

With a pang, she realized her mother might not have been pleased to have a grown daughter so forward in the public view. Well, that could be another reason to be grateful for her present conditions: Aunt Charlotte supported women's rights to speak, and even vote, at least in school meetings where their interests were so deeply concerned.

With that in mind, Almyra turned her quill to inking the sermon into her own journal, adapting the words of the Parable of the Sower. Women sowed seeds in many forms of gardens, though not often in fields. Or did women work in the fields more if their farming lives demanded it? She must ask Susannah for perspective on this. Nobody seemed to object to Susannah assisting in the stables.

Halfway through, she paused to wonder whether her uncle would send word of the expedition into Canada, or simply return as soon as or sooner than a letter might arrive.

At the noon meal, she asked Aunt Charlotte. "The messenger that you and Miss Farrow sent north—how will he find Uncle Eliphalet? Do you know in advance where he will stay?"

Her aunt lifted an eyebrow. "Not at all. But three men traveling together on horseback will be noted. Especially as they cross into

Canada, which I think they must have accomplished yesterday. I know your uncle did not care to stay overnight in Newport."

"Why not? What is the town like?"

"It's a rough place, barely settled, and any ministers there are often away, tending multiple parishes. I believe Captain Young advised that any lodging house in the town would include men who receive the forged currency from across the border. Naturally, your uncle prefers not to advertise the presence of his group among such individuals as long as he can avoid it."

Almyra pictured a rough crowd of frontiersmen, garbed as in the engravings of the ladies' journals. "Do they carry rifles, and wear furs?"

Aunt Charlotte finally laughed. "In May? Even in Newport, I imagine those winter garments have been set aside. And it's not a frontier in terms of defense—even during the war against the British, Newport must have been too small to bother. But I believe there are few walkways for ladies, for instance, and barely any civilized advantages such as millinery or tea rooms. Remember, my dear, even the railroad has not reached Newport yet. I daresay the town will change when that finally takes place."

"Will they be safe as they pass through? What about Isaiah, that is, Mr. Hutchinson?" She realized she'd fallen into a habit of thinking of the dark-skinned man by his first name and vowed to correct the habit. Just because she'd been slow to learn his surname didn't mean she should fail to respect him.

"I am sure they will be safe. Mind you, Mr. Hutchinson is likely to feel great relief when they all enter Canada where enslavement of Negroes was abolished twenty years ago."

Almyra shared Aunt Charlotte's exasperated sigh. If the province of Canada and all the British Empire could insist on the dignity of Negro men and women, why could not America? There was a sermon in that, if she could find the pertinent passages in Scripture.

Her aunt was speaking further. "I should think, upon reflection, that Captain Young draws the most risk, as his military bearing must be obvious. Criminals passing counterfeits would notice him at once." She added reassuringly, "But only to disperse, I'm sure of it. No, I should think if the roads are not all mud, they may reach Stanstead Plain after a long day's ride, and they will lodge there for several shorter expeditions to the mines before they proceed to other towns. So our messenger should find them in Stanstead. Which, I understand is quite prosperous in its way, with its own newspaper. And," she sighed, "far more raw immigrants arriving all the time. But it is the county seat, and has a Customs Office, your uncle said. So I daresay it has a good number of sheriffs, or whatever they are called there."

How strange to realize that another nation lay only a day's ride away. A long day's ride. Whether or not they'd crossed the border before the first evening, they must surely be in Stanstead Plain today. And the messenger—when would he reach them?

Aunt Charlotte rose from her seat, signaling the end of the meal. Perhaps Susannah, with her understanding of horses, would be the better person to consult about the messenger. Somehow the entire matter felt uncertain, and a stiffness in her aunt's shoulders echoed Almyra's unease. "Then you believe they are all safe?"

Her aunt frowned. "Trust God to watch over his flock, Almyra. You may wipe clean the plates, and then perhaps you'll present to me your Sunday service plan, so that I may advise you on any details still wanting attention."

Almyra squelched a sharp prickle of inner annoyance at this instruction. Of course, her aunt had years of experience with Uncle Eliphalet's Sunday services. Perhaps this even made up part of their usual routines. And even if not—a humble heart would not object to guidance. Alas, she feared perhaps her heart lacked some humility.

At mid-afternoon, with a few corrections made to the sermon and several to the psalmody and hymns, Aunt Charlotte declared Almyra's preparation excellent and suggested an outdoor stroll for the sake of health and good spirits. "In the meanwhile, I shall peruse today's correspondence."

A quick glance at the pair of envelopes on the table confirmed the letters were only for Aunt Charlotte. Good, no more urgent summonses for Uncle Eliphalet. And no more news from Boston for Almyra.

Outdoors, her steps turned automatically toward the inn and its stables where Susannah might be caring for horses. Between home and the inn, however, Almyra realized she hadn't pursued her own intent to teach the youngest Hall daughter something more of Scripture. What other tale might interest little Polly? Joseph's coat of many colors, perhaps.

So instead of going directly to the livery beyond the inn, she first visited the household end of the main structure, rapping at the door and then, after a moment, letting herself into the oddly quiet kitchen.

"Mrs. Hall? Polly?" No reply. Hesitantly, she walked in further. The room was warm, and a kettle on the stove bubbled, its lid jittering.

Suddenly a door behind her swung open with a gust of damp and cooler air, admitting Susannah's frazzled and puffing older sister, Jane, carrying a basket of potatoes. "I was only down cellar for a moment," Jane protested, then seemed to realize it was Almyra standing there. "Oh, I heard the footsteps and thought Mama was back. Are you looking for her?"

"Not exactly. That is, I wondered whether Polly might like to hear a Bible story." This sounded a bit lame even in Almyra's own ears. "I didn't mean to intrude, I thought perhaps someone was in the kitchen."

"No, Mama and Polly took the wagon to Upton Center earlier. I daresay they won't be home until closer to suppertime. And you didn't need anything? For yourself?"

Under Jane's sharp gaze at her skirts, Almyra suddenly realized what the question meant. "Not at all," she replied sharply. "I'm quite well, thank you."

"Ah. That's good. It seems you might be the only woman within miles around who can say that, in this season of drafts and chills and more." Jane pushed past and set the basket on the table. "You're welcome to peel potatoes, though, if you've nothing else to do."

"Thank you kindly, but I believe I'll go look for Susannah in the stables."

"You go right ahead." As Almyra turned, she heard Jane mutter, "There's a lot of that about."

What on earth? Was one sister jealous of the other? Never mind, this wasn't her affair. She slipped back outside in relief, and circled toward the livery shed.

Susannah's voice, cheerful and bold, carried over the rustles and thuds of animals in their stables. "For all I know, they're looking at more sheep. Lambing's more than half done, and I think Mr. Sanborn hasn't achieved the flock size he wanted for this season. Perhaps Almyra can inform you better, Mr. McBride."

McBride? What was Solomon doing here? Almyra pressed forward into the dim shadows to see her brother-in-law hastily standing erect from his casual leaning position against a dusty half-wall and brushing himself off. Even in the low light, she could see a bright flush on his face.

A glance at Susannah showed a similar blush. Oh dear. Perhaps Susannah didn't realize Solomon's married status. She wouldn't be the first young woman in North Upton to find the handsome political operative too charming for everyone's good.

Annoyed, nearly angry, Almyra dipped a shallow bow from the waist and said, "Well, if it isn't Mr. Solomon McBride, come north from Boston society. How goes my sister, your wife?"

Susannah spun away, toppling a pail of grain in the process and bending to deal with the mess. Solomon merely gave a rakish smile, lifted his hat brim in salute, and said, "She sends her warm regards to her little sister, who does not write to her often enough. Which of course is one reason I have arrived, to investigate and carry assurance back to her." He paused, evidently seeing that his coaxing wasn't going to work. In a lower voice, he added, "My other reason is to meet with Mr. Sanborn, but I failed to notify him of my plans in advance. Miss, err, Miss Hall here tells me he's not in the village at present. And Mrs. Sanborn, I gather, is seeing to a young wife's needs in some other home."

"I'm sure she's very much in demand," Almyra replied. She hesitated. How much should she tell Solomon McBride about Captain Young's expedition? She didn't like this situation. "Perhaps you'd call at my aunt's home and join us for a light supper in an hour or so? Aunt Charlotte may be able to tell you more."

With a nod of understanding, Solomon tipped his hat again in thanks and said, "I appreciate the invitation. I shall hie me to the store and examine the goods there, in the interim."

Though he left immediately, Almyra watched to make sure he'd reached the road and headed away before she turned back to Susannah.

"He's an outrageous flirt," she said bluntly. "It's not your fault."

Susannah gave a forced laugh, her face still red as she wielded a pair of brushes on the side of a heavy-bellied horse tethered in front of her. "He's not the first, won't be the last," she said quickly. "I don't mind it. Usually Matthew's here and interrupts things. I was trying to send him off, when you came in."

That clearly wasn't the case, but what point would there be to arguing? Instead, Almyra asked, "Then where is Matthew?"

"Went with Mother and Polly to Upton Center. Something about a freight shipment, some items for her simples, some for the inn, and she wanted him along. It all came by train to St. Johnsbury and the wagon driver didn't want to come up to the village, so he left the bundles in the Center instead."

That speech took long enough for the flush to calm, and for words to slow down to normal. Almyra nodded and asked, "Did Solomon ask directly about where the men have gone? What did you have to tell him?"

"No more than what you overheard. He doesn't know about the others."

"Ah, good. My aunt will know how much to reveal, I believe. You haven't heard from them, have you?"

Susannah looked over sharply. "No, have you?"

"Not at all. I hope our messenger has reached them. A man's freedom is at stake. I'm worried."

"How far did the messenger need to ride?"

"Past Newport, across the border to Stanstead Plain. And then find them. They could be out at the mines already." Oh dear, had Susannah even known about the mines? Perhaps that was too much to say.

But there was no indication of surprise or curiosity. Instead, after a pause to calculate, Susannah simply said, "I doubt even a fast horse would have reached there before this morning. You'll be waiting a while longer, most likely. Finding them, and then getting the reply in return."

The return time hadn't occurred to her before. Almyra wondered whether her uncle could persuade the Boston lawyer speedily. Must he travel to Boston himself? Suddenly the pieces of the plan to assist the trial seemed spread too far apart. Perhaps, after all, engaging Solomon McBride in her father's business might be necessary.

She pulled her thoughts back and asked Susannah, "Have you ever seen Newport? Or crossed the border into Canada?"

"Ha, not I. I've plenty to keep me working right here." Susannah cast a sideways glance toward her. "You won't mention about your Mr. McBride being in my barn, with me on my lonesome, will you? My mother's sensible enough, but it's not something I'd want my sister Julia holding over my head."

"Never a word," Almyra pledged.

A sudden loud clang from the bell in front of the inn made her jump. Susannah tossed her currying brushes aside. "Can't be the stage yet, but someone's here."

They hurried out into the sunlight and around to the front of the inn. A thin but elderly man, easily past sixty, stood uncertainly next to a dark-brown horse that was slurping from the water trough. Upon seeing the two of them, he swept off his beaver hat and gave an old-fashioned bow that nearly tipped him over. Susannah grabbed his elbow and assisted him back to his stance.

"Th-thank you, young m-master," he began, then corrected himself, "young m-miss. Your pardon, m-miss. I'm weary from r-r-riding. Could you d-d-direct me to the house of M-Mister Alexander? The m-m-minister?"

Almyra stepped closer. "I am just about to return there, sir. Can I escort you?"

"Yes, th-that would be very k-kind of you." He bobbed his head, birdlike. As Susannah released him, he turned back to her. "I m-may need a r-room," he added. "I will know soon. M-might you have one available, m-miss?"

"Certainly," Susannah said. To Almyra she gave a quick smile "Do you want me to walk with you?"

"Thank you, no," Almyra replied, understanding the offer. "I'll be fine from here to there." She turned to the elderly gentleman, who wore a coat clearly tailored in Boston or some other city, and fairly recently at that. She bobbed a polite nod of her head as she said, "My name is Almyra Alexander, sir. Might you share yours?"

"M-Miss Alexander, m-my very great pleasure. And m-my name is Foster P-Pierce. At your service."

Almyra froze and looked at Susannah. Had she too recognized that name? Foster Pierce, the notorious head of the counterfeiting gang that her uncle said had dispersed some years ago? There could be no coincidence in this arrival. And perhaps there was some danger after all.

She forced a smile, and said, "Welcome to North Upton, Mr. Pierce. Susannah, perhaps I'll accept your company after all, since you can walk Mr. Pierce's horse for him, while the two of us stroll to the parsonage. It's only a short walk," she reassured the man.

Though why in the world she felt she should reassure a man with such a terrifying reputation, she really could not have said. Only that she wished Uncle Eliphalet, or even Matthew, or Mr. Sanborn, was in the village at this moment.

From Susannah's sharp glance and quick movement toward the horse, she knew her friend had grasped that the situation troubled Almyra, whatever might be the reason.

The man offered her his elbow in a courtly fashion, thanked her, and said, "I'm afraid I'm g-getting a bit p-past this sort of r-ride. You see, I started y-yesterday, from C-Canada. A town n-named for yours, I b-believe. Upton, in the p-province of Quebec. And you m-must be the m-minister's daughter?"

"His niece," Almyra said through numb lips as she set her hand onto the offered elbow and confirmed the fine weave of the coat fabric. "And I'm afraid he's not at home at this hour. But my Aunt Charlotte will know how to reach him, as soon as you share your concern with her."

A flash of brown eyes under the bushy white eyebrows conveyed both concern and annoyance, maybe even anger. Well, it wasn't her fault Uncle Eliphalet wasn't home. If anyone was to blame—it was this man, Foster Pierce.

## ~ 19 ~

Walking at a slow pace along the road, her hand secured at Mr. Pierce's elbow, Almyra lowered her gaze from the bright sun in her face. This afternoon, mid-May felt closer to June than to April, as the scent of warm earth battled with that of thawed horse droppings along the road. In these few years of country life, she'd come to appreciate the release from winter's rigor far more than she ever had when living as a child in Boston.

But this was no moment to think about the weather. What should she do about Mr. Pierce? How could she protect Aunt Charlotte, but also discover what brought this man to North Upton? Uncle Eliphalet's words came back to her: "Surely he's too old for such idiocy now. He's a government leader in the Parliament up north."

Her fingers told her two things. From the fabric of his coat, this Mr. Pierce spent well on his garments, so perhaps he still profited from the counterfeiters operating north of the border. And from the thinness of his arm and the way he trembled slightly as he stepped, his physical strength could not be much. She reassured herself with this detail. She and Aunt Charlotte between them would be more than a match for the elderly criminal. That is, government leader.

His labored breathing prevented conversation, and Almyra began to worry about the man's health. Did all old men struggle like this? She glanced behind them, confirming that Susannah still followed with the man's horse about twenty feet behind them.

As if reading her thoughts, Mr. Pierce paused and murmured, "A breath here, if you don't m-m-mind."

She waited for him, letting a look of concern take over her own features. "Are you all right, sir?"

"Right enough." He panted slightly, gripped her hand with his other as if to emphasize the need to pause and continued to draw breath, gradually becoming easier in his stance. "Age is a f-fierce opponent. But

I have d-d-determination on my side, you see, and I m-must speak with your uncle."

Almyra repeated, "He's not at home just now, sir. But perhaps my aunt and I can assist. We are, as much as possible, his partners in his endeavors."

That sharp glance evaluated her again. Mr. Pierce's lips pressed out and in again as he considered her statement. He seemed to reach a decision. "Banking. I n-n-need to d-discuss banking with your uncle."

At that moment, Mr. Sanborn, John and Alice's father, emerged from the village store, a sack in his hand. Thank goodness. She'd pictured him off with his sheep. Now she could muster his support.

"Mr. Sanborn," she called out. "Would you care to walk with us? I am bringing Mr. Pierce to my uncle's house, and I think you might be able to assist him with your conversation."

Behind Mr. Sanborn, through the open store doorway, she noted Solomon McBride peering out in curiosity. He tipped his head to one side and pointed to his chest. Need me, too?

Almyra shook her head, aware that the man holding her against him noticed. She turned and spoke quietly to him. "Mr. Sanborn is aware of the banking issues that concern my uncle. Mr. McBride, inside the store, may not be as informed."

But her caution was swept aside by Mr. Sanborn's own action, for he turned and beckoned to Solomon, then approached Mr. Pierce to offer a hand in greeting. "It's an honor to meet you, sir. As it happens, Mr. McBride and I were just discussing this matter. If you'll permit, the two of us will accompany you and Almyra, and perhaps she and her aunt will indulge us with tea at their table."

"Of course," Almyra replied. What else could she say? Her hand on Mr. Pierce's arm gathered more information for her. He didn't like the interference, and then changed his mind and opted to agree. Hmm. She made a mental note to utilize this method again in the future—when opportunities for appropriate holding of a gentleman's arm arose.

Susannah caught up with them, leading the horse along the edge of the road. She sized up the conversation and suggested, "I might take the horse back to our livery stable, until your business is done. You need only send word, and I'll bring him back."

"Th-thank you, young m-miss," Mr. Pierce agreed, without his gaze leaving Mr. Sanborn and Solomon. "M-much ap-p-preciated."

Minutes later, the odd grouping sat around the dining table where Aunt Charlotte insisted they settle. Small inquiries about weather and travel occupied the three men. Almyra hurried to assemble a tray of cups and the teapot. Aunt Charlotte had understood at once the identity of this stranger to the village, which Almyra could detect from a momentary narrowing of eyes and clenching of fingers—and which, she suspected, Mr. Pierce also observed and interpreted. Well, it wasn't her fault that he had a terrible reputation. How could the people in Canada elect him to their Parliament, considering his criminal past?

Mr. Sanborn rose to help Almyra set down the tea tray and to pull out a chair for Aunt Charlotte. "You ladies will join us, I'm sure, since you may be able to convey something of our absent minister's concerns and will want to provide details to him when he returns."

Aunt Charlotte nodded, gave a small bob from the waist toward Mr. Pierce, and said, "Indeed, I would value hearing what brings you to North Upton, sir."

Mr. Pierce, looking more elderly but not as frail, now that he'd removed his coat, held up a hand. "When all have their t-t-tea," he said.

Almyra nodded and set out the last two cups of tea and passed the plate of shortbread squares that Aunt Charlotte had retrieved from the pantry. Then she took her own seat and gave a small smile to Mr. Pierce. "We will do our best to assist you, sir."

The ambivalence of that polite phrase struck her. Assist a criminal? Or assist a political leader from across the border? A twitch of Solomon's lips suggested he too noticed. Well, of course, since he too was a political operative in his labors for Mr. William Seward, already being discussed as a potential presidential candidate.

Mr. Pierce took a sip of tea, cleared his throat, and began. "I have r-r-ridden today from Hardwick, where I met with a Miss M-Martha Johnson."

Almyra gasped in surprise, then realized Mr. Pierce had noticed. She pressed her lips together, inhaled slowly through her nose, and attempted to look interested but not concerned.

Their guest continued, "She c-conveyed that an abundance of f-f-forged bills in the r-r-region is inter-f-fering with efforts to f-fund the Abolitionist m-movement." His gaze circled the table. "N-naturally, as an ardent op-p-ponent of slavery m-myself, I was gravely dismayed to hear this, and I have already taken some action to redeem the situation."

Almyra noticed that Mr. Pierce's stammer relented as he reached the part he must have rehearsed in advance, his position statement. A sermon could function the same way: small introduction, then significant explication.

"Naturally, again, although I m-myself am a redeemed m-man, and c-called by God to good works that my district v-values highly, I am able to communicate with others who have not yet m-made such a choice. I w-wish to assure you that I have d-demanded g-guarantees that any r-remaining bills of, shall we say, uncertain p-p-provenance, will not be r-released in N-New England for the foreseeable future."

He paused, waiting for comments. Mr. McBride said, "I had heard of your Parliamentary position, sir, and am surely relieved to hear that you can put your influence to such good use." Almyra heard the double meaning: influence in politics, and influence as the notorious former leader of the counterfeiting gangs across the border.

Mr. Sanborn fingered his chin, clearly assessing this further. He asked, "Why would you bring this announcement here, sir? Much appreciated, of course, that it is."

The elderly man's eyebrows rose. "It's c-clear to any observer that the l-leaders of the r-rising support for abolition are the m-men of the cloth. Miss Johnson excepted, though of course her m-menfolk fill that r-role. I understand that M-Minister Alexander is the c-connection between the c-county seat here in Upton, and the p-p-passionate and p-professional leaders in St. Johnsbury d-driving the m-movement forward." He looked around the table, then recited smoothly, "Doctor Jewett, Judge Paddock, the Gilman brothers, need I say m-more? I have no intent to p-personally c-correspond with those, but I am assured," his diction smoothed out again, revealing to Almyra that he'd formed these words ahead of time, "that the minister of this village is able to immediately share word with those p-persons."

Mr. Sanborn nodded, jumping ahead. "And you'd hope that a quick mention of your intent would forestall any summoning of a sheriff's posse that might otherwise be motivated to head north across the border."

Almyra lifted a hand, and Mr. Sanborn nodded that he saw this. But rather than allow her to speak, he continued in his own deep, slow tones. "With full consideration for your efforts, sir, I'm afraid I must inform you that a posse left St. Johnsbury earlier this week, with that very intent. I'm afraid I don't yet have word of their success."

The canny glance Mr. Pierce shot toward Almyra convinced her this was not news to the elderly former counterfeiter. "I rather think that p-particular group has become d-distracted in Stanstead Plain, where they m-made one or two arrests, and c-could be c-c-concluding business shortly. Though m-my own information c-could, of c-course, be faulty." He gave a courteous nod toward Mr. Sanborn.

Almyra sat rigidly in her seat. Stanstead Plain—where Uncle Eliphalet, John Sanborn, Isaiah Hutchinson, and Captain Young must be staying. She saw the realization reach her aunt also. To prevent the clever Mr. Pierce from drawing more from this, she leaned across and asked Aunt Charlotte, "Is there more hot water for the teapot, aunt? Should I refill it?"

To her satisfaction, the distraction worked well, as her aunt immediately rose and said, "I shall set the kettle on. Pray continue your discussion, gentlemen."

There. Although a lift of Mr. Pierce's eyebrow suggested she hadn't been entirely successful at diverting him from other information, Almyra simply offered a small smile of her own and turned to Mr. Sanborn.

"Mr. McBride will join us for supper, I believe, as he has news to share about my dear sister in Boston. Will you also join us, sir? Perhaps you'd care to share our board?"

With the fresh intensity of all her senses, she noted Aunt Charlotte overhearing this and turning toward the pantry, even as Mr. Pierce interrupted.

"I b-b-believe I'll stay this night at your local inn," the visitor announced. "I r-rode from Upton, Canada, to Hardwick yesterday, and then from Hardwick to here, today. Though I'll take m-m-my supper there, perhaps you gentlemen would c-care to join me for a c-congenial beverage afterward. We m-m-might then discuss further what I hope may be our agreement to moderate the c-c-course of future events. With the m-minister's ap-p-proval, I trust, when he is again in residence."

Slow nods around the table confirmed that this "deal" was not yet complete, but nearly so, and also asserted the closing of the conversation, though Mr. Sanborn added to Almyra that he'd decline supper this time, for the sake of checking his lambs, and in hopes that his wife might return home soon.

Interesting. With Mr. Sanborn at his side for the walk back through the village to the inn, there seemed no need for Mr. Pierce to have someone's arm to lean on. Not so frail, if he walked beside a man, was he? In frustration, Almyra realized the former counterfeiter had deliberately sought her own arm as a way to gather more information. How annoying.

Solomon McBride strolled off to Uncle Eliphalet's study, where he settled in a comfortable chair, one hand rubbing his forehead in apparent thought. Almyra carried the cups to the kitchen. Her aunt, dicing onions, gestured toward a half dozen large potatoes, and Almyra moved smoothly into assisting with the supper. Diced ham with potatoes and onions should do nicely for the two of them and their last guest.

Now Almyra wondered, *Why did Solomon want to speak with Mr. Sanborn? It surely couldn't have been related to Mr. Pierce, could it? Would the two of them conduct other business after the meeting at the inn?*

If she were a young man, she could sit with them and hear firsthand the final arrangements all around. However, she realized suddenly that her Sunday morning was racing toward her.

She finished peeling and slicing the potatoes. Then, so that she would not drop any of the threads of the moment, she went to her own desk for a moment, ignoring Solomon's curious glance. On a scrap of paper, she wrote: When will we hear from Stanstead Plain? Are they all safe? Who did the posse arrest? Would Uncle agree to Mr. Pierce's request? Will Judge Paddock? Was Susannah safe with Mr. Pierce at the inn? How did Martha Johnson know Mr. Pierce? Does Solomon know about the Boston court case?

Having thus arranged her most pressing thoughts and given herself fresh warning of Solomon's possible duplicity—such a terrible thing to consider about one's sister's husband, but she knew it to be his nature—she placed her list of questions inside the pages of her Bible and ostentatiously carried the leather-bound volume out of the room and off to her chamber for later consideration.

Assisting Aunt Charlotte with supper must come first.

Almyra knew it was wrong. Sitting on an upturned wooden box in the loft of the tavern, a handkerchief held to her face to keep from sneezing in the settling dust, she wondered for a moment whether most criminals began this way: making excuses for misbehavior. But with Uncle Eliphalet gone, she felt responsible for actions taken in his name. Really, these men should not be making any agreement until her uncle returned. Clearly, they didn't feel the same way. Or else they felt the times pressed them forward with pardonable urgency.

And that, Almyra told herself, explained why she'd asked Susannah to help her into position, to listen to the evening conversation with a pardonable sense of urgency and responsibility.

Suppertime shared with Solomon McBride and her aunt had brought no significant information to her. Aunt Charlotte pressed for long-stale details of the trousseau that Almyra's sister Janet brought when she'd married Solomon nearly two years earlier, and cleverly coaxed Solomon into admitting that Janet was with child. Then, of course, she had exclaimed, "You're becoming an aunt yourself, Almyra."

With enormous effort, Almyra produced whatever smiles and nods the conversation required. This included an amazed appreciation for the Boston lifestyle, concern for Janet's health, pleasure for the young couple's oncoming joy, and a daughterly wish that Solomon would convey her regards to her papa in Boston.

Throughout the meal, however, she'd seethed with inner impatience. Her aunt had squelched Almyra's one attempt to shift the conversation to the visit from Foster Pierce, either for the sake of mealtime manners or because Aunt Charlotte preferred not to risk divulging Uncle Eliphalet's mission north of the border.

After Solomon finally departed, Aunt Charlotte, clearly worn out from all the bustle, had claimed the start of a headache and retreated to her chamber. Almyra prepared a pot of mint tea for her, carried it in, and kissed her aunt's forehead with a wish for swift recovery.

"I'm like Judas," she told herself now, listening to the small talk below about weather and roads. "I gave her a kiss and betrayed her trust."

Wasn't she upholding another trust, however? That was the best she could reply.

A pause in the conversation below, accompanied by the scrape of chair legs as the men rearranged their positions, called her attention to the changing tones of voice. Mr. Pierce took the lead, "As I explained, I have already n-notified my former ac-c-quaintances that their b-business p-practices are m-misfiring here, and they would do well to send their p-printed matter down the N-N-New York route, express to that city without p-p-pause for c-commercial distribution in n-n-northern N-New England. What I r-require from you gentlemen is," ah, here came that smoothed delivery again, "assurance that you will quiet the interest of the authorities, including your bank and your judge."

Mr. Sanborn's deep slow voice challenged the visitor. "You mistake the American custom, sir, if you believe we can instruct any such person in whom to investigate or when to cease doing so."

"I m-m-make very few m-mistakes, gentlemen, and this is n-not one of them. I c-c-comprehend influence very well. I agree that the p-presence of your m-m-minister would help on this, b-b-but if you w-wish my assistance c-clearing up the p-presence of c-counterfeits on this side of the C-C-Canada line, you m-m-must do your share."

Solomon McBride cut in. "It would give me great pleasure to inform Judge Paddock that we expect the flood of forged bills to wane in the immediate future. Whether he then pulls back the urge to send a future posse, that we cannot guarantee. But I think Mr. Sanborn will agree with me that if the bank, not to mention our funding subscriptions, ceases to be plagued by these artifices, it is far less likely to demand the efforts of law enforcement."

Without seeing the men's faces, Almyra couldn't tell enough about who was leading and who was following. She knew Mr. Sanborn could get very angry at times, and she braced for one of his usual thumps of his fist on the table.

Solomon must have assessed the mood and considered it safe to proceed. "Mind you, sir, Mr. Sanborn is entirely correct that the authorities are independent of what is said here. That said, good news is always welcome and has its own potent effects." A brief silence told Almyra that Mr. Sanborn must have shown enough willingness, in his face or with a nod, to stop further argument.

Apparently Mr. Pierce thought so, too. Chair legs scraped as he rose. "Then I b-believe we have informed each other of our n-n-news and intents, and there is a warm b-bed waiting for these aging b-b-bones. Gentlemen, a g-good night to you. I shan't expect to see you in the m-m-morning, as I'll be m-making an early departure for N-Newport and b-b-beyond."

Newport and beyond? Did that mean Stanstead Plain and the nearby communities, where Uncle Eliphalet and the others were probing the ongoing fraudulent coinage and printing as Isaiah Hutchinson assayed the copper mines? Almyra recollected that Stanstead Plain was a day's ride from the town of Upton, Quebec, which seemed to be Mr. Pierce's home location. Was the region all one piece, in terms of counterfeiting? More urgently, would Mr. Pierce's mission cross paths with her uncle's?

She had only time to make a quick decision to write to Miss Farrow about this, when the two remaining men below resumed.

"Keep your voice low," Mr. Sanborn growled. "I've no faith in that man's discretion about our other business. Tell me at once, do you need shelter for someone, or more documents for escorting men northward?"

Almyra knew the Sanborn family and the Gilman brothers, owners of the big mills in St. Johnsbury, had assisted in the past so that fugitives from the South, so that anyone of dark skin, imperiled by the harsh fugitive laws, could journey safely. But those travels had ceased, she believed, as the dangers escalated. Oh, why couldn't Solomon's political colleagues halt such persecution? It all came down, as it always did, to the dire need for the abolition of enslavement.

She bent closer to the edge of the loft to hear a rustle of papers, and Solomon's hushed reply.

"That time's gone past us," came the hoarse whisper. "The battleground today is entirely at the frontier, in Illinois and Kansas.

Here, your brother's newspaper report will give you some notion. Meantime, there's a plan out of Boston to enlist settlers from New England who'll not only work the land out there, but cast their votes for a Free state, even perhaps two such states. You met Eli Thayer when he stopped here, I know. So my news from Boston is this. Last week, Thayer completed organizing the Massachusetts Emigrant Aid Company to send anti-slavery settlers westward. Wagons, tools, supplies, he and his sponsors will ensure such support. So I, that is, we, all of us, need you to pass word, and send young men to Boston to enlist." His voice rose in enthusiasm. "This is our new battle front. One where we are uniquely equipped to succeed."

"Hush."

At Mr. Sanborn's sharp command, Solomon fell silent. Almyra sensed them listening. She clutched her handkerchief more tightly to her face, barely breathing. I will not sniff or sneeze, she told herself, as the urge to do both kept rising.

When Mr. Sanborn began again to speak, she dared to sniff into the fabric, as she strained to hear more.

"You already have my sons out there. We're short of hands in this village already, for the farms and mills. What more do you want?"

If he'd been in his own kitchen, he'd be banging his fist, Almyra was sure.

"We want St. Johnsbury. And Lyndon. And even Barton Landing's young men. I ride tomorrow for Hardwick and Craftsbury. I need you—Mr. Seward needs you—this nation needs you to convince others to send their sons and brothers. Should we fail, God help us all. We may yet see a civil war erupt in Congress, which is increasingly un-civil, day by day. It's the money, man—the Slave Power won't see fit to release profits."

A deeper growl from Mr. Sanborn raised a shiver in Almyra. If she'd been at the table with him, she'd have pushed her chair back in alarm.

"Don't you think there's profit here, too? Or lack of it. If the price of wool drops any lower, I'll be slaughtering my sheep for mutton. And the Gilmans in St. Johnsbury, you think they'll be pleased to have their young workers head westward? When they need every hand not just for scale construction but for engineering the machines that process cotton? Oh yes, even here, cotton is king, as the Slave Power proclaims. My daughter's gone off to Illinois to assist my brother's enterprise." Almyra heard the newspaper sheets rattle. "And to fight the sale of rum there … rum made by slave labor in the far-off islands, or do you think the Illinois Maine Law Alliance will succeed in closing down that loop of profit and commerce?"

Solomon said something so quietly that Alymra couldn't catch it.

Mr. Sanborn roared, "Of course Gilman suffers when he stands for abolition. So do we all."

The door from the house banged open, and Almyra heard Matthew. Oh my, he and his mother must have returned long since—but she hadn't seen him when Susannah had boosted her up the ladder to the loft.

Matthew asked, "Trouble here, gentlemen? Short of cider, perhaps?"

Solomon's voice shook a bit. "Another mug wouldn't be declined on my part, Matthew. I won't dare ask for rum, all things considered."

"No," Matthew said evenly, "we've no rum in this establishment. Nor whiskey."

Chair legs scraped. Mr. Sanborn's voice came more clearly. He must be standing. "I've had all I can swallow," he said, his double meaning clear. Then he added with obvious reluctance, "I'll pass along your news, McBride. Whatever it takes to fight this blood-red sinfulness, it's worth the cost. But take it to the bigger towns, would you? North Upton's reaching a limit for what we can give, give, and give."

Almyra heard Matthew set a mug on the table. "You're welcome to carry it to your chamber," he said.

Dear heavens, was Solomon staying in the other loft room? Would he see her as he climbed up to there?

The mug must have gone to use straight away. As it clunked back down on the table, Solomon said, "Good thing I've a ground floor room this time. You brew a potent cider, Matthew. I'm for my bed. You'll wake me at dawn, if you don't hear me stirring by then?"

"Indeed. You and Mr. Pierce, the two of you. Mrs. Hall says there'll be something hot and ready here at the table to fit you for your rides."

Almyra waited for all the scrapes of chairs and tidying to end, with the lamp quenched and Matthew's step, then the closing of the door to the house. The inn's two bedchambers sat beyond the tavern room, overlooking the stable yard. Good thing she planned to go out the front way and quietly walk back through the village.

Fumbling on the ladder in the darkness, her head spun with all the news and information. She must reach Miss Farrow as soon as she could to spread word as needed and to seek counsel.

Her morning sermon suddenly seemed too tame for the time. Planting seeds? Tending gardens? Instead, she should speak of courage. Pharoah's daughter. Esther. She thought of the book of James: "Doth a fountain send forth at the same place sweet water and bitter?" Which waters were her own?

If her uncle should be delayed in his mission, she'd prepare for another Sunday. She, too, could join this battle.

~ 21 ~

When she woke at dawn on Sunday morning, Almyra's mind danced with the thoughts that she'd fallen asleep with. *Mr. Thayer's call, through Solomon, for young men to settle in Kansas, to prepare to cast ballots for a free state in the enormous territory. And the cost that Abolition could exert in Vermont, most especially for the Gilman machinery manufacturing.*

No conversation she'd heard before had ever pointed out that the northern states also benefited from cotton plantations with their enslaved workers. She longed to ask Aunt Charlotte and Uncle Eliphalet about this, as well as Mr. Sanborn himself, once he'd calmed down.

But without a deeper understanding, she could not carry this into her preaching. Uncle Eliphalet's insistence that she work from one of his own sermons, carefully thought through and adjusted to her own mode of speaking, seemed generous and not overbearing, now that she found the pulpit only a few hours away. She must do this well—both for her uncle's sake, and to show that a woman could preach the Word of God with propriety and good sense.

First for this morning—her clothing.

Almyra smiled, thinking of how her mother would have fussed over the correct outfit for the day, one that spoke of elegant fit and good posture, while also hinting at the solemn force of the ministry. The years living in North Upton hadn't treated Almyra's Boston skirts and waists well: worn seams, an occasional lost button replaced with an imperfect match. But Aunt Charlotte's skill with letting down hems and adding ribbon trim helped.

One more swipe with the clothes brush ensured that her skirts lay smoothly over her petticoats and made the wool band along the hem look fresh. Should she wear gloves? Yes, the long ones with the open fingers—but those should go into her reticule for now, along with the pages of her sermon. She carried her best lace collar with her to the kitchen, knowing her aunt would have the knack of pinning it neatly in place.

"Turn around, my dear, let me see. Yes, that will suit well. Mind you don't crush the back of the skirt as you sit for your breakfast." Aunt Charlotte gestured to the steaming meat pie she'd already cut open. "There's a light frost on the ground, but the day will warm quickly. Thank goodness it isn't raining, so your boots won't suffer."

"I wish we could know what the men are pursuing in the north," Almyra said after a few bites. "It seems so strange to go on as usual, when they may be confronting counterfeiters or other dangers."

With a shake of her head, Almyra's aunt dismissed the notion. "It's more likely that Isaiah has been laboring for the mine speculators with his assaying chemicals, assisted by John Sanborn, while your uncle and Captain Young are attaching new friends all around. Of course, they must all attend a worship service this morning. Unless your uncle is preaching in some lodging house to a gathering of working men. But if they are in Stanstead Plain, I'm sure they're making for a proper church for the next few hours."

"Have you ever seen Uncle Eliphalet do such a thing? Preach without a pulpit?" Surely every town in Vermont had a meetinghouse.

"In the earlier years, yes, of course. Not just for lack of a meetinghouse, mind, but when a minister had left or been sent off, yet the church wasn't prepared for a successor. When we were younger, we often traveled half of Saturday to reach some village in need."

Almyra nodded. "My father has done something similar, but across further distances. He was called to Philadelphia several times, and he has invitations to the capital when Congress gathers."

Her aunt patted her hand. "There is much to admire in Charles's preaching. I think he and your uncle offer many similarities, as brothers, but their different paths have shaped their outlooks and forms of speech. You must send for some of your father's sermon drafts, you know. Learning from both your uncle and your father will widen your own approach, I'm sure."

Would her father share his written notes with her? How had she never thought of asking? "I'll write to him this evening," she promised.

A thump at the kitchen door startled them both. Almyra jumped up to see who'd come calling so early on the Sabbath. Something heavy seemed pressed against the door. She pushed outward and heard an agitated bellow from a sheep.

Aunt Charlotte laughed. "Latch the door securely. I'm sure Mr. Sanborn must know he's lost one. By the time we have your cuffs and collar pinned, the animal will have wandered or been herded back."

This, Almyra thought, would never happen in her father's city positions. She could describe it for him when she penned her next letter. A mix of guilt and loss tossed her for a moment. The guilt that she so rarely wrote to him now, and loss, because his new marriage clearly occupied his time and thoughts. Oh Mama, she reflected, would you bless his new life? I think you would, from Heaven. But it is harder for me.

Enough! Such notions would not make her a better speaker from the pulpit. Instead, she mouthed the start of her Scriptural passage: "Behold, a sower went for to sow; And when he sowed, some seeds fell by the way side, and the fowls came and devoured them up." Or the sheep? She smiled. "But other fell into good ground, and brought forth fruit, some an hundredfold, some sixtyfold, some thirtyfold." And then the difficult portion about who would receive more, and who would discover that all he had was being taken from him.

She added aloud, "'But he that received seed into the good ground is he that heareth the word, and understandeth it.' How clever women are, Aunt, to hear this and know it applies to both man and wife."

"Certainly," her aunt replied, "it is always so in Scripture."

Almyra mused aloud, "Miss Sarah Grimke might expound further, charging wives and mother, sisters and daughters, with further obligations. As she has in terms of the overthrow of slavery."

"And you shall preach such Gospel also, my dear, but not today. Be kind to your neighbors and give them food they can recognize that they may call it good and be sustained."

"Why, Aunt Charlotte, you are propounding a Gospel of the Kitchen."

Laughing together, they checked that the sheep had gone its way, and they exited the house, while the May sun, high over the village already, lit the morning with hope.

By the time they reached the church, Almyra wished she had not eaten any breakfast. She concentrated on posture, and walking from the door to the wooden railing that marked the start of the preacher's area at the front of the church. Aunt Charlotte remained standing near their family pew, nodding and smiling and occasionally clasping someone's hand as the neighbors arrived. Almyra set her pages down onto the lectern, opened the heavy Bible to the page of her Scripture passage, and closed her eyes a moment. What if she let Uncle Eliphalet down? Would he simply discourage her from the ministry, or would he, could he, send her back to Boston and the life of a daughter preparing for marriage?

She forced herself to swallow from a dry mouth, and to open her eyes. If she gazed only at her pages, she could do this.

Aunt Charlotte took her seat. It must be time to begin. Almyra opened, "This is the day which the Lord hath made; we will rejoice and be glad in it."

The sunshine through the tall side windows cast a warm light on the congregation. Though the faces blurred, she realized they looked to her expectantly. *Rise to the occasion,* she told herself firmly, and continued the service she'd planned.

Not only were the faces blurred—so was her sense of time, and of the responses around her. At one moment she managed to focus on Jeremy Hopkins's wife and small child. She'd known Jeremy, enough to say hello to, before he'd married; how could there be already a child old enough to bring to Sunday worship? Time in its larger sense also made no sense today. At least the sermon itself, so thoroughly rehearsed, felt real and proper. Time crawled, then leapt forward, then crawled again.

A face in the back row, constant and steady, became her anchor. At first she only saw the wide eyes examining her, not distracted by the small movements and breathing of several dozen others in the sanctuary. She reminded herself to tell a story, as the Lord had told stories. "The same day," she said, "went Jesus out of the house, and sat by the seaside." Almyra saw those eyes widen at the notion of a young man placing himself on the shore of a sea, a wide expanse of salted water filled with mystery. She did not raise her arms from the desk—a minister maintained an erect and steady posture and present the holy words without raising his arms, without making foolish facial gestures—but she allowed her voice to rise as if it were light reflected from that sea, reaching out to the woman on the back bench. I want you to hear this as if it were new to you, she thought, and she tongued the passage clearly. "And great multitudes were gathered together unto him." See them, feel how they press forward. "And he spake many things unto them in parables." Dear Lord, she knew that face.

It was Susannah.

For a moment the breath fueling her sermon faltered. Mrs. Hall of course sat on the bench also, but Almyra hadn't paid attention to her. She'd attended the morning's worship service before, though not always. But never, ever had Susannah been there as far as Almyra could recall.

A stirring of breath around her warned her she'd paused for too long, so that others wondered why. She gripped the desk for a moment, then lifted her voice again. It flooded into her: the sudden knowledge that laying out the story in all its specific warning provided the footboard, the stirrup, the very ground for everything she valued. Loyalty. Respect. Freedom of every person. Abolition, and Temperance, and Justice.

When she said about the seeds, "Some fell upon stony places," she saw Susannah mirror her own regret. When she brought up the triumph of the passage, for the seed that "fell into good ground, and brought for fruit, some an hundredfold," she marveled at the miracle of a seed's journey toward harvest, toward feeding the people around it, fulfilling its purpose. "Who hath ears to hear, let him hear." Susannah's face glowed in response. I am bringing food of the spirit, Almyra realized.

She blinked, looked down at her page to remind herself of the next portion, almost committed to memory by now, of the listener who "heareth the word, and anon with joy receiveith it." If her mother were here, sitting in a front pew next to Aunt Charlotte, her mother's mouth would purse in disagreement—her mother would never indulge in joy, only in pain and self-pity and gusts of sour anger.

"Tribulation and persecution," Almyra warned. Her gaze fell again on Susannah, and her heart lifted. A friend. Susannah might never have sat to study her Bible, might not ache for discussion of moral purpose, would not consider that the evil of the Slave Power demanded a personal commitment to battle.

But Susannah was here. For Almyra's first sermon. She was a true friend.

At the final "Amen," Almyra placed her pages into her reticule in haste. Uncle Eliphalet always stood at the church door, to greet each person by name as they left the church, and she must do likewise. She saw Susannah slip out of the church without waiting, but it didn't worry her. The open doorway glowed in bright sunshine. She stood just inside it, thinking of how the church became a well of living water, and the people who drank from it could then go out into their gardens, into their lives, and grow like the seeds on good soil. Aunt Charlotte came to stand at her side, with a murmur of, "Well done, my dear," and an example of straight shoulders and a kind smile for all.

Small words of approval from others warmed Almyra, and she could not refrain from blushing, until her cheeks felt as hot as if she perched next to a woodstove. She paid close attention to how her aunt greeted each person and tried to employ matching levels of formality and appreciation. So many bobs of her head.

At last, Aunt Charlotte offered both her hands to clasp those of a woman wearing a long well-cut woolen jacket over skirts surely resting on hoops. It took a moment for Almyra to make sense of who this was: Miss Farrow, all the way from St. Johnsbury in time for the church service.

"I learned recently that your uncle had been called away and made an impetuous decision to listen to his niece deliver a sermon. You'll pardon me, I hope, for failing to notify you in advance."

Almyra followed her aunt's example and took Miss Farrow's gloved hands in her own. "Indeed, I am only delighted to see you, ma'am."

Her aunt cut in. "You'll join us for our noon meal, I trust? Almyra won't provide an afternoon sermon, since this is her first occasion."

"Your first." Miss Farrow beamed. "One would never have guessed that from your delivery. Perhaps we may converse further over our meal on the implications of the parable. I look forward to it."

One of Alice Sanborn's brothers, William, who had a mill at the far edge of the village, waited to escort them out and close the door. Even William, often short with his words, spoke to Almyra: "I wouldn't have guessed you could stand at your uncle's place so well. He'll be back with us for the next Sabbath, I trust?"

"And also your brother John," Almyra agreed. "Do you hear from Charles? A new letter from Alice?"

"You'll need to ask my mother what the latest is." William shook his head as he released the door. "I confess I'm fair knackered these days, and grateful to pause for a day of rest." He lifted his hat to Aunt Charlotte and Miss Farrow and headed down the road.

Spring bird calls and a warm breeze welcomed Almyra, and she felt her usual self settle back into place. There would be time later to contemplate her morning's effort. Instead, she scrambled to catch up with the others.

"Miss Farrow," she asked, "have you heard from my uncle or the others yet?"

"Not yet. But yesterday I had a short note from Sarah. I've brought it so you can read it for yourself. And," Miss Farrow turned back to Aunt Charlotte, "a separate concern on which I hope you can assist."

"Of course. Whatever I can do. What does this concern?"

Miss Farrow paused to look appraisingly at Almyra before she answered Aunt Charlotte. "The Hall family," she said quietly. "And their herbs and medicaments."

Almyra drew in a long breath. Even with the strength of preaching sustaining her, she felt so much younger than these strong women. Nevertheless, she spoke, "Then, I presume, we will wish to ask Mrs. Hall to also join our gathering."

~ 22 ~

Almyra's hurried mission to find Mrs. Hall at the inn failed. Mrs. Hall had left to visit her husband and sons at the family farm in Waterford. It seemed she did this every two weeks or so, though Almyra hadn't noticed it before. Polly and Jane didn't always go, but this time they had.

So instead, Almyra asked Susannah to come. There wasn't time to explain much. Still, she waited long enough for Susannah to step back into the Sunday skirt she'd worn earlier.

On the way back together, she struggled for the right words to thank Susannah for listening so intently to her sermon. But the truth of how she'd felt—supported, needed, useful—seemed too big to speak into the moment. So instead she said simply, "I was glad to see you in the church this morning."

Susannah slanted a skeptical glance at her. "I can't make that sort of time often. Jane stayed at the house with Polly. You wouldn't want her coughing while you spoke." She added, "I found it interesting. You tell the story better than, well, differently from, your father. Or Mr. Hastings, back in Waterford."

They'd reached the house and had run out of time. Almyra wondered whether it was a good thing or a shameful, overly dramatic thing, to tell a Gospel story well. But she had only a moment to remind herself that she needed to be Martha, not Mary, at this moment—that is, she needed to help her aunt feed this small multitude of women.

As it happened, Miss Farrow didn't reveal her mission until Almyra and Susannah, easily working together, had cleared the dishes from the table. There had been ham pie, brown bread, and apple compote. Mrs. Sanborn also had joined the group in the sunlit kitchen, regaling the group with recent birthings.

"And then, if you please, he took the baby in those huge hands of his and peeled back the blanket from his little damp head, and asked me whether that dark hair came from his wife's insistence on coffee instead of tea while she was with child. Can you imagine. Of course, the fool's been bald for so long he's forgotten what his own head of hair looked like—but I recall him from graded school, and that baby is the spitting image … but a good sight cleaner."

Amid the cascade of laughter, Almyra refreshed the hot water in the teapot and smiled at Susannah, sitting next to Mrs. Sanborn. Such an unusual gathering: the three women and Susannah and herself, not for a sewing circle or book discussion, but to consider something important that required immediate action. Why else would Miss Farrow ride early on a Sunday morning to North Upton?

Now Miss Farrow passed Almyra the promised note from Sarah, assuring her there was no need to return it. Almyra set it carefully aside to enjoy later.

Miss Farrow leaned toward Aunt Charlotte and began, "I must first ask your indulgence, yours and Almyra's in particular, for a conversation that doesn't strictly pertain to the Sabbath. I wanted very much to attend your first sermon, Almyra, so I beg you'll indulge me in carrying this subject to the table today."

"By all means." Aunt Charlotte smiled. "I can't imagine Our Lord would object either—when there was a choice between a rule and a healing, I believe he always selected the healing, regardless of the day of the week. Almyra, would you agree?"

Almyra nodded. "Even to the point of reminding his disciples to pay more attention to their words, than to their strict eating habits," she noted. It felt good to be asked. She saw Susannah's lifted eyebrows, and blushed. A person could quickly appear "puffed up" like this.

Mrs. Sanborn pursued the Sabbath point. "Babies arrive on every day of the week. Recall the rhyme, 'The child that is born on the Sabbath day is bonnie and blythe, good and gay.' We might consider this a birth of sorts, Rachel. Lay your troubles on the table and we'll try to set them right."

Rachel? Well of course, Miss Farrow must have a Christian name— but Almyra had never heard it before. She tucked away the new knowledge. She said, "I too have a concern that doesn't relate to the Sabbath, Miss Farrow, and I may raise it later."

Miss Farrow nodded. In the afternoon sunlight, she blinked her dark brown eyes. Her age showed at this moment, the creases in her face, and gray threads in her tightly coiled braid. But so did her concern, and her sharp mind, as she began to speak. Almyra marveled that a woman who'd spent her childhood enslaved had become so highly educated. Had Judge Paddock seen to Miss Farrow's education in childhood? Or was her wisdom gained in adulthood? Somehow, Almyra had never thought about this before. Well, she would ask Aunt Charlotte later.

"So you see," Miss Farrow continued, "because the Judge keeps careful records of births, marriages, and deaths for the county—he considers it part of his responsibility—he has confirmed what I had only suspected. The number of women dying who are with child is shocking, especially on the hill farms."

"I can't be everywhere," Mrs. Sanborn said defensively. Aunt Charlotte and Miss Farrow reached out simultaneously to enfold Mrs. Sanborn's hands.

"You're a marvel, Abigail, and without your efforts, there's no doubt there'd be fewer healthy babies and mothers around North Upton. I heard you rode all the way to Hardwick last winter, for a breach birth," Miss Farrow said.

Aunt Charlotte concurred, saying, "There's no doubt you're doing all you can, and more than many. That's not the issue at all, is it, Rachel?"

With a shake of her head, Miss Farrow replied, "Indeed it's not. Let me ask you something. I know Mrs. Hall hasn't resided in this village for long. Do you advise women to consume her strengthening tonics when they are gravid?"

Susannah shot a glance at Almyra but remained silent.

"I always have, even before she resided here," Mrs. Sanborn confirmed. "I used to send letters to her, with names of women she might call upon. Her tonics can make such a difference, especially when a woman is swelling during winter and has no greens to depend on. Beans and bacon can only go just so far. And farm work can't stop, you see."

"And, if you'll pardon the indelicacy, at what point after a woman's courses have ceased would you wish her to begin to consume the tonics?"

"Immediately." Mrs. Sanborn looked at Almyra. "This may be new to you." She hesitated. "You're aware of how." She stopped and looked at Almyra's aunt.

"She knows," Aunt Charlotte confirmed. "She's young, but she's a woman herself. Moreover, as a minister, she must be aware of the paths of marriage and bearing children. And Susannah assists her own mother, of course." Susannah nodded, still silent.

Unspoken in this moment was the difficult truth Almyra and her aunt had recently reviewed: that if Almyra pursued the ministry, she'd be unlikely to marry and have children. Though perhaps she might do so later in life—at the cost of her ministry.

Miss Farrow pressed onward. "At a guess, Abigail, how far along are the women when they come to you?"

"Many never do," Mrs. Sanborn pointed out. "If they've borne children before, they may not even call for me or anyone else to assist with the birth. Often their mothers or older daughters assist. However, some write to me in the last month, worrying and asking whether I can oblige." She nodded toward Almyra. "Or they're young and afraid, with the first child to come, and too shy to say so, or not realizing until it's almost time. Petticoats and hard work, you see."

Actually Almyra didn't quite see, but she didn't want to sound less educated. Especially since Susannah's slight nod seemed to agree.

Now Miss Farrow reached her point, leaning forward to emphasize it. "That, I think, is the trouble. Especially in the homes where the menfolk drink strong beverages and the women keep their questions to themselves for fear of an argument or worse."

"But how can they drink strong beverages?" Almyra had to ask. "Doesn't Vermont's version of the Maine law, the temperance law, stop that?"

Aunt Charlotte winced. "You must perceive human nature more clearly," she told Almyra. "A man whose habit leans to strong drink will continue to do so, regardless of the law. Under the law, the tavern keeper fails to profit from those beverages. But there have always been others to make them and sell them. Even some who brew at home."

Red-faced, Almyra nodded. She struggled to recover her sense of being nearly a woman grown, and close to becoming a seminary student. "I see. So, Miss Farrow, are you seeking a way to reach out to these women? The ones with harsh husbands?"

Their guest lifted her hands, first one, then the other. "I think we must do so, but bear in mind that such a marriage is often not obvious beyond the house doors. So instead, it's a matter of making Mrs. Hall's tonics available more widely. Dr. Jewett already trusts them and suggests their use. I did think about suggesting a peddler's cart."

Susannah smiled. But Almyra felt shock at the notion and saw this reflected in Mrs. Sanborn's face and Aunt Charlotte's.

"Fear not, I know it's not a reasonable idea," Miss Farrow said quickly. "Although in Europe, I understand, it is sometimes the case that a woman drives a market cart. But here among the rough roads, mountains, and storms, it can't be considered."

Susannah spoke up at last. "I carry quite a bit when I ride out to the other towns. Though weather and time may work against me."

"Yes, of course. And I know you bring more when you or your mother happen to come to town with a wagon. I must ask, Susannah. If we could pass more work about your mother's tonics, could she—and you—meet an increase in demand?"

Susannah only nodded this time.

"Thank you. So I propose instead that we assist Mrs. Hall by having broadsides printed for her tonics, and distributing them to shopkeepers, postal clerks, and the like."

Ah. Almyra asked at once, "What would it cost?"

"The Judge will cover the expense," Miss Farrow replied. "If we can distribute them. I suggest that in addition, we begin to firm up our links with women in the other hill towns, like Peacham, Wheelock, and further. Letters should go forth also."

Mrs. Sanborn and Aunt Charlotte now leaned across the table, lit with fresh energy. "And thus," Aunt Charlotte said, "firm up the connections for other uses as well. Such as to circulate literature on the abolition of slavery, and the necessity for action."

The three women beamed at each other. Almyra said to Susannah, "I might talk with Miss Johnson of Peacham, the one we visited, about extending this westward to Hardwick and beyond."

"Excellent." Miss Farrow patted her hand. "Your own father is a minister in both Boston and the nation's capital, is he not? I see his likeness in you, my dear, as you will extend the work of freeing this nation from sin out to the scattered farming communities on which our liberties depend."

Again that glance from Susannah, half amused—really, Almyra must consider seriously how to avoid an inflated reputation based on a single morning in the pulpit. However, she must also consider Uncle Eliphalet, as she occupied his place at this moment. What would he say?

"I think," she answered slowly, "drawing women together behind the cause of abolition is both urgent and prudent. In Boston, I know, there are ladies' anti-slavery societies, who raise funds as needed, from their needlework and writings. But let us be clear, we are discussing tonics for the health of woman and child, are we not? I would wish to avoid further promoting the other kind."

A shiver ran around the table. Fear? Disturbance? Something the older women knew about the tonics intended for women to regain their monthly courses, against what nature and marriage intended. Almyra resisted looking to Susannah for support.

Again, it was Miss Farrow who leaned forward in sympathy. "I'm sure you're correct, Almyra. And you do honor to your uncle with your thoughtful caution. We shall indeed focus on the tonics that support health and strength and easy birthing."

"What about the plants?"

Everyone looked baffled by Susannah's question.

"Mother will need more herbs," she explained, a tad impatiently. "It's planting season. If we're to make more tonic as we see demand increase, we can't be the only ones setting these into the garden. As it is, Polly's harvested around the edges of many an ill-kept and forgotten herb bed or scrap of pasture, where I know she shouldn't, just to bring home enough."

Almyra laughed. So this was the secret, the reason the small child so often scurried around the village in the shadows of evening. "Do you know there are parables of harvest, too? Mrs. Sanborn, what about more seed all around?"

In a flurry of suggestions and plans, the talk turned to gardens, and the sunlight in the room seemed brighter all at once.

Yet Almyra wondered whether Uncle Eliphalet would consider that she'd taken a firm enough stance. Enslavement was sinful. So was a death induced after a baby had quickened in the mother's womb. She couldn't help thinking about that girl who'd used Mrs. Hall's potion too late, bleeding and then dying herself.

Now she recalled the way Mrs. Sanborn had once said, when all the girls—Alice, Sarah, Almyra—had been much younger, that women must speak for liberty of all kinds. At the time, Almyra had enthused about linking abolition and temperance and a vote for women. What more might this little convocation add?

Under Susannah's inquiring gaze, she blushed again. She offered aloud, "I can carry seeds with me as I make visits that my uncle suggests. I am learning also to ride, and to drive a wagon. Though Susannah will always do so better than I."

She rose to make a fresh pot of tea, while Susannah began to explain about several kinds of mint, and which were of benefit. Ah, there could be a sermon in this.

Almyra smiled at the familiar thought, then poked more wood into the stove's firebox to start the kettle heating.

A rap at the kitchen door interrupted them all. It was Mr. Weeks, the postmaster. "Telegram," he called as he knocked again. Aunt Charlotte rose from her seat.

# ~ 23 ~

Mr. Weeks apologized for bringing the envelope on the Sabbath. "It came last night, when I'd already closed up the store," he explained. "My wife received it at the house, and, well, you know how it can be when you have grandchildren who need tending on a Saturday night. She never thought to mention it until just now."

Almyra bit her lip, holding back both frustration and fear. Any telegram meant urgency, and surely this one came from Uncle Eliphalet. She wanted to say aloud, "It's a man's freedom at stake," and fault Mr. Weeks's wife for adding more risk to that, but any such words would only mean more time before Aunt Charlotte could read the thin page.

She clenched her hands into fists but hid them in her skirt. The sounds of the kettle coming to a boil set her back into motion, sluicing out the teapot, adding fresh tea leaves and then the hot water. Everything in its ordained sequence. No, this was not for a sermon, this was people she cared about far from home.

At the table, Miss Farrow perched with straight back, alert, as if she could rise up and fly if needed. Mrs. Sanborn spoke quietly to Susannah.

At last Mr. Weeks departed, and Aunt Charlotte unfolded the telegram. Almyra walked the teapot to the table, without taking her eyes off her aunt.

"They are all well," Aunt Charlotte said at last. "But I'm not sure I understand this. Who is Grame? And what should I do?"

"Perhaps the Reverend Leonard Grimes," Almyra speculated. "In Boston. He leads a Baptist church for colored people there. My father knows him well. Aunt, will you read it to us all, entire?"

Aunt Charlotte returned to her seat, and Almyra pressed close, to look at the paper. Her aunt read aloud. "RHDana agrees. Tell Paddock and Grame plates confiscated Upton Bank and Wells River. Rider to sheriff two days." She added, "It was sent from Branston, Quebec, by telegraph to St. Albans, Vermont, then to St. Johnsbury."

Almyra shook her head. "It can't be my father's friend in Boston. Is there a Grimes associated with Judge Paddock?"

Mrs. Sanborn, pouring tea all around, paused. "Not Grimes, but Graham. One of the directors of the bank in Upton Center. Could that be?"

"I should think so," Almyra replied. "Perhaps the telegrapher made an error. And plates, that would mean plates for printing forged bills. Counterfeits." Only Susannah looked confused by this, and Almyra nodded to her. "The bad pennies your mother receives from stage passengers. There are bad bills also and printing them uses flat sheets of metal called plates, which mark the proper designs onto paper."

"Upton Bank?" Mrs. Sanborn's voice rose. "Then any bank items now might be fraudulent. It could crush the bank, and even the farms. What should we do?"

The clink of a spoon against a cup startled Almyra, and like the others, she stared at Susannah, who'd made this unusual interruption. "If they've confiscated the plates," Susannah said calmly, "there won't be more of those bad bills printed. We only need to do what the telegram says. Let the bank directors know. It sounds like they have someone to carry the plates to the sheriff, and then I daresay a posse will head out to seek the criminals, crossing the border if needed."

"No! They mustn't," Even as she stood and exclaimed. Almyra realized her mistake. Of all the persons at the table, she was the only one who knew of the agreement between Solomon McBride and Foster Pierce. Now receive the wages of sin, she told herself—because, having listened to the men's collaboration illicitly, hidden in the loft, she could only explain herself if she reported what she had done.

Confession was good for the soul, she'd heard her father say. But to tell of her exploit would also put Susannah into trouble, all out of proportion.

She had to say something: Her aunt, Miss Farrow, and Mrs. Sanborn all stared at her. Susannah, gathering a hint of the issue, held a hand over her own mouth, eyes wide.

Aunt Charlotte seemed to suddenly understand. "Oh, Almyra, you mustn't be afraid for your uncle. I'm sure he meant that someone else would make the ride. Perhaps John Sanborn, if he can be spared, or even a hired messenger. It's quite all right, your uncle knows better than to attempt such a ride at his age." With a dismissive smile, she offered a dish of sweet biscuits to Miss Farrow.

Perhaps Almyra wouldn't need to confess to her aunt, at least not with Miss Farrow and Mrs. Sanborn listening. She forced a smile of her own. "Of course, Aunt, forgive my foolishness." Seated again, she gave a tiny nod toward Susannah, who dropped her own hand. Would Susannah follow her lead? "Miss Farrow, I wonder whether Susannah and I might drive you to St. Johnsbury, either this afternoon or in the morning. She is teaching me to handle the horses with a buggy, and I should be grateful for the practice."

A tilt of the head suggested Miss Farrow hadn't been as easily reassured as Aunt Charlotte. Nonetheless, Judge Paddock's housekeeper said agreeably, "I accept, Almyra. And Susannah. But it's late already, perhaps too late to travel today."

Susannah disagreed. "I would hazard that we could be there and back again with still some light, as the evenings are now so long. I must help with tomorrow's stage at the inn, where my mother and sisters and I provide the sustenance, so I should much prefer to collaborate today on this effort. If it pleases you, ma'am."

Ah, she did understand. Almyra watched Miss Farrow think about the offer. Thank goodness, she appeared to decide in its favor. "Allow me a few minutes to make my farewell to your aunt, and I'll prepare to travel with you young ladies. My own horse can be led behind us. Perhaps, in the name of good speed, you might go to prepare your conveyance?"

Susannah immediately offered to let Matthew know, and to prepare the buggy and both horses. Almyra would escort Miss Farrow back to the inn in a few minutes.

While Miss Farrow slipped out to the "necessary" for a moment, and Aunt Charlotte began gathering up dishes, Almyra retreated to her chamber to exchange her best Sunday garments for ones that would endure a dusty journey.

As she straightened her workday skirt over her petticoats, Mrs. Sanborn came into the chamber, intent and low-voiced. "I've raised three sons and a daughter. Tell me quickly, what has you upset?"

"The part about the sheriff," Almyra admitted. "I can't explain now. But Foster Pierce is involved, and the judge, and even my uncle, so I must reach one of them if I can and pass along warning right away. I think Mr. Pierce is in St. Johnsbury."

"No riding north for the border yourself? Your word, please, Almyra, and quickly."

"I promise. I'll only deliver a message." She didn't dare ask for a guarantee in return that Mrs. Sanborn wouldn't alert Aunt Charlotte.

A sharp nod from the older woman, however, signaled some level of agreement. "I'll be watching for you and Susannah to return this evening," Mrs. Sanborn warned.

Minutes later, with a parcel of bread and cheese in a satchel and a quick embrace from her aunt, Almyra nodded to Miss Farrow, and they stepped toward the inn. A light buggy with a horse harnessed in front and another on a lead rope already waited at the roadside.

By the angle of the sun, it was about three o'clock. The bright and nearly cloudless sky felt reassuring, and Almyra dared to hope her mission might succeed.

The closer they came to the buggy, though, the more it baffled her. Clearly, only two people could sit in the two-wheeled carriage. Then she realized that Miss Farrow's horse, the one on the lead rope, wore a sidesaddle.

"Take your choice," Susannah called, from her perch in the carriage. "Miss Farrow of course rides here; will you sit with her and drive, or shall I do so and you settle on her horse?"

How had she not realized this would be the case? She could have bundled an extra pair of petticoats under her skirt for padding, but without them, riding the horse would be agony.

Her distress must have shown in her face, for Miss Farrow laughed and said, "Ride with me on this bench, Almyra. As it happens, I'm somewhat tutored in driving a buggy. When I resided in Rhode Island, it wasn't permitted. Then the Judge removed to Vermont, and I made sure to seek the experience. You may exhibit to me what you have already learned, and your friend shall also call out further instruction if needed."

With that settled, Susannah leapt down and assisted Miss Farrow up, then let Almyra figure out her own climb into the structure. At least it had four wheels instead of two, so it didn't sway as she mounted. Her skirts swayed and slid, to a mortifying extent.

Miss Farrow allowed Almyra to focus on the reins and making small occasional taps with the long buggy whip. After some time, Almyra asked, "Is Judge Paddock in residence?" To justify the question, she added, "Do you need to reach home in time to prepare his supper?"

"That's a question unworthy of your intelligence, Almyra, since you already are aware that I might have waited until morning to return to town. As it happens, the judge takes his Sunday dinner at his daughter's home, so I generally enjoy a Sabbath of rest and other occupations of the mind."

Almyra murmured an apology as she lifted the reins higher to prepare for a curve ahead. She felt her face burn with embarrassment, in part for a clumsy question and in part from the implied compliment. It tied her tongue.

A low laugh from her companion only increased her discomfort. The horse seemed to notice, too, and slowed. Should she tap his haunch with the crop, so close to the curve?

As if aware of this thought, Miss Farrow said quietly, "Let him find his own best pace around the curve. He may hear something that you haven't. Just take up the slack in the reins."

Almyra did so, wondering whether another rider might be coming toward them. But after the curve, the track widened and the horse picked up his pace again.

From behind, Susannah called, "Make sure to halt before the slope toward the four corners. Miss Farrow should drive that part."

Showing an uncanny ability to guess Almyra's next question, Miss Farrow then said, "Considering the time of day, there is a good chance the judge will arrive at home about the same hour that I do. Do you wish to speak with him, Almyra? Does this explain why you and your friend wished to accompany me?"

She might as well be forthright. "We, that is, I, mostly, must convey some news to Judge Paddock. It's important."

After a moment, Miss Farrow said quietly, "Then I'm sure you will have an opportunity to do so. But would you like to tell me now, in case the timing doesn't suit?"

"It's about, umm, Mr. Pierce. Mr. Foster Pierce. You might have heard he came to North Upton yesterday." She hesitated.

Miss Farrow nodded. "Then I think you should wait and try to tell the judge directly. Your news might need privacy."

Relief loosened her tension on the reins, and the horse flicked his ears, inquiring whether this was an instruction. As Susannah called her name, however, Almyra had already realized the location and taken up the slack, along with saying a firm "Whoa" to the animal. She should have asked his name before she started driving.

There was no brake on this simple buggy, Miss Farrow pointed out as she took the reins, so the harness and the horse must do the work of holding it back on the slope downward. Much of the rest of the way toward town, Miss Farrow gave explanations. Her words reshaped the instructions Susannah had provided, and Almyra paid close attention. The horse's easy trot slowed to a walk as the road entered the town.

Then, suddenly, Judge Paddock's stately home loomed in front of them, and there were other people and conveyances all around. Susannah followed them to the stables behind the house and had swung off her mount and into position to hold the buggy's horse while Miss Farrow and then Almyra climbed down. This time, Almyra paid more attention to keeping her skirts in position. Was the judge home yet?

Before she could find out, however, Susannah reminded her that she should assist with watering and then walking the horses for a few minutes. "Let Miss Farrow go ahead,with her bundle. But it's better to have two of us for two horses."

How could she best explain to the judge about the counterfeiters' printing plates coming, and ask him to hold back on sending out a sheriff?

Then, as she took the lead rope that Susannah offered to walk the horse that had followed the buggy, she glanced into the stables and noticed a horse already in one shadowy stall. Did the judge keep his own horse? Surely if he did, it would have been discussed when Aunt Charlotte was here before?

Oh, how could she have forgotten that Solomon McBride had mentioned talking with Judge Paddock? She looked regretfully at her creased and dusty skirts. Well, "Needs must," as Aunt Charlotte might say.

The five minutes of pacing with the horses, however, settled her thoughts more clearly. Almyra looked at Susannah already leading the unhitched buggy horse to a post, and realized that having a friend with her made a difference.

Now, if only she could hold her courage in place through the conversation ahead.

# ~ 24 ~

Voices and the sounds of horses and carriages came faintly from the road on the other side of the house. Susannah's very small adjustment of the second horse's tether, after Almyra had linked it to a second post, felt satisfying. As Susannah turned toward her, Almyra linked an arm through her elbow. "Now we make sure the menfolk will work with us," she said cheerfully.

Susannah eyed her with skepticism. "On which part? You haven't explained why we are here. To earn someone's approval for the ladies' group? Or has this something to do with those printing plates you were all talking about?"

"Neither. But there isn't time to explain. Only," Almyra turned to face the young woman at her side, noticing that she too had made time to change from her Sunday skirt, "you might already know I speak very passionately about what I believe is right. And for this negotiation, I need to stay calm instead. Would you signal me if you note that I'm flying too high, talking too loudly?"

"How? By raising a hand, like in school?"

Almyra shook her head. "Best to be less direct. Just drop something on the floor and then bend to pick it up. Can you do that?"

Susannah nodded. She swallowed hard, then said, "How must I adjust my manners? I've never entered a judge's home before."

"As long as we don't carry manure on our shoes, I think we'll be fine." Almyra smiled as Susannah lifted her feet, one after the other, with an edge of panic. "There'll be a mat by the door to wipe them. And I imagine Miss Farrow will serve us tea."

Susannah whispered, "Was she really enslaved in Rhode Island?"

"Yes. she was. But good manners means we don't mention it unless she brings it up first. You'll be fine, just follow my lead, the way I have followed yours."

They reached the doorway and let go of each other. Almyra stepped up, tapped on the door, and pushed it open. Susannah followed.

Miss Farrow, already pouring hot water into a teapot, pointed them toward the next doorway. "I told them you were here," she said in a low voice. "Go ahead in."

Almyra recognized the narrow shoulders and slim waist from behind, and halted an instant at the sill, her balance sorely tested. It wasn't Solomon visiting the judge after all. Why was Captain Young here? Had he abandoned her uncle and John Sanborn and Isaiah Hutchinson in Lower Canada? What did Judge Paddock have to do with all this?

The judge, already on his feet at the far side of the parlor, nodded courteously. "Miss Alexander," he said. "And will you introduce your companion?"

Captain Young also stood, turning toward Almyra, something urgent in his expression. Was he trying to warn her?

Feeling for the right level of deference, Almyra offered a small bow from the waist. "Judge Paddock, and Captain Young," she acknowledged. "How kind of you to allow this interruption. May I present my neighbor, Miss Hall? I am certain you are acquainted with her cousin Sam, who drives the east–west stage."

Susannah gave an equally small bow, which pleased Almyra. Working at a tavern and in a stable didn't make her friend feel that any deeper deference was needed toward these two men. This is what *liberty* should mean, Almyra thought in a flash, then set the notion aside for a future sermon as she stepped forward. "Might we join you gentlemen at the table for a brief conversation?"

Captain Young sprang to his feet and pulled out a chair for each of them as Miss Farrow brought in the teapot and two more cups. When Almyra began to sit and the captain slid the chair neatly forward, his strong and warm hand pressed firmly and briefly on her shoulder. She did her best to keep her face calm, and looked across at the judge while Susannah in turn was seated. Oh, dear, not only did he look stern, but also much worn, perhaps even ill. Miss Farrow seemed to notice Almyra's discovery, for as she circled behind the judge, she looked meaningfully at Almyra and laid a finger to her lips.

What should she do? She'd come to make sure the judge wouldn't react to the captured printing plates by sending north a sheriff, and to explain the uncomfortable truce with Mr. Pierce. Had the captain himself brought the etched metal plates? Nothing sat on the table.

The only option was to seek more information. And to gain some, one must first give, she decided swiftly. She leaned forward a bit, looking into the judge's face. "Sir, I believe you've forwarded the cause of abolition quite steadily, and I thought perhaps I might let you know that my mother and some other ladies of North Upton and I are considering forming a ladies' anti-slavery society to assist the one that your Gilman nephews are supporting here in St. Johnsbury. Your family sets a fine example for charity and moral endeavor, sir."

Judge Paddock sat up straighter, clearly pleased. "You must invite my daughter Constance to your society, Miss Alexander. She will be much interested."

"I shall do so at once, sir. Of course, you are also kindly supporting other endeavors in Upton, I understand. Do you still sit as a director of the bank?"

Ah, she'd touched the area Captain Young wished to manage. He slid nimbly into the conversation. "The justice and I were just discussing how well the bank is doing. The directors are about to issue a report that confirms its solid basis and ample assets."

If word circulated that a printing plate for the Bank of Upton could be used to forge currency, it would damage the bank, whether or not counterfeits ever circulated, How could she signal the captain that she understood why no metal plates sat on the table before him?

"That is such welcome news," Almyra said. "I quite understand that the bank is responsible for the underpinning of the town. And Upton, of course, is the county seat, a great responsibility."

Captain Young's shoulders relaxed just a bit.

"Indeed," said the judge, "one could hardly praise your town sufficiently. It has done well." He gestured toward Captain Young. "Though Captain Young tells me there are continued deliberations about moving the county seat to St. Johnsbury instead, now that the railroad has arrived here. Your uncle must come to see me, to share his insight on the proposal."

"I'm sure he will, sir." What should she say next? She glanced at Susannah, who looked back at her but didn't say anything. Almyra fumbled, "The ladies might like to offer their viewpoints also."

The judge in turn seemed startled at such a notion. A small clink of Susannah's tea spoon tumbling to the floor reminded Almyra that the involvement of women in political decisions might be discussed among the ladies at home, but might still be considered wildly inappropriate by this aging leader.

Captain Young seemed to feel the same way. "No doubt Constance would convey their interest to her father," he quickly inserted. "Now, I'm sure you young ladies have shopping to do here in town. Judge Paddock, might I be excused to escort your guests into the town?"

"Of course, of course." The judge turned to Miss Farrow, still standing near the doorway to the kitchen. "Rachel, bring me the tonic, if you please. The one Mrs. Hall made up for me." He seemed to realize the connection of names and asked Susannah, as she stood, "Would that be your family, my dear?"

"Yes, sir, my mother." Susannah kept her response brief. "Thank you, sir, for welcoming us and our news."

"Always a pleasure." The judge placed both hands on the table and lifted himself cautiously to stand, in courteous farewell. "Captain, you will find me in my study when you return to the house."

Miss Farrow didn't follow them outside—she only nodded as she opened a cupboard in the kitchen where a number of bottles, amber, green, and brown, suggested the judge must often require diverse remedies. Almyra nodded in return, feeling that Captain Young could barely wait to get her and Susannah out of the house.

When they reached the horses, however, she stopped and turned to him, her fists on her hips. "The plates?" she demanded. "Did you bring them with you? What is taking place? And where are my uncle and the others?"

"In the other Upton," Captain Young said at once. "Upton, in Canada. Except that Isaiah remains lodged in Stanstead. The copper assays are complete, and your uncle is investigating a possible coin manufactory near Upton. But Isaiah's discoveries have complicated everything."

"Why? What did he discover?"

Captain Young bit his lip a moment, his sideways look at Susannah suggesting he wasn't sure whether to tell both of them. Then he leaned forward and whispered: "Gold."

Susannah gasped. She whispered, "Can we go there? To see it?"

Almyra allowed a moment for the captain to smile and shake his head, as he whispered back indulgently, "Wait a bit. Isaiah is sure to bring you something to see."

Enough sidetracking. Almyra repeated, "Where are the plates?"

"In my pouch." He patted the flat leather wallet attached by a strap over his shoulder. "When we've confirmed that the Upton Bank one hasn't sent bills into circulation, I'll destroy it. That's our best hope. We think the Wells River false currency went to New York, however." Captain Young looked grim. "It would help if we could confirm this and take action before the bills work their way north as a claim on that bank."

Almyra asked, "Would Foster Pierce know?"

Shocked, the captain admitted, "He might. But I don't expect the chance to ask him."

"I think he's here in St. Johnsbury if he hasn't already left for Newport. He was in Upton already. I, er," she glanced sideways, seeing Susannah tense up, "I might have overheard something of his plans."

"In this very town? The grand old man of the Canada counterfeit gangs? Are you sure?"

"I am sure he was in Upton and headed this way. If he were still in town, where would he be?"

Susannah came up with the first answer. "The mill," she said. "The Gilman mill, where machines are designed and made. Sure as a penny, that's where."

A penny might be counterfeited, too. But Almyra didn't say that. Instead she turned to Captain Young. "Can you escort us there? Now?"

Almyra expected to hear the roar of the Sleepers River, its rapids and falls, all around her at the Gilman Mill. Yet the structure where their carriage paused was some distance from the waters, linked to the mill's power by rapidly moving leather belts. Captain Young did his best to leave them in the carriage to wait for him, but Almyra ignored his intent, placing her shoe neatly on the metal peg behind the wheels and climbing down nimbly. Truly, she was mastering how to gather and grip her skirts properly for such a maneuver.

Susannah jumped down without fuss, and tethered both the carriage horse and the one the captain rode. She looked to Almyra, who nodded and slipped an arm around her waist.

When Captain Young began, predictably, to object to the "ladies" accompanying him, Almyra pointed out, "We'll draw far more notice than you, and the supervisor is sure to be eager to direct us all. Let us discover whether Mr. Pierce is still on the premises."

Assured that their quarry must still be in Mr. Gilman's offices, the three of them followed a man in shirtsleeves and a leather apron over to another structure on the lot. Inside, coal smoke swirled, blown back from a forge; a massive chunk of metal driven by more belts rose up and down, hammering the red-hot items placed within its maw. Were some of these for milling cotton? Almyra recalled what Mr. Sanborn had said about New England's profit from enslavement.

But such noise. How could anyone think under such conditions?

At the far end, however, a counting room stood with sturdy double doors. Once inside it, Susannah stayed by the doorway, eyes wide, hands to her ears. Even in here, the noise felt like a force against her chest. Nevertheless, Almyra lowered her shoulders, shook out her skirt, and stepped forward. She could see Mr. Pierce at a long wooden table, talking with a younger man.

The counterfeiter—no, she must try to think of him now as a Canadian politician—looked up, recognized her, and immediately stood, though she saw it cost him some discomfort to do so. He said something to the younger man, who spread a cloth over the stacks of currency on the table, then also rose to his feet.

Almyra suddenly realized that Mr. Pierce and Captain Young were not acquainted, and she made the introduction. The younger man, a bookkeeper, said he was Ulric Norris, then excused himself for a moment.

Captain Young pulled the plates out of his pouch. Almyra pressed closer, curious to see them. They were larger than she'd expected, with hard knurled edges and elegant swirls etched onto them. The backward writing still flowed gracefully, and she could see some differences between them.

Mr. Pierce stiffened at the sight. "I have n-nothing to do with such items," he spat angrily. "T-t-take them away."

"Sir, I beg your pardon, I am well aware of that. I only need a word of your advice, if you'd be so kind."

Almyra reached out to take the old man's hand. It wasn't proper, but someone had to stop him from working himself into a rage. "Our partnership," she reminded him. "The captain has already mollified the judge and avoided another posse. Will you assist him, just for a moment?"

He snatched back his hand and glared at her. "You t-take too much upon yourself, young lady. I m-may resemble your grandfather, or some such, but I have worked to become a m-man of service to my p-people. Have the c-courtesy to respect that."

With a deep curtsey, Almyra responded to this demand in her most feminine voice, "Then I trust you will wish to serve them again in this small favor, sir."

Whether it was this gesture of manners or a delayed echo of her plea for partnership, Mr. Pierce finally gave a short nod to the captain. "Your question?"

"Sir, I'm aware these have nothing to do with you," the captain said quickly. "They come from, well, from someone north of the border, and are drawn on two local banks. I only want to be sure they haven't been used yet for printing."

For a moment, Almyra thought Mr. Pierce would refuse. But instead he gestured at the table. "Set them down."

He picked up a loupe from next to the covered currency, and lifted it to his eye, examining the two plates. A low growl came from him as he did this. Almyra wasn't sure the man even realized the sound could be heard by others. It made her shiver. She never wanted to be this man's enemy, no matter how much indeed he resembled some grandfathers she'd seen in the past.

At last he set the loupe aside and looked up at Captain Young. "One's n-never been used," he said. "The other, I r-r-recognize because I've already seen the p-p-paper from it. In fact," he gestured to the other end of the table, "some of the b-bills are here. I'm assisting this Mr. N-Norris in sorting out the bad c-c-currency from this lot, which arrived last n-night from Illinois."

Captain Young stiffened. "Would you be able to advise me, sir, as to whether these bank bills are most likely to have all gone west?"

Mr. Pierce frowned. "F-f-follow your n-n-nose. What use would they be if k-k-kept c-close to home?"

To Almyra, that sounded like an irritated but confirming assent. She edged closer, trying to determine which plate was for which bank, but the captain was already wrapping them again in their length of fabric.

It seemed to Almyra that, having done some of the persuading, she should also do some thanking: "Mr. Pierce, it was very kind of you to help us."

The old man snorted. "L-little l-lady, I am not p-particularly k-k-kind, even now. You and the c-c-captain m-might wish to know. Ch-ch-Charles Gilman is a d-d-director of the Bank of N-Newbury. And there is n-no bank of W-wells R-River."

Turning abruptly, he uncovered some of the stacks of paper on the table and resumed his sorting. The bookkeeper materialized next to him, as if from thin air, though he'd probably been around the back of a desk somewhere. Captain Young added his thanks and received no reply besides a dismissive nod from the bookkeeper. He looked at Almyra, shrugged, and turned back toward the door.

Susannah lowered her hands from her ears and bent toward Almyra. "Did you find out?"

Almyra waved toward the outdoors, and when they reached its blessedly ordinary level of noise, she told Susannah, "He knew something, all right. Captain Young, which news went with which bank?"

His slender face looked drawn and tense, as he replied, "Upton's plate was never used. I'll see that it's destroyed. And the other plate also, but I must send word immediately to Alan Pinkerton so that the banks in Illinois can be warned." He looked back toward the structure they'd left. "I should have asked them when. When the bills went out there."

Hesitantly, Almyra asked, "Might John Sanborn be returning to Illinois when he and his friend finish the assaying? Perhaps he could carry word for you. Then you could feel confident, and not be as worried."

With a warm smile that lit up his tired face, Captain Young thanked Almyra for the notion. "Although I suspect the mails are quicker, I am grateful that you consider how to speed my efforts." Once again, he brushed a hand against her shoulder, surprising her. She caught Susannah's half smile and stepped back.

"We are on our way home to North Upton, sir. It's been a pleasure to see you again. Do let my aunt and uncle know when you are next in the area." There, that put things back to where they should be. Suddenly she recalled, "You once asked me to ask Miss Farrow to watch for the Gilmans driving north out of town. Does this have something to do with your question then?"

Captain Young stopped smiling, shook his head to close the conversation, and took his leave, firmly but quite courteously. Susannah, with a worried glance at the sky, suggested that they begin the drive back to Upton at once. "It's later than we meant to depart, and it looks like rain coming in."

For the first hour, there was so much to discuss and fill in for each other. Susannah kept reminding Almyra about the gold that Isaiah had assayed in Canada. "I've heard sometimes it's in the water, and sometimes in rocks," she said. "I wonder which kind this is. And what it means for the counterfeiters. Do you think they can make gold coins from what they find?"

"Perhaps they could," Almyra said dubiously, "but it wouldn't be a counterfeiter's project, would it? Because gold, no matter what it says on a coin, is valued by the weight."

"My mother always says there are three things that matter: your money, your good health, and who you marry." Susannah nudged Almyra. "Captain Young looks at you more often than he needs to. Would you marry an officer, if he asked?"

"I doubt I'll marry anyone." Almyra explained yet again about the ministry. "In September I'll begin a year of final studies at Peacham Academy, before attending the Seminary in Springfield. Then I can preach properly. To marry would mean to give all that up."

Susannah paused a moment, then speculated in another direction. "I wonder whether a military man might wish to open a livery stable after his discharge. If he had a wife who could be a helpmeet."

They giggled together, though Almyra felt a pang at realizing that Susannah had the liberty to "set her cap" for the gentlemanly Captain Young. Not I, she told herself firmly. There is something else I want more. Still, there was some sting in the knowledge.

A few minutes later, after they'd crested the hill at the four corners and turned the horse toward North Upton, the first drops of rain began to fall. Susannah handed the reins to Almyra and pulled out a woolen blanket from under the seat, to spread over their laps. "I suppose our bonnets will hold up for a little while."

But the bonnet straw, once soaked, would require great care in reshaping. Almyra sighed, foreseeing an evening of attention to her clothing rather than her books. Perhaps Aunt Charlotte would assist.

Impulsively, she asked Susannah, "Do you wish to be like your mother? I mean, when you are a married woman?"

Susannah wrinkled her nose. "In the kitchen half the day? With children always wanting something, and a husband at home taking up half the bed or more? No, thank you. Why do you ask, would you wish to be like yours? Married to a minister?"

"That's my Aunt Charlotte," Almyra corrected, and then said, "Actually, I suppose it was my own mother also, in Boston. You know she died two years ago?"

"I know that," Susannah admitted cautiously. "And she was also married to a minister?"

"My father," Almyra confirmed. "But he was, he is, so different from Uncle Eliphalet. He loves to travel and see his friends, senators, and even the president. And my mother wasn't a bit like Aunt Charlotte—she had her own seamstress, and she went to balls. And she was very slender, too."

Susannah grinned. "Not at all like your aunt, then."

The horse slowed, his ears twitching. They both noticed. "Someone else is on the road." There were muddy puddles all along the center of the road. Susannah pulled to the side and let the horse pause. The buggy rocked slightly in place as it settled.

From a narrower route to the right, a rider, not a carriage, came out into the main road. He was leading a second horse, and wore a hat pulled down low and a high cravat, making it difficult to see his face.

That worried Almyra. She whispered to Susannah, "Do you have a stick?"

"Only this," Susannah whispered back, twitching the buggy whip. "Let me talk, not you."
As the rider came closer, he lifted his hat briefly in courtesy. But Almyra still couldn't see much of his face. A thick brown beard covered most of it, and the small strip around his eyes seemed tanned by the sun, yet in the twilight, even that was uncertain.

"A good evening, sir," Susannah said in a level tone. "Headed for St. Johnsbury?"

The man cleared his throat. "Ma'am, your obedient," he said quietly.

"Must be just another five miles or so?"

"Maybe six," Susannah agreed. "God speed, then."

Almyra felt the man's eyes rake across both their faces, but he didn't look threatening, and he walked his horse and the led animal past them, tipped his hat again, and was almost gone from sight in another moment.

Susannah hissed like a kettle coming to the boil. "The horse he was leading," she said to Almyra, still whispering just in case. "That's one of the ones that went north from the inn. With your uncle."

Almyra gasped. "How can you be sure?"

The horse in front of them pricked its ears back at the anger in Susannah's voice as she spoke more loudly. "I might not have as much schooling as some, but I know a horse when I've saddled it. That hind quarter with the scar over the off leg—didn't you see?" She slapped the reins, called out "Get up, there," and encouraged their horse to a vigorous trot. "I need to let Matthew know, right away."

Almyra clung to the side of the buggy as it bounced. "What does this mean? Do you think something's happened to them? Are they hurt up in Canada?"

Susannah leaned forward, urging the horse to its best pace for the mud underfoot. "Who knows? But didn't someone say they are trading horses instead of currency up there with so much forgery? Maybe they just traded it for supplies or something."

"Then how would they ride back home again?" Almyra leaned forward. The sooner they reached Matthew, the better. Though she didn't like to suspect an elderly man, she had to wonder if this had something to do with Mr. Foster Pierce.

~ 26 ~

What a relief to arrive in their own familiar village. Susannah drove the horse into the muddy yard behind the inn, pocked with foot and hoof prints and ruts. Matthew came out of the stables, setting aside a shovel, and held the bridle of their horse while Susannah swiftly uncoupled the harness. Almyra climbed down, careful not to make the buggy tip while also managing her skirts.

Already, Susannah was rattling off the news. "And I know it was one of the horses we sent north with Mr. Alexander and the others, the one John Sanborn was riding. I'd know that scarred rump anywhere. We have to send someone to St. Johnsbury, to the sheriff, to get it back."

The horse stamped in sympathy with Susannah's agitation and splashed mud on all of them. Matthew spoke quietly, rubbing his hand over the animal's long face. "There, fellow, that's fine, she's not angry with you. Easy, boy." Without changing his tone, he went on, "Stage was delayed, should be here in this evening. Best to send your message to the sheriff with Sam. It'll get there sooner. And it's not our horse, remember, it's one from the stage, so Sam's the one to tell first."

Almyra came closer and tried to keep her own voice even and calm. "But Matthew, if the horse has been stolen from John Sanborn, doesn't that mean they might have been attacked? Or it could have been taken when they were staying overnight somewhere. What should we do? What if they are hurt? Or just can't get back home? Maybe all of their horses were stolen."

Her voice was rising despite her intentions, so she stopped, clenching a hand over her mouth, and stared at Matthew, willing him to have an answer. A reassuring answer, or an action she could take. Thinking of Alice Sanborn's brother being injured, or worse, felt terrifying. And Uncle Eliphalet, was he safe? What about Isaiah Hutchinson—did Canadians really treat Negroes as freemen, or had someone kidnapped him? And he'd found gold in the assay.

Matthew was still talking, this time to her, and she hadn't been paying attention. "Step away, Almyra, step back, that's the way, I can see you're worried and so can the horse, easy, boy, that's right, come on Susannah, pull that free so I can walk him."

Susannah hung up the harness segments in the stable and beckoned to Almyra for assistance pushing the buggy off to the side. Matthew's words seemed to have calmed her.

For Almyra, however, the shocking set of possible events she'd just described raced in her thoughts. She did her best to help Susannah, then said, "I think I need to go home to my aunt straight away. Maybe the stage will bring some news, as well as the mail. Or my aunt may already know something."

"If you find out more," Susannah said over her shoulder as she stepped into the stables, "come tell me."

A star sparkled in the east; the rain clouds had vanished, the evening sky hung tender with final shades of gold and pink, and the air carried a scent of freshly turned earth. Someone in the village must have started plowing or digging during the mild afternoon. Almyra walked slowly, shaking out her limbs from the tense ride, and trying to decide what to say first to Aunt Charlotte. And how to say it. Did the presence of the horse really mean something had gone wrong up north? And what was she supposed to convey from the trip to town, which had almost slipped her mind in all this commotion?

Aunt Charlotte met her at the kitchen door. "There's supper in the warming oven," she said right away. "Eat, and then you can tell me all about it."

It seemed a good idea. Better to be calm and well fed, and to organize her thoughts before sharing her own agitation with her aunt—and perhaps, Almyra thought as she spooned up a thick mutton stew with buttered biscuit on the side, perhaps she had this wrong.

The room began to cool, as the darkness blacked the windows. A rattle of hooves and creaking of a carriage could be heard through the small gap at the bottom of one. Aunt Charlotte rose to close the window and to poke a few small splits of wood into the firebox, saying, "We might as well remain in the kitchen since your uncle won't be home tonight. But I do expect him by suppertime tomorrow. Also, that probably was the stage, at last. If there's any letter for us, I doubt that we'll see it before morning since Mr. Weeks closed the post office hours ago."

Almyra fastened on what seemed most important in all this: "You expect Uncle Eliphalet tomorrow by supper? How can you know that?"

Her aunt smiled gently. "Because that's what he told me when he left. That no matter what, he'd be here by Friday evening, to spend Saturday preparing for his Sunday." She paused, and then said, "He has never broken his word to me, Almyra. I hope that if you ever marry—yes, I know, you will first serve the church—that you give your heart to the same kind of man. Even at the worst of times, we have chosen to take care of each other."

The worst of times. Almyra knew that must refer to the early years of their marriage when one, two, three babies died not long after their births, and then the child who'd drowned before his third birthday. She'd seen the stones at the cemetery but hadn't dared to ask. Now she said, "Do you each still mourn?"

"Of course we do. But it gets a little softer, a little more distant each year." Aunt Charlotte smiled again. "Especially since you have come here, my dear. You've brought us home to each other in a new way."

Almyra put a hand over her aunt's. "And you've given me a home that my mother couldn't. I understand much more now than I did two years ago."

The wood in the stove settled, and the iron ticked as it changed temperature. Aunt Charlotte rose to move the kettle onto one of hot places. "Chamomile tea tonight, thanks to Mrs. Hall. Now, Almyra, begin at the beginning."

Almyra set her bowl aside and said, "I think I must begin at the end instead, Aunt. As Susannah and I were driving home, when we had almost reached the village, a rider emerged from a trail, perhaps the Wheelock one, leading a second horse. Susannah is certain it's the horse that John Sanborn rode north. We have told Matthew, and he said he would let Sam know. That horse was a stage horse, and Sam can tell the sheriff. But what has happened? Why would that horse be on a lead rope on the road to St. Johnsbury?" Fingers curled together, biting her lip, she stopped herself from reciting all the possible answers that frightened her, and waited for her aunt's response.

Aunt Charlotte nodded but didn't begin to speak. Instead, she rose, poured steaming water from the kettle into a teapot, and brought it back to the table. She set out a cup for each of them and moved her chair close to Almyra's.

"My father was also drawn to the Bible," she began. "Not a minister, but a man who sought the hand of God in all around him. Every hopeful psalm in Scripture, he committed to memory, and taught them to all his children." She pursed her lips a moment. "I suspect he knew all the psalms of despair, as well, but he was in most ways a merciful man, and he did not ask us to learn those by rote. Though sometimes he recited pieces of them."

The tea had steeped enough to pour some for each of them. Almyra held her hands around her cup and waited. Her aunt had never spoken of her childhood before. Somehow the topic never arose.

"You have only seen North Upton as a sheep-farming village of fields and gardens. In my father's time, it was little more than a few structures along the river surrounded by thick woods. My father cut trees all day, every day except the Sabbath. We had two oxen, and they hauled the trunks, with him guiding, to the sawmill several times each day. Anyone new arriving here always expected to cut their own timber for a cabin, but they soon realized how much they needed and wanted boards, and the sawmill prospered. So did my father." She smiled wistfully. "I could have been a very spoiled child, but both my parents insisted that their children work hard, and I had no notion of any sort of wealth until my father's death, when each of my eight brothers inherited some three hundred acres of good farmland."

Fascinated though she was, urgency and fear ticked in Almyra's chest, with time passing and a sense that anything could have happened, north of the border in wild places where criminals might thrive. She set her cup down, as her hands trembled. Her aunt extended a hand to hold one of Almyra's.

"One day, just at dusk, my father's oxen came back to the house, dragging one half-hitched tree trunk and nothing else. They were thirsty and hungry, of course, and my mother made sure we cared for them, starting with taking off their load, before going to the table for what was then a quick supper of soup and biscuit. We often had soup in those days. Mother kept a stock kettle always simmering on the hearth." She squeezed Almyra's hand. "No cookstove until I was nearly grown. But a good brick baking oven.

"At any rate, Mother insisted that we all say grace together and eat our supper. Wherever our father was at that moment, she said, he intended us to carry on and do what was right, and at suppertime, it is right to give thanks and be sustained with a meal."

"But was your father injured? Was he waiting in the woods with an axe wound to a leg or arm? Had a tree crushed him?"

"We said all those things to Mother, and more, but she refused to change her mind. Now I know she was thinking all the way through eating her soup."

Soup. Almyra recalled how amusing she and her friend Alice had thought soup was, back before Aunt Charlotte transformed herself into a cheerful and generous cook. "And then did she seek help? Did she ask the others in the village to go find your father in the woods?"

"It was September," her aunt resumed. "I should have said that, at the start. Because it matters that in September the evening starts earlier, but not too early. Mother rose from the table quoting Psalm 119, 'Thy word is a lamp unto my feet, and a light unto my path.' She gave my brothers a task: to fetch the rope and harness we'd taken off the oxen, to cut a six-foot branch, and to bind together some shorter ones as a basic sort of sled that they or, if needed, an ox could pull."

"And you and your sisters? What did you do?"

"One sister," Aunt Charlotte corrected. "She was older than I, and usually tended the baby, so Mother could complete her efforts. My sister Ruth and I took the only cotton fabric in the house then, our warm-season petticoats, and we cut and tore them according to Mother's directions into long strips, which we packed into a bag. There was a crock in the kitchen to hold the cooking fat, and we emptied it into the only tin pail that we had. Then my sister rocked the baby to sleep, while Mother and I wound and tied the strips onto the long stick and plunged the wrapped end into our pail. Mother said I was to carry it like that so the cotton would keep soaking up the fat, and I did, with the long end leaning on my shoulder. Following Mother and one of our oxen and my brothers into the night forest." She paused to take a long shaky breath. "I've never been so frightened. Back then we had wolves, you know. Close to us at night. I was sure we'd be eaten. But of course our racket and thumping must have driven the wild animals far from us."

"And your father? How did you find him? Was he hurt? Was he …." Almyra couldn't say the word "dead." Wouldn't she somehow know if that had happened? Wouldn't her aunt be a tragic person, someone who wept often and felt lost?

"Mother had a plan." Her aunt's eyes closed for a moment. Then she continued, "We were to follow the drag marks from the oxen hauling that tree trunk for as far as they were clear. And then my brothers were to climb the tallest trees around us and look for smoke against the evening sky."

"What? I don't understand. Smoke from the village?"

"No—in the other direction. Mother knew that my father always carried the makings for a fire: a flint, a good stone, some dry tinder from old bark. If he could, she knew he'd start some sort of fire to signal us. And to keep away," she swallowed hard, "any wolves."

A second cup of chamomile tea seemed called for. Almyra filled both their cups. She whispered, "Did you find him?"

"The problem was, any remaining standing trees near us were in bristling thickets and uneven ground. There were good reasons not to have cut them yet. So it took a while for my brothers to find ones that took them high enough. And the best climber, Edward, was also the best at striking a spark, so Mother kept him on the ground near her. She waited as long as she could, not wanting to make light that might compete with any signs in the sky. And when Myles finally called out that he could see some smoke, and pointed out the direction, we all began to scramble that way. Mother stopped us. I took my torch, which is what the cotton soaked in fat amounted to, and held it out dripping in front of me. It took hardly any time for Edward to set it blazing. And then, of course, we could see the oxen drag marks again and pick out the ones that went in the direction Myles indicated."

Almyra's hands were clenched together. She didn't dare interrupt.

"Yes, we found him." Aunt Charlotte seemed to have trouble speaking. But it seemed to be laughter, not tears, stopping the flow of words. Hysteria? Should Almyra fetch the smelling salts?

Before she could decide, her aunt resumed.

"He'd been up in a huge pine tree, limbing it a bit—you know what limbing is, yes? Taking off some of the bigger branches with an axe so they won't catch on other trees when you cut the trunk? Yes, well, a limb had come down crossways and pinned him against the trunk. He'd dropped the axe in the process of trying to release himself. And there he hung, like some sort of bear without hair, caught in place but perfectly whole. There was just one very big difficulty left." Aunt Charlotte pushed back her chair and beamed into Almyra's face. "He'd set a fire, to let Mother know where he was. Which meant, of course, he'd set the tree itself smoldering, and he was hollering for my brothers to come get him loose before the treetop burst into flame."

With her hands pressed to her mouth, Almyra couldn't say much.

Her aunt nodded, still bubbling with laughter. "Edward scrambled up in time with the axe, and all was well, other than a smoldering pine tree in the midst of the forest far enough from home to make things difficult, but close enough to worry everyone about setting the woods afire. Mother had to sacrifice her own petticoat, which we soaked in a nearby spring, and Myles carried it up and wrapped the tree in the soaking wet cotton."

"And nobody was hurt at all?"

"Well, not exactly. While we'd been so busy, the ox had turned and walked home on its own. With the barn not fully open, it made a terrible ruckus, and finally knocked loose the door so that Ruth thought it was a bear and climbed up into our cabin loft with the baby, kicking over the ladder after she did so, to make sure no bear could follow her up. The ladder landed in the kitchen, and broke two of the table legs. Father always said we'd turned a perfectly ordinary woods event into two broken legs."

At last Almyra laughed, too. And when the two of them finally quieted, Almyra repeated from the psalm, "'A light unto my path.' Aunt, do you think Uncle Eliphalet is simply stuck in a pine tree, so to speak? And will we go to find him?"

"We'll wait right here, and not imagine a bear, and be sure that on the morrow we accomplish both washing and baking, my dear. You have no idea what we'll be called upon to accomplish when the men return, and we had best be prepared. Which also means," Aunt Charlotte said gently, "that it is time a certain buggy-driving young lady made her way to some rest. As will I."

In spite of abundant washing and baking tasks, the next day dragged. Almyra sped to the window or door each time the sound of a horse or carriage echoed outside.

But the first sign of the men returning was not until supper had been served and eaten, with Uncle Eliphalet's portion set aside for him. Now Aunt Charlotte, too, kept looking up at any sound in the road. At last, without any hoofbeats or wagon squeals, a light tap sounded at the kitchen door. Aunt Charlotte jumped to open it.

It was Susannah, in her Turkish pantaloons with a heavy cloak tossed over. "My mother sent me. We need you both at the inn, straight away. She said to tell you the explanations can wait. It's life and death."

Almyra leapt to her feet and helped her aunt pull on a woolen jacket, then seized her own. Susannah led them at an undignified trot down the road. "Hurry," she said repeatedly. When Aunt Charlotte stumbled, they each took one of her arms and kept going.

They burst through the house door into the kitchen and found two of the men, Uncle Eliphalet and John Sanborn, seated at the table with grim expressions. Aunt Charlotte drew a huge breath, half sob, half relief, and said, "Who is ill?"

On his feet now, Uncle Eliphalet clutched his wife's hand a moment, then gestured toward the front parlor. Almyra dreaded what might be there. Was it Isaiah? Wounded from some wild border escape perhaps? She followed her aunt, braced to uphold her if needed, and wished she'd brought smelling salts along.

Someone was lying where the bleeding young woman had, making terrible sounds, and Almyra's heart sank, along with her stomach. But she couldn't see enough, because two men, crouching, blocked her view. Both were dark skinned, and one was making sounds that at first she thought were sobs, then realized the man meant them to be encouraging. "Come on, come on," he was coaxing.

Aunt Charlotte dropped her jacket into Almyra's arms and rolled up her sleeves. "Is there an apron?"

Almyra recalled where to find one in the kitchen and fetched it; she realized Isaiah Hutchinson had just followed her out of the front parlor. His face was beaded with sweat and his breath ragged. "We came as quickly as we could," he said. "Her pains didn't start until we were up on Sheffield Heights, so we took the Wheelock trail down. I'm not sure it saved much time, as it's so rough."

This explained little, but Almyra didn't stop to ask more. She seized an apron and, on impulse, asked her uncle to light a lantern. Whatever was happening in the front parlor, more light must be of use.

Aunt Charlotte knelt next to Mrs. Hall, her hands out of sight. "Tie it around me, Almyra, I can't let go. Then go find Mr. Sanborn. See if he knows where his wife is. Fetch her here, as quickly as you can."

The young woman on her back wailed, a high cry of pain, and the other man crouching in the room obeyed Mrs. Hall's directions, moving to the young woman's shoulders and taking her hands in his. With the added lantern and more light, Almyra realized the man looked familiar. Could it be Benjamin Blake? The man she'd met so briefly in Peacham, before the Canada expedition had been thought of?

Yes, it was.

"Almyra! If you please—we need Mrs. Sanborn, as soon as you can find her."

Her aunt's urgency cut through the confusion, and Almyra stood and turned toward the kitchen. Susannah waited there, looking like she'd rather be anywhere else on earth. Her sister Jane stood at the stove, stirring something. Heaven only knew where little Polly was; Almyra couldn't bother asking just now.

John Sanborn and Uncle Eliphalet sat with their hands to their faces, only John peering for a moment through his fingers. Almyra ignored him. Grabbing Susannah's arm, Almyra said, "We must fetch Mrs. Sanborn, and they say to ask her husband where she's gone."

"Then come on," Susannah replied at once. They sped toward the out-of-doors, but Susannah paused to seize an unlit lantern from a hook in the hall. "If he's not where we first look, we may need this."

A half disk of moon hung above them, offering enough light to readily cross the road and rush up the track to the Sanborn barn. Susannah seized the bar of the door and lifted it, and they both called, "Mr. Sanborn. Are you there?" Only the thick air of sheep and bedding reached them, and the rustle of disturbed livestock. Susannah fastened the door shut again. Without needing to talk, they hurried to the nearby kitchen door and rapped loudly.

This time Almyra was the one who pulled it open. "Mr. Sanborn. Mr. Sanborn?"

From a seat near the parlor stove, the neighbor rose up, startled and concerned. "Almyra. What on earth? Is there something amiss at the parsonage?"

"No," she gasped, "it's someone at the inn. They need Mrs. Sanborn. Where can we find her?"

From the doorway, Susannah spoke up, not nearly as breathless. "It's an early birth, sir. There's nobody as skilled as Mrs. Sanborn for it."

Mr. Sanborn's dismay showed clearly. "I took her to St. Johnsbury this morning. She planned to stay the night, and I'm to fetch her tomorrow."

Almyra thought quickly. "Is she assisting someone there, sir?"

"I don't believe so. She's staying with Miss Farrow at that farm at the four corners, where there's a winter's worth of embroidered goods to sort before they are sent to Boston. For the ladies' anti-slavery society there," he added.

"Then we need to fetch her, I think. If we can."

Mr. Sanborn looked at her incredulously. "I can't be away for the night. We're still lambing. I'm only taking a short rest before I go check the flock again."

Lambing, birthing, riding. Wait, there were two people not doing anything much. Her uncle and John Sanborn, Mr. Sanborn's son.

"Thank you, and good lambing, sir," Almyra managed. She spun toward Susannah and tugged at her arm. They fled out of the house as one, nearly running along the muddy track.

When they burst back into the Halls' kitchen, Uncle Eliphalet rose from his seat, though exhaustion grayed his face. "Where is she?"

"Halfway to St. Johnsbury," Almyra replied. "With Miss Farrow."

"Jane! More of the hot wet cloths, and a clean basin." That was Mrs. Hall in the front parlor. At least Almyra didn't smell the stench from the other young woman who'd died of her bleeding. But she also didn't want to look in the front room again.

"I'll fetch her," John Sanborn offered. "Is there a buggy I can hitch up?"

"Not this time," Susannah pronounced crisply. "The buggy that's here is rickety, especially in the dark. I'll ride there, and she can ride my horse back again."

"I'll keep you company," Almyra agreed.

"Not in the dark for either of you on a horse," Uncle Eliphalet objected. "Between the trail and the wild animals, it's not safe."

Almyra and Susannah shared a look of exasperation. "We've driven there and back," Susannah pointed out. "We know the way."

"I won't allow it." Now Uncle Eliphalet spoke with fierce authority. "There's too much risk."

A wail from the front room made the opposite point. "Life and death," Almyra said softly.

Jane came back to the cookstove and resumed stirring. "Mama says they'll need a wet nurse if the baby is born alive," she said over her shoulder. "She says when you find Mrs. Sanborn, tell her that, too."

"Why is Benjamin Blake here?" Almyra finally asked.

Her uncle replied, "It's his wife and child."

A tense pause was broken by John Sanborn speaking to Uncle Eliphalet. "The carriage is still here. Not clean. But still here."

Uncle Eliphalet frowned. "It's heavy enough. But I doubt that you could drive it safely, John. You're as weary as I am."

The solution seemed obvious, but it took Almyra a precious ten minutes to persuade her uncle. She and Susannah would drive the carriage. John would ride in it, along with some sort of rifle he'd brought east from the Nebraska Territory, and rest a little if he could. Isaiah, equally weary, would wait with Uncle Eliphalet. "It's only to the four corners," Almyra reminded her uncle. "We'll be there in an hour, and back in two."

As it happened, however, after one look at the interior of the carriage, with its bloodstains and sour-smelling linen and blankets,

Almyra determined to ride inside with John to spend the hour cleaning what she could. She borrowed a sack from the stable while Susannah hitched up a horse that hadn't traveled that day. Everything could be stuffed into the sack and then left at the farmhouse at the four corners to pick up another day. Perhaps someone would even wash them. Faint hope, but perhaps.

With Susannah's unlit lantern and John's rifle, there wasn't much room for even the two of them within the carriage.

Susannah mounted the front bench. "Ready?"

John Sanborn boosted Almyra up into the dim and reeking interior, clambered stiffly after, and rapped on the partition that separated the passengers from the driver's bench in the usual signal, "Ready."

Clearly, Susannah didn't wish to lose another minute, as she urged the horse to a rapid trot, and they jounced off into the moonlit night.

## ~ 28 ~

In the darkness of the carriage interior, John pulled himself into a corner of the bench. The windows held no isinglass, only loose leather curtains that flapped as the horse trotted. Amyra tugged one curtain back on the side where some moon glow might penetrate, but it slid back as soon as she let go of it. John said, "There should be a strap to fasten it. Perhaps I can find it."

"I can't feel one," Almyra said. "Are you sure?"

"No," John admitted. "We rode with them closed, considering we had both Benjamin and his wife in here."

She could hear him fumble in his pockets, and a moment later he pressed a length of what felt like twine into her hand and asked whether it would do. A minute later, she'd tied it, and the bundled curtain dangled, flopping, from the ledge over the opening, leaving both sides open for the silvery light.

She couldn't see him in detail, just the shadowy bulk of him, oddly reassuring. As she opened her sack to begin work, a gleam on the rifle made her ask, "Is it safe?"

"As safe as any such weapon." In an instructive tone, he said, "There are two rules for managing a firearm. One, always assume it is loaded, just in case. Two, never point it at any creature you're not willing to kill. In militia practice, the officers also remind you never to let go of your weapon, which is wise even now."

Almyra smiled and nodded, then realized he probably couldn't see her. "Then please do not release your hold on yours. Nonetheless, Mr. Sanborn, Susannah and I saw Captain Young's horse being led toward St. Johnsbury by a man we didn't know. We were afraid it had been stolen up in Canada. What happened? What did you find out?"

"Mister Sanborn? When I'm the brother of your friend Alice? Must I call you Miss Alexander now? Things have certainly changed in this village!"

She could hear the teasing in his voice. "John, then. Please will you tell me?"

He sighed, a long deep tired sigh.

"Let's begin with the horse. You must realize by now, with the need to return using a carriage, for the sake of Benjamin's wife, we had more horses than we required or even could manage well. The man you saw lives near the border and wanted to visit friends in St. Johnsbury. He escorted the spare horse in exchange for some traveling funds."

"I should have guessed, from the horse being here. If it had been stolen, why would someone bring it south?"

"Precisely. Now, as to the reason we brought the Blakes south with us. What do you know about slave ownership in Canada?"

Almyra fumbled to marshal her thoughts while she continued to stuff scraps form the floor into the sack. "There isn't any," she began. "Negroes have fled to Canada for freedom for many years."

"Yes, and no." She heard him stretch his legs, and one brushed against her sack. "Upper Canada's abolition movement has limited slavery there but did not eliminate it until twenty years ago. Lower Canada, where we traveled these past few days, protects fugitives from our United States. But again, until the British Commonwealth broke apart slavery in 1834, it remained possible in pockets, especially on large farms."

Almyra cut in. "I met Benjamin Blake in Peacham. Mister Johnson, who lives in that village, told me Benjamin's parents were enslaved by a family in Potton, in the Eastern Townships of Lower Canada."

"That is correct. And Benjamin continues to work for Jasper Blake there out of a sense of obligation since Jasper provides housing for Benjamin's aging parents. Your connection to Adam Blake enabled us to call at the farm, for which we certainly thank you." Amusement bubbled in his voice. "Mister Adam Blake was sore disappointed that you did not accompany us, however."

Almyra choked back a giggle. "To the point, sir. How did Benjamin come to leave there?"

"In a sense, he already had done so, for he and his wife have a home some miles from the farm, shared with her parents. At Upton. Upton, in

Canada." He moved again, apparently uncomfortable. "Almyra, what do you know about that other Upton?"

After a pause, she admitted, "Nothing, except that it shares the name of this one."

The carriage slowed and they both listened in case something was wrong. Then they heard Susannah call to the horse, which resumed trotting, but more slowly than before. The moon brightened, and for a moment Almyra saw John Sanborn's face clearly, the fatigue etched in it, the rough beard from days of travel, and yet somehow that air of reliability that had always drawn her.

He met her gaze for a long moment, a half-smile softening his own. "When you have drawn enough of my own narrative from me," he said, "I'd be honored to hear yours. Not only this week's, but more."

Her chest thumped and her breath caught. But before she could reply, the carriage slowed again and began to take a turn.

Susannah called out, "We're here."

Before the carriage had even quite stopped, Almyra had the door open, the sack of filthy garments out, and leapt down lightly, just missing a large puddle that reflected the half-moon. "I'll go in," she called up to Susannah. "You do what the horse needs. I can be swift, I'm sure of it."

The house door hung wide, and a broad-shouldered man stood there. Almyra darted forward. "Mister Wilson? I'm Almyra Alexander, the minister's niece, from North Upton. There's an urgent need for Mrs. Sanborn there, and I need to make a request of Miss Farrow as well. May I come in?"

Inside the house, Mrs. Wilson rose from a seat at a table heaped with what looked like narrow woolen blankets. At the far side of the table, Mrs. Sanborn was already pulling on a heavy shawl. Miss Farrow spoke first. "What is it, Almyra? Is someone injured?" Her usually calm voice shook.

"It's a mother with pains that have come too early, and she's giving birth," Almyra summarized. "And they said to tell you that if the baby survives, there's a need for a wet nurse."

Miss Farrow asked, "To tell me? Why me, in particular?"

"The mother is a Negress," Almyra explained. "Would that make a difference?"

"Not to the kind of milk the baby will need," Miss Farrow said, an edge of anger in her voice. "Many's the black-skinned mammy who has wet-nursed white babies in the South. As you must know."

"I do know," Almyra fumbled. She couldn't see how to say more without offense. She stumbled over the words, "I think my aunt might have thought you'd know someone whose milk has come in, and who would …." She stopped. This was ridiculous. "No, I must be wrong. That can't be why Aunt Charlotte asked me to ask you. Forgive me, please, Miss Farrow." She swallowed hard, fixed by Miss Farrow's glare.

Behind her, John's calm voice showed she wasn't the only one who'd opted to jump down and enter. "I believe, Almyra, that you have this confused, which is understandable." Miss Farrow's sharp gaze didn't seem to bother him. He added quietly, "The ladies felt you'd be better able to reassure the new mother, Miss Farrow, because you share some of her experience. She's a child of enslavement from Canada, and even under the best circumstances, we all understand how frightened she must be."

At this, Miss Farrow flung on her own shawl, made a brief apology to Mrs. Wilson, and headed out the door with Mrs. Sanborn at her heels.

Almyra brushed a hand against the stack of woolens. "I'm so sorry," she began.

Mrs. Wilson cut her off. "Go. Take them to North Upton. This can wait." And with perfect manners added, "Give my regards to your aunt, if you please."

Susannah and Mr. Wilson must have watered the horse since they were leading it in a wide circle to turn the carriage. As soon as it came to a halt, the four of them, Almyra, John, Miss Farrow, and Mrs. Sanborn, climbed up and sorted themselves within the tight space as best they could. Almyra's face flamed in the darkness, as she realized she'd taken a seat next to John.

After a long silence, Miss Farrow asked, "Well, Mr. Sanborn, now is the time for an explanation. How does there happen to be a woman born from enslavement, in North Upton this night, giving birth?"

"There again," John Sanborn began, "I must start from an unusual piece of history. You ladies, being considerably more experienced than Almyra, will already know something about the other town of Upton, the one in Canada."

Mrs. Sanborn smothered an exclamation with her hand, then lowered it and said in an almost calm voice, "The town where our Tories retreated, when America declared its independence from Britain."

And Miss Farrow added, in disgust, "And where enslavement lingered, despite the laws of Lower Canada."

"Exactly. And Mrs. Benjamin Blake, late of Upton, Quebec, lives in a hamlet of free persons who have found little option but to work for a very low wage for a landowner there who expects to open a copper mine. Her mother, father, and grandmother, as well as her sisters and brothers, all do the same. They sort the stones and open passageways into the earth, and more."

The air in the carriage felt thick with dismay and anger. Almyra realized this included her own anger. That young woman, in such pain, with Mrs. Hall and Aunt Charlotte attending her—in what ways had she been forced to labor, north of the border, in a nation that Almyra had always assumed meant the free terminus for American fugitives?

Mrs. Sanborn thrust her head out the open window. "Susannah, we are all snugly packed in here, and more speed shall not bother us."

"Very well." The horse changed pace, and the carriage moved more swiftly. Almyra looked to be sure John held his rifle securely. She felt his other hand brush her shoulder in reassurance, and once again, for what felt like the hundredth time in one evening, her face flamed in the darkness.

Miss Farrow asked, "Who might wet-nurse the babe, should it survive?"

Mrs. Sanborn replied, "The Hopkins girl seems to have plenty. And she could use some distraction. I believe she'll do."

After a long indrawn breath, Miss Farrow said, "Almyra, I believe I was overly sharp with you. I don't doubt your good intentions."

Yet there'd been just long enough now for Almyra to realize how offensive her own question had been, and she choked out, "My words and thoughts were both wrong, ma'am. I beg your pardon."

"Not at all necessary but thank you." And that was that.

A hint of discomfort remained, however, and John found the first way to deal with it. "While we are all here, let me conclude my account of the principal purpose of our journey into Canada this past few days. We found few who'd talk about where the counterfeit currency is being printed, and in the hamlet where we'd been told the main operation took place, only women and children, no men. So I am not sure we accomplished our task of trying to shut the spigot of the forged bills of trade."

Since everyone in the carriage seemed to understand this pronouncement, Almyra decided to describe her own efforts—without explaining how she'd happened to overhear the negotiations among Foster Pierce, Solomon McBride, and Mr. Sanborn, John's father, in the tavern room of the inn. She skipped directly to the meeting of Captain Young and Foster Pierce in the counting room of the Gilman Mill instead, with the printing plates, as well as the stacks of currency at the mill.

"Foster Pierce would do that for this region? Identify the use of the plates, and assure that the ones saying Wells River will go west to the frontier, rather than flood our region?" Mrs. Sanborn put it all together quickly. "Why? What does he get from this?"

Thank goodness for the darkness in the carriage! Almyra tried to sound as though this were a natural reason. "He says that he is a redeemed man," she relayed. "He is willing to be helpful through his old connections."

An air of doubt hung among them, with Miss Farrow saying nothing, and Mrs. Sanborn giving an entirely unladylike snort.

John Sanborn added quietly, "It's something I've seen from time to time on the frontier. Many a man goes bad with greed. But a few, especially as they age, have other thoughts."

Almyra added, "He has difficulty speaking, and he often seeks support when he walks." She didn't mention her own doubt about the times Mr. Pierce wanted an arm linked to his own—her suspicion that he used such connections to more clearly determine the response of another person. It was bad enough to believe he'd taken some advantage of her. She didn't need to tell everyone she'd been fooled by an old man. But it did seem important to pass along one more thing. "I believe he said he was headed soon to Upton. The one in Canada."

The carriage slowed. How quickly they'd returned to North Upton! John passed his rifle to Almyra, and she held it uncertainly, pointed toward the roof. He climbed down and assisted the ladies, then took the weapon from Almyra with one hand and offered her his other.

"You're not going inside yet," Susannah declared firmly. "Now that you know how to take care of a horse, you can help me with this one."

She began to separate the horse from the carriage, and Almyra realized John was laughing. "You'll be better able to manage a circuit ministry if you have such skills," he teased. "Or come West, where every woman needs to be able to manage a horse, without losing her standing as a lady."

Matt met them inside the livery stable, and immediately took John Sanborn aside for a low-voiced conversation, then tugged him toward the inn. Susannah handed a cloth and a pair of brushes to Almyra and set to work wiping and oiling the harness. How frustrating not to be able to listen to the men's discussion; Almyra felt exhaustion seeping into her muscles, although she bit back a complaint that rose to her lips. After so much attention in the carriage, she felt abandoned.

Susannah circled the horse's head to come closer and asked quietly, "Do you think we brought the others here in time?"

"I don't know. We'll find out when we go inside."

"I'm never going to bear a child. Between my mother and Mrs. Sanborn, I've already seen too much of it." She tipped her head to the side and asked, "Do you know, can a woman be married and not bear children?"

"Only if God so wills it," Almyra replied. "Or perhaps your mother knows some remedy to stop a woman's courses, but it might be harmful in the long run."

They wiped and brushed the horse's coat together, and Susannah demonstrated how to lift each hoof to check for stones or bruising.

Almyra finally cleaned her hands on a cloth and swallowed a sense of dread. "Let's go inside and find out."

## ~ 29 ~

Almyra and Susannah entered at the back of the tavern and walked through the quiet and empty rooms, edging around furnishings in the shadows. Opening the door into the house, they were met by thick warmth, far too much for their garb and recent exercise. Almyra shed her shawl at once.

She did not see either Jane or Polly in the kitchen. The stove chittered with heat, water thumped in a kettle, and a glow around the edges of the firebox door gave a bit of light. Lamplight from the front parlor also flickered at the further doorway.

She paused to sniff the air and to listen. The foul smell she'd experienced with the woman who failed to survive wasn't present, though she caught the scent of blood and a whiff of outhouse aromas. A rhythmic creak on the floorboards of the far room signaled a rocking chair in action. Beyond that, she only heard whispers.

Susannah sank into a kitchen chair, fatigue finally revealed in her slow movements. Almyra longed to do the same, but first she had to know what had happened to Benjamin Blake's young wife.

She tiptoed toward the front parlor and edged around the frame of the door. The room seemed very full of women, though Benjamin Blake himself was no longer present. Aunt Charlotte, no longer kneeling on the floor but perched on a chair, noticed Almyra, set a finger to her lips, and rose, beckoning her into the room.

Still, she hesitated. Mrs. Sanborn and Mrs. Hall, head to head, were crouched between the young woman's legs. Miss Farrow sat in the rocking chair near the woman's head, leaning over a bundle on her lap and humming quietly.

Almyra realized her aunt was trying to lift one of several basins on the floor. Finally she moved forward and took that basin, straining to handle the weight of the contents, and at her aunt's nod, she carried it out to the kitchen. Her aunt followed with a second basin filled with red liquid and something else. Almyra tried not to look. Susannah seemed asleep at the kitchen table, her head on her arms.

Almyra whispered, "Is Mrs. Blake going to live?"

"If God wills it," her aunt replied. A faint tired smile added reassurance. "The baby was so early that the birth wasn't very hard. The others are packing her with compresses now, to try to prevent infection."

"And the baby?" Almyra held her breath for the reply.

"Too early. Much too early. But living, for now. Tomorrow one of Mrs. Sanborn's friends who bore a baby of her own earlier this month will come to be a wet-nurse for a few days. We'll see. Sometimes a tiny scrap of life can persist. It is, you know, in the good Lord's hands, but there could not be a better group of women to make an effort. Your friend's wife came to a very good place."

Was Benjamin Blake her friend? Almyra felt too tired to dispute the notion. She hadn't even told her aunt yet about Foster Pierce in St. Johnsbury, or Captain Young, or what she'd learned from John Sanborn.

"Uncle Eliphalet," she managed to say aloud.

"Home, and asleep," Aunt Charlotte confirmed. "And Matthew took Benjamin also to rest, after the baby came. It's a boy, you know."

This seemed magical in its way: a baby boy born from the fears of this day. If only it could survive.

Aunt Charlotte brushed a hand across Almrya's shoulders and said, "We'll go home now, my dear. Let me just tell the others." She walked back to the door to the front parlor, whispered something, and returned to lift Almyra's shawl. "Put this on, and we'll go to our own beds. There will be time tomorrow morning to hear each other's news."

They tiptoed together across the kitchen. Almyra supposed Susannah would stir eventually and go to her own bed or be sent there by Mrs. Hall. It seemed wrong to leave the basins not yet emptied, but someone else would have to tackle that.

As they reached the door to leave, John Sanborn came quietly from the inn. He nodded to Aunt Charlotte and offered to walk them home. Her aunt declined, but he held the door for them and stepped outside.

"Almyra, I wanted you to know," he began. As quietly as if they were all still in the kitchen, he said, "Matthew gave me more details about Mr. Pierce, and what my father agreed to. I'm sure I'll see you tomorrow, with him, and we can work out what must follow."

Aunt Charlotte said firmly, "Not until noon. A certain young lady is headed for bed. And so am I."

Still, John's reassurance helped warm Almyra, and with an arm linked in her aunt's, she reached home and found her way to her chamber. After dropping her skirt over a chair and fumbling to unbutton and untie her other garments, she crawled under a blanket and did not wake for hours, until the aromas of bacon and biscuit roused her.

It was indeed almost noon, by the window's light. She swept up her hair, paused to brush mud from the hem of her skirt, then tucked her creased clothing back together as best she could and followed the urgency of her rumbling stomach.

In the kitchen, Aunt Charlotte stood at the cookstove and four men sat at the table, deep in conversation. Almyra went directly to her aunt and asked, "The baby?"

"So far, so good," her aunt replied. "Bowls and forks, please, Almyra, and some butter from the cellar."

As she turned to fetch these items, Almyra scanned the seated men. Her uncle of course, and Mr. Sanborn, John's father. Matthew. And Benjamin Blake. It surprised her that Captain Young wasn't on hand, but perhaps he'd been delayed. And where was John?

"Who'll let Judge Paddock know?" That was Uncle Eliphalet.

Mr. Sanborn replied, "Miss Farrow can tell him should it be necessary. But I understand he's not well, and perhaps the bank should simply examine all its currency without making any fuss. If Pierce holds to his guarantee, there should gradually be fewer forgeries circulating north of Boston."

Benjamin asked, "Should I then pass word to the Johnsons in Peacham?"

The other men agreed, and Uncle Eliphalet added, "Remind them to speak in turn to Kiah Bailey in Hardwick. The more funds we raise for these efforts, the more cautious all should be."

Almyra and her aunt joined the men for the meal. For a few minutes she only paid attention to eating. Then her uncle caught her eye.

"I understand you did very well on Sunday, niece. I've heard nothing but praise for your efforts. Well done, my dear."

She spoke her mind, "Perhaps I might not take the extra schooling at Peacham Academy? Do you suppose I might apply directly to the seminary in Springfield?"

Uncle Eliphalet looked to Aunt Charlotte, who said only, "I think the idea merits consideration. Perhaps after the Sabbath."

Her husband nodded to her, then reached across to pat Almyra's hand. "None of us are in any hurry to see you leave. Be patient." He turned back toward the men. "Now, at what point should we consider moving Mrs. Blake and the baby to Peacham? Benjamin, is there room there for your family? I'm sure you'd prefer to have them at one of the locations where you spend time, and I know that is not North Upton."

But Benjamin Blake was shaking his head. "Sir, I'm afraid Peacham is not the best place for them. We didn't intend to spend more than a few days there and had hoped to be back in Canada very soon." He hesitated, looked among the puzzled faces at the table, and sighed. "I don't want my son taken into servitude, sir."

"Here in Vermont? How is that possible? Even the state's constitution forbids enslavement. This should not be a consideration, man."

Benjamin looked agitated. "Sir, if you'll pardon my saying the opposite, that restriction only applies after the age of twenty-one years. My wife and I, we've heard of towns that take the children into custody until then. Brattleboro would be one such place."

Uncle Eliphalet looked to Mr. Sanborn. "Is that so?"

Mr. Sanborn hesitated. "I might have heard something. Also, perhaps St. Albans over by Lake Champlain. Miss Farrow or the judge would be more certain."

Almyra was shocked but cut in anyway, "We might for now presume the worst. After so much risk, and with such a blessing last night, that this child lives, may we not defer to Mr. Blake?" Seeing cautious nods around the table, she asked, "Benjamin, where did you plan to raise your children, then?"

"In Canada, Miss, but not in Upton if we can help it. Perhaps Stanstead Plain or nearby seemed safe enough, though."

She pressed onward. "You don't have that home prepared as yet?"

Benjamin shook his head. Almyra felt for him—so much fear, so much worry. She turned to her uncle. "Might his wife and child stay in North Upton until he has prepared a place for them up north?"

Uncle Eliphalet looked at Aunt Charlotte. She said, "I will ask among the women later. But I would think it possible."

This seemed to satisfy the men, whose conversation turned almost at once to Mr. Sanborn's report, based on what his son John had told him, of conditions to the west, in what seemed about to be the Territory of Kansas.

"And the final House vote takes place later this month," Mr. Sanborn continued. "There seems small doubt that it will pass. Word's reached me," he didn't say how, but Almyra remembered Solomon McBride's argument, "that Eli Thayer of Massachusetts is seeking settlers to head there to help vote its standing into free, not slave. As you may note, I've no further sons to send there." She heard the bitterness in his voice, and knew the others must, also. "Still, we can carry word to others. He says he'll provide a wagon and supplies for anyone willing to go."

This part, she already knew. She touched her aunt's elbow and whispered. "May we go to see the mother and baby? And talk with the others?"

Aunt Charlotte agreed. They set a pot of tea and a plate of sugared cakes on the table for the men and donned their shawls. Matthew noticed and excused himself, as did Benjamin, and the two of them strode off ahead. Mr. Sanborn said he'd follow shortly.

The air through the window felt mild, and the sun shone brightly. Already the village road seemed less muddy. Someone in a distant field dragged a harrow across it with oxen. Birds sang. For the first time in weeks, if not longer, Almyra felt hopeful. She wondered whether John Sanborn would be at the inn and recalled again that nobody had mentioned Captain Young's whereabouts. Her aunt shook her head when asked. "I have no idea. But there is something else I need to discover."

"What is it?"

"Why that young woman's baby came so early. There must be a reason."

Almyra asked, "Doesn't it just, sometimes, happen? From a fall, or a rough ride, or something in God's hands?" She felt awkward saying it that way, but wasn't that what childbirth involved? Either you were blessed, or not. Either the child survived to become an adult, or it died in the first few weeks, or even the first few years, from some illness.

Aunt Charlotte pursed her lips. "We asked Benjamin last night. He said she'd been well enough protected, and was still working without a fuss, sorting stone and samples for the Nichols company exploration up there. He said the other women knew she was with child, and made sure to cosset her, with a seat, and shelter, and plenty of healthy food and drink. And the ride south, in a sprung carriage, seemed easy enough as well." She shook her head. "I am not satisfied. Nor was Mrs. Sanborn last night."

The two of them increased their pace. Almyra wondered, *Was anything as simple as it seemed?*

Another aspect to explore in a sermon or homily. She skipped for a moment with eagerness, recalling that her aunt and uncle had agreed to consider speeding her into seminary sooner rather than later.

Aunt Charlotte, focused on reaching the inn with speed, did not notice or scold.

$$\sim 30 \sim$$

Mrs. Hall's kitchen air again pressed a wave of heat and dampness against Almyra's face. It must be to keep the baby warm. Or the mother. Or both. Two kettles and a washboiler simmered on the cookstove. The basins, she was relieved to see, had vanished, along with their mysterious and odorous contents. Now she could smell mint and something unfamiliar.

Behind her, Aunt Charlotte guessed, "Raspberry leaf tea. It may help the milk to come in."

Jane turned from the dry sink to nod. "For both of them." She gestured toward the front parlor.

Curious, Almyra followed her aunt. Surely Jane didn't mean Mrs. Hall, did she?

In the front room a new cluster of women sat around an improvised bed where Benjamin Blake's wife lay, both ends of her propped up to make an arc of her body. Mrs. Sanborn seemed to be examining something under the woman's petticoat, while crooning in a reassuring tone. "And the flow is almost done, I think. You're healing well, Flora."

At Flora's head, Mrs. Hall held a cup to her lips. "A little more, for the baby's sake. Yes, that's right."

Almyra thought the woman in the rocking chair seemed familiar, and guessed it was one of the Hopkins sisters, from the freckles on her wide face. She held her own baby with one arm, asleep in her lap. With her other hand, she held a folded cloth against her chest. Almyra quickly looked away from the exposed skin. Aunt Charlotte, on the other hand, stepped directly across to assist. Then, as the woman in the rocking chair adjusted her shawl, and lifted a cup of tea of her own, Aunt Charlotte carried the cloth to Mrs. Hall, who appeared to dab it someplace on Flora.

"Now we'll see if we can coax your babe to suckle, with the sweet taste already there," Mrs. Hall suggested.

This complicated set of maneuvers surely meant the baby still lived, and Almyra watched just long enough to see Mrs. Hall lift an impossibly tiny swaddled bundle from a box toward its eager mama.

That sufficed. Almyra backed out of the room. She didn't precisely feel ill, but off balance. Was this what childbed and motherhood required? Absurdly, she wondered how women on the frontier managed without a village of neighbors and treatments. At least if she never married, she'd never have to submit to such indignities.

Back in the kitchen, she saw Polly come in with a basket of what must be dandelion greens. She admired them, then said casually, "I suppose Susannah is out in the stables?"

Jane said with scorn, "Where else?"

"I think I'll just go see how she's doing, then." With relief, she exited the kitchen, grateful for the cooler air of the hallway. She crossed into the tavern and noticed soiled dishes and tankards on the tables. She should be neighborly and gather them up for Jane. Perhaps on her way back.

Outside, she inhaled the familiar fragrances of farm life waking to the warmer seasons. Already, the sunstruck heap of manure near the stables sent forth a powerful aroma of its own.

An unfamiliar horse, taller than usual and with a pale coat, stood in the doorway to the stables, held by a tether at each side. Matthew continued to examine its hooves while he greeted Almyra.

"Looking for Susannah?"

"Yes, but also, Matthew, where is Captain Young? And did Miss Farrow leave already?"

"Captain Young escorted Miss Farrow back to St. Johnsbury this morning." Matthew shot her a curious glance. "Is there something you wanted to tell him?"

"No, I only wanted to ask something about when they traveled from Canada. My aunt said something that made me curious."

Matthew shrugged. "I don't expect him again for a few weeks. Perhaps you could ask John Sanborn." He nodded toward the farm across the road. "Isaiah told me that they leave tomorrow by train. I expect I'll take them to the station in the morning."

Susannah ducked under one of the tethers, her pantaloons exposing her ankles as she did so. Almyra closed her eyes a moment; this day seemed full of things she didn't want to see or hear. A verse from the Book of Matthew occurred to her: "But blessed are your eyes, for they see; and your ears, for they hear." Then I am feeling over-much blessed, she thought.

She felt Susannah grip her shoulder. "What is it? Do you feel faint?"

Almyra tried to smile as she opened her eyes. "I just had the sun in my face for a moment. Susannah, it seems all the menfolk are departing, and we shall be able to resume our own actions. That is, I believe we had some underway before so much confusion arrived."

Her friend laughed. "Riding lessons? Driving lessons? Or do you mean the handbills to circulate for my mother's strengthening tonics?"

Almyra frowned. "I wonder. Would your mother's tonics prevent an early birth like the one with Mrs. Blake?"

"Ask her," Susannah grinned. "She will be pleased to tell you, no doubt. Which reminds me, she's going to scold, since I haven't yet cleared off the tavern tables. I'd rather clear a stable any day," she confessed.

"Come then, many hands make light work." Leaving Matthew to his task, which now seemed to involve a peculiar tool applied to the hooves of the horse, they re-entered the tavern and stacked plates. Susannah produced a basket for the emptied tankards. Cautiously, making as little noise as possible, they opened the door to the overly warm kitchen, and Polly ran between them as they carried in their balanced stacks.

Their caution failed to avoid the notice of Mrs. Hall, who looked like she'd start to scold, then realized Almyra also had an armful. In a low voice she said, "Good girls, bring them over to Jane. And kindly stay with her to help her wipe them for the next meal."

A cloth in her hand, Almyra turned sideways to look at her aunt, Mrs. Hall, and Mrs. Sanborn, each with a cup of tea at the wide scrubbed table. She supposed the other woman, the wet-nurse, must still be in the front parlor.

"How is Mrs. Blake?" she whispered.

"Stronger," Mrs. Hall confirmed. "She'll be sitting up by the morrow."

"And her baby?"

The three women exchanged glances. Aunt Charlotte murmured at last, "Everything rests in God's hands. He's a beautiful little boy, but he's not breathing well. So small, so early." The others nodded, clearly distressed.

Almyra finished wiping a bowl and stepped a bit closer. "Was it the journey in the carriage? Was it too rough for her?"

Mrs. Sanborn shook her head. "They didn't hurry until her pains began. It was a gentle journey until then. No," she said slowly, "but I've seen something similar. The way the baby droops a bit, and the shape of the feet."

Mrs. Hall nodded. "I thought the same. Lead, do you think?"

Pursed lips and narrowed eyes signaled agreement among them. But what did that mean? Almyra asked, "From something like those bad pennies?" She recalled Mrs. Hall saying the false coins were made from lead.

"Lead water pipes, I would have guessed," her aunt inserted, "but Benjamin says they only have a dug well, with a pail."

An idea came to her. Almyra asked, "What about copper?"

Mrs. Hall said, still keeping her voice low, "Water lines aren't made from copper. Nor is a water pail. It would be far too costly, and too soft."

"But copper ore," Almyra mused. "We know she and her family were sorting the stones and dug soil where Isaiah said the new copper mines will be set. Could that be?"

After a moment of thought, Aunt Charlotte reflected, "That would give new meaning to the phrase 'bright as a new penny.'" Grim nods of agreement met her statement.

Mrs. Hall finally said, "We don't know enough, Almyra. But it could be. At least, it's enough to be suspicious of, and we'll send word north with the Blakes so that women working with the Canadian ore have some warning. For now, we need to try to save this one babe."

"If God wills," Almyra's aunt repeated softly.

Almyra wiped the last bowl, and Susannah stacked them. They set the forks and spoons into a wooden tray. Mrs. Hall rose to fetch two more cups and began to pour for the two of them. Susannah brushed a hand across Almyra's shoulder as they sat side by side at the far end of the table, smiling in relief.

The gesture, the touch to her shoulder, recalled John Sanborn's comforting touch in the carriage, and after he'd helped her down. Soon, he'd be back at the Thetford-area copper mines with Isaiah, and it might be months until she'd see him again.

Copper mines. She whirled in alarm, looking first at Susannah, then at Mrs. Hall, then at Aunt Charlotte. "Copper mines. The ones in Thetford." Her words were too loud, and everyone hushed her at once, but Susannah was the first to realize what she meant.

"They haven't left yet," Susannah exclaimed, also too loudly. "Come on, we'll go tell them."

Whispering toward the others, "We must, please pardon our voices," Almyra jumped from her seat. With Susannah close behind, she leapt for the door to the inn's yard, tugging her shawl around her as she ran.

# ~ 31 ~

They ran up the track toward the Sanborn farm. A haze of green to either side of them said spring had truly arrived. Almyra clutched her skirt and petticoat with both hands, trying to keep them out of any puddles and free her feet. Susannah ran ahead, then stopped at the barn door. "In here?"

Almyra shook her head, veering toward the steps at the kitchen door. "Mr. Sanborn. John." She pounded on the door, then flung it open.

John Sanborn's father Ephraim sat on a chair, pulling on his boots. "What is it, Almyra? Is someone hurt? Did your father send you?"

"No, sir," she gasped, trying to ignore a pain in her side from running. "I must talk with John, please. Immediately."

Susannah now stood beside her, and echoed, "Immediately."

Ephraim Sanborn frowned. "He and Isaiah walked up to the spring, to clean it out some. I expect they're on the way down by now."

Almyra had no idea where the Sanborn spring would be. Somewhere on the ridge, perhaps. She asked, "Is there … is there a way to call them, sir?"

"I could shout a bit," Mr. Sanborn said slowly. "Might bring them down sooner." He stood up. "We'll give it a try. But not too much, or someone will think we have a fire."

With Susannah, Almyra darted back down the steps. Mr. Sanborn looked toward the fields by the river, and the rising slope beyond. He cupped his hands around his face and called, "Johnny. Johnny."

Almyra strained to hear any response. The sheep in the barn began to call back, baa-ing and thumping. Mr. Sanborn cleared his throat, then tried again. "John. Come on down."

A faint shout replied. "There you are, girls," Mr. Sanborn said. "They're on the way. You just wait here for them. I'll be in the barn if you need me."

The river water flowed brown and frothy, still high with meltwater and rain. In summer you could wade across, but not now. Almyra tugged at Susannah's arm. "The bridge."

They walked downriver quickly and reached the crossing, just as John and Isaiah came close enough to call out, each carrying a shovel, half running. "Who's hurt?"

"Nobody yet." Susannah's shout and Almyra's call of "Hurry, please," clearly confused them, but the men kept up their pace and thudded across the wet boards of the bridge. The girls rushed to meet him.

"Copper mines. Babies. You have to do something," Susannah burst out. Isaiah stared, and John's eyebrows flew up.

Almyra almost smiled, then seized John's elbow. "Listen," she said urgently, "there's a woman that Mrs. Hall and the others are tending, and she's given birth way too early."

John was clean-shaven today, shorn of his western beard, and Almyra could read both concern and a hint of amusement in his face. "Yes, we know that. Even though we are only menfolk. My mother does explain some things to me, you see."

Susannah hissed with exasperation. "She didn't explain why it happened, did she?"

Isaiah spoke up. "Wasn't it the ride from Canada that startled Mrs. Blake?"

Almyra said impatiently, "It was a gentle ride until her pains began, when they started to hurry. Listen," she repeated, "the women tending her think it looks like what lead water pipes can do. Bring the baby early, and not formed quite right."

Now both men looked grave. "Lead water pipes are common enough," Isaiah mused.

Susannah cut in. "They didn't have pipes. Just a dug well and a pail. Oh, why won't you both listen?"

Almyra released John's elbow and took Susannah's instead. "She's right. What they did have, what might have done the damage, is they've been sorting copper ore, both rocks and dug soil, at the place you visited up north, Mr. Hutchinson. Where you did the assays. And copper's a metal just like lead. And what if the mines near Thetford are poisoning all the women who are with child? You have to do something!"

John Sanborn exchanged glances with Isaiah, then looked back to Almyra. "Silver's a metal, too," he mused. "People use silver teaspoons all the time, without harm. Why should copper be any different?"

"But people, our people, don't live beside silver mines. And what about dust in the air, and copper in the water?"

Isaiah rumbled slowly, "Might be something to think about. Mineral springs have effects. Metals in streams might, as well." He nodded. "I could assay the water, I'm sure of it. But Miss Alexander, the Vermont mines are barely started. It's mostly men so far, besides a couple of women in the cook sheds."

"But she's right," John mused, "the Canada operation's entirely different. With all those freed colored people needing work, it's already families living there. Still," he backtracked, "must be a dozen things that could have caused this particular babe to come early. And the mother's well enough, isn't she?"

What seemed obvious to Almyra didn't seem urgent to these men. She gave an unladylike stamp of one foot. "Bearing a baby so early is not a sign of health. Susannah, say something."

Her friend looked up at the sky for a moment, pulling her thoughts together. Then she said, "Look, what my mother's always taught me, about tonics and medicines and such, it's what goes into you over the long haul that shapes your health. That's why we," she glanced at Almyra, "that is, the womenfolk around here, we're eager to teach what we already know. About plants, and even about what people eat. Who is going to teach your people at your copper mines to be healthy? Who is bound to watch over them?"

Almyra saw the masculine aspect at last. "It's part of freedom," she spelled out. "To take responsibility. And you don't have to be elected, or designated, or even ordained, to have that responsibility. If you know more, you're obliged to teach others."

The long silence as the two men looked at each other told her she'd reached them. That they understood. She took a deep breath, and let it back out, as she met Susannah's gaze and nodded.

Isaiah spoke first. "Miss Alexander, I understand you're aiming to train as a minister of the Word. I imagine you'll make a good one. I have a sense you've just preached us a short, strong sermon."

Almyra looked at John for confirmation. Like Isaiah, he was half smiling, half serious. "We'll do it," he told her. "We understand what you're teaching."

Everyone seemed to sigh in the same moment. Then Susannah warned, "We'd best be getting back. Almyra and I have mothers—that is, a mother and an aunt—who feel responsible for us, and that's going to mean a scolding if we stay out here when there's a meal to prepare."

The four of them walked back to the farmyard, and the men set their wet but empty pails by the barn door. "We'll walk with you," John said. "Might be it will spare you some chastising." He smiled at Almyra.

"And I should pay my respects, with Benjamin off in Peacham. How is his wife today? Is she …" Isaiah hesitated.

"She's strong," Susannah answered. "My mother says she's strong enough. But," she swallowed hard, "a person can't say that about a babe. Not yet."

"I understand."

Without effort, their group sorted itself—John and Almyra walking together, followed by Susannah and Isaiah, who somehow were already discussing horses. Almyra blushed to realize they were actually describing the breeding of foals. How embarrassing.

John nudged her gently. "Don't listen. Tell me instead about this path of yours, to become a minister. It's true, then, that there will be places in Vermont for you, as a lady? I've never seen that."

"Uncle Eliphalet says there have been several. The training will offer some challenges, as I should like to attend the Wesleyan Seminary in Springfield, and I'm not sure they've trained girls. But they must." Passion raised her voice, and she blushed again. Being around John Sanborn seemed to wrong-foot her often.

"Indeed, they must," he agreed, without laughing. "I shall look forward to learning about your progress." It was his turn to hesitate, and he turned partway toward her. "Would you write to me? And allow me to write back to you?"

"Oh yes!" Without thinking, she placed a hand on his arm. "I would like that very much, John."

He covered her hand with his own for a moment, his eyes directly meeting hers. "So would I," he said quietly. "Very much."

They reached the end of the track, the edge of the main road, with the inn just across from them. He removed his hand, and she pulled back hers, but the moment lingered as they waited for Isaiah and Susannah to catch up.

He smiled widely, and she noted the flash of that gold tooth she'd noticed when he first came home, along with the deep creases from his smile, and the friendly crinkling around his eyes. "You know, Miss Almyra Alexander, out West things are quite a bit different. A woman minister won't be any surprise in the Kansas Territory, or even in Illinois, I daresay." He leaned closer and whispered, "I have even heard that a woman preaching the word of God in Illinois may be a married woman."

Laughing, she tapped his arm as a Boston woman might scold a flirtatious man. "You'll have to investigate and write to me all about it."

As a group of four, they crossed toward the other buildings. Susannah and Isaiah veered away toward the stables. John paused.

"I don't have a reason to go into the house," he admitted. "And I should be packing."

"For the mines at Thetford?"

He shook his head. "I'll escort Isaiah that far, and set him rolling with this new responsibility you've reminded us to take. Also I believe he's buying a bit of land up north, to go with his assay work in the new region. But I'm for the West once again. I'll escort a group of settlers that Eli Thayer is assembling, and then my uncle Martin expects my assistance." He touched a hand, very briefly, to her shoulder. "A free Kansas depends on each and all of us."

Almyra nodded. "I understand," she told him. "And I'll begin writing to you tomorrow, after you've departed. You'll leave me the addresses for posting them?"

"I will," he said. And with one more smile, one she swore she'd hold in her heart, he turned and walked back toward his father's house.

## ~ 32 ~

Full summer reached North Upton the second week of June.

Beset by the aromas of blossoms and the calls of small birds, Almyra found it harder and harder to stay at her table. She inked the final paragraph for her letter to the Rev. Miss Antoinette L. Brown of Wayne County, New York, congratulating her on her ordination and mentioning Mr. Parker's recent sermon on the spiritual development of the human race. Mr. Parker faulted men for refusing to allow women the vote. She found his argument cogent and meant to share it with as many preachers as she could.

This added labor, she told herself again, would be to her benefit in August, when she'd apply for entrance to Vermont's Wesleyan seminary in Springfield. Every name she could cite then to show her connection to others already ordained must be an advantage.

The absence of support from her father seemed a bitter return to her efforts. Unlike Uncle Eliphalet, he seemed to think her fit only for marriage. It must be, Almyra felt, the influence of his new wife. This seemed doubly unfair, since this "step-mama" had not even met Almyra. Which, upon reflection, at least saved time. Who could spare the days of entertaining Boston guests, when there was so much to be done right here?

Aunt Charlotte called out from the kitchen: "You have time before the noon meal, my dear. Why not take a walk? Go say hello to Susannah, enjoy some sunshine."

Almyra wiped her pen clean and set the page aside. She would review her writing and post the letter tomorrow. Sometimes wisdom meant waiting a bit.

In the kitchen, she brushed a kiss onto her aunt's cheek, inhaled the aroma of a chicken pie, and agreed. "But I won't be out long. I'll come back and help you finish preparing for Uncle Eliphalet and Mr. Johnson."

They exchanged smiles. Uncle Eliphalet's discovery of how much he and Mr. Johnson of Peacham both shared and disagreed about seemed to have lit much joy, as well as argument. This visit, after several letters, boded well for new friendship.

With a light shawl over her head, Almyra slipped out into the green and gold embrace of the day. Dandelions seemed to have spread around the village, from Mrs. Hall's garden of medicinals, and she tried not to crush any of their bright blooms.

The road to the cemetery was steep and difficult. At least in this season no ice slowed her, and she didn't fear any wild animals, so close to the blacksmith's barn that a smoky resonance of burning coal rose up with her.

Because Benjamin and Flora Blake did not live in North Upton, there was only a small stone, marked Baby. When they could, she knew they meant to move the tiny body in its wooden box to their Canadian homestead. She plucked a dandelion and set it on the stone, said a short prayer, and moved back a few rows to where Jerusha Clark's marker stood. She hadn't known the young woman—this was Alice's friend, from before Almyra lived here—but Alice sometimes mentioned Jerusha, and Almyra could write that she'd paid a visit here.

One more prayer, and she started back toward home. The stage pulled away, headed east, as she reached the main road. She hadn't driven or gone riding on a horse since John Sanborn had left town; there'd been no call for it and Susannah's errands hadn't fit her own timing. Soon, she promised herself. The friendship must be nurtured, and she enjoyed Susannah's sharp wit and quick comprehension. Though, truth be told, she didn't miss the rub of that sidesaddle at all.

She waved to Matthew, who had a sack of mail in hand, taking it to the store to be sorted. He called out, "Have they reached Illinois yet?"

Of course, he meant John Sanborn and the party of Eli Thayer's New England settlers, bound to homestead in the Kansas Territory and cast their votes. She replied, "Too soon. But if there's a letter, I'll let you know."

Over the noon meal with Aunt Charlotte and Uncle Eliphalet, they began plans for a summer Sunday school for the children of the village. Her aunt asked, "Will Polly return in time?"

Mrs. Hall had taken Polly with her to their home farm in Waterford, near East Village, and Jane and Susannah were managing the meals at Matthew's inn. Almyra counted the days,and said, "Yes, I believe so. But she may not read much. I have never seen her at the school."

"We must place her with the smaller children, then, and tell her perhaps that she is our assistant, a little older than the others around her. She is a hard-working little thing."

Almyra agreed. She stepped into the front room to fetch paper and ink and brought them back to the kitchen table to list the children they anticipated and begin to form the classes.

Uncle Eliphalet pushed back his chair. "Luther should be sorry he missed this fine meal. But he was in a hurry to get back to his wife. He has to be in Hardwick tomorrow."

Hardwick. Almyra hadn't thought of that town since she'd heard Foster Pierce mention it, which now felt like a very long time ago. She looked up at her uncle and asked, "Do you hear how the bank is going?"

"Well enough, I'm sure," he said with some surprise, then realized the intent of her question. "No more than a handful of bad currency since then. So far, the Canadians seem to have kept their agreement to send their dastardly papers elsewhere. But it's early days to be sure."

She mentioned this in correspondence to Alice and Caroline, who might see such currency out in Illinois. She recalled that the printing plate that Foster Pierce had inspected indicated a fictional "Bank of Wells River." She must add this to her next letter.

"Uncle, may I ask another question before you leave the room?"

"Of course. What is it, Almyra?"

"The copper mines. I know pennies are made from copper, and I've heard you say we need our own currency, without all the Spanish coins and such. But surely that can't use all the metal from so many mines, can it?" She knew she should have asked this sooner, but the moment never seemed right before.

Uncle Eliphalet smiled. "Copper pennies, and copper cooking pots and kettles are what most women know for the metal's use, so your description is not surprising. But most copper, until a few years ago, went to sheathing the bottoms of wooden ships so that they might endure the ravages of salt water and its organisms. Now, however," he gestured east, toward St. Johnsbury, "now the pressing use for copper is for railroads. The locomotive engines require boiler plates made of this metal. And although the railroad hasn't yet altered lives in North Upton, it is changing them across the nation."

He paused, then added, "Were it not for the railroad, there would not be telegraph lines in so many places, like Branston, in Quebec Province. Recall, Almyra, that the telegraph enabled me to reach Mr. Dana and commend to him the representation of Anthony Burns in court."

How vexing that she'd never thought to ask further about that Boston case. She asked now, "Was Mr. Dana successful? Has Mr. Burns been released?"

The grave expression warned her of what was coming. "No, he was sent back to the South, and is sitting in a jail in Richmond, Virginia. It seems likely that when the furor calms, he will again be sold into enslavement." Uncle Eliphalet continued in a lower voice. "But you, niece, are I think acquainted with at least the name of Leonard Grimes, the African pastor in Boston? He continues his efforts on behalf of Mr. Burns. Some of the funds we all raise go toward his work. Do not give up hope."

One of the Hopkins boys rapped at the kitchen door with a handful of envelopes. Uncle Eliphalet accepted them with thanks and sorted them. "Two here from the Conference on church matters. One for you, my dear, from your sister," he said to his wife. "And who might this be for, and from?" He smiled as he passed the last to Almyra.

"Ah, from Alice. At last," Almyra slipped open the letter eagerly and sat again at the table, to pore over the cramped lines that crossed and recrossed the page.

She exclaimed to her aunt as she read portions aloud. "More than a hundred students at the school. And the Superintendent has noticed our Caroline. He wishes to have more qualified teachers who can use the signing language. Well, then surely Caroline will be valued there. Listen, Aunt, The children wake at half past four each morning, and they must each complete five hours of labor each day, in addition to their study, prayers, and meals. But she doesn't write what kind of labor. I will ask her straight away." She fingered the page, following the sentences separated by enthusiastic long dashes. "Alice has met two men from the state legislature, because her Uncle Martin sometimes brings them to the subscription office. She has more than doubled the subscription for his newspaper since her last letter. And she says," Almyra looked up to meet her aunt's gaze, "oh, isn't this just like Alice, she says she wants to go to the Kansas Territory before the end of the year. That she wants to write for her uncle's newspaper under the same A. Sanborn, and try her hand at moving people to stand up for abolition in more ways."

Aunt Charlotte sniffed. "As if those of us here are not doing our part also?"

"No, I am sure she does not mean to slight our efforts. But she means to be where the decisions are being made, and she says that must mean Kansas Territory this year, as the settlers pour in."

From the front room, Uncle Eliphalet called out, "I should think she'd opt for Washington, then."

He returned to the kitchen. "Your sister's husband," he began. "Yes, Solomon McBride. While you ladies were applying your efforts in other arenas, I took him aside for a long conversation. You know he's forwarding Eli Thayer's project? Yes, I thought you might realize that. But what neither of you ladies would have heard is this: He has hope of moving William Seward into backing the new Republican Party with its strong abolitionist stance. There's to be a convention in Michigan next month, and from there, it's only a matter of time until candidates for higher office can be recruited."

"Uncle Eliphalet, must one go to Washington, then, to see abolition succeed? Will you also feel called to go there?"

Almyra waited a long moment, and feared she'd been too direct. At last her uncle growled, "I'll leave that to my brother. Now then, I have letters to write."

Her uncle's brother was, of course, Almyra's father. Did this mean that in order to take a strong role in moving the nation away from its besetting sin, Almyra should attempt to resume some sort of closer daughterly duties?

She looked up to see her aunt eying her quizzically. "I believe I noticed you writing a few letters of your own."

"Yes. Yes, I am. There are other women speaking for abolition from the pulpit. I thought we should know each other and correspond. And promote each other's words."

Aunt Charlotte nodded. "I follow your thinking, my dear, and find it wise. We shall show your uncle and your father that even from here, women may bring correction to the nation's trajectory. Which reminds me, now that Mr. Johnson has called on your uncle, I believe it's time for us to make a ladies' visit to Mrs. Johnson and her daughter. And of course Miss Farrow. Perhaps your friend Susannah can help us once again."

Almyra said, "Of course we shall." She left the table, letter still in hand, to prepare a list of visits and actions. Perhaps she should call for a Ladies' Anti-Slavery Society in North Upton.

What would John Sanborn think when she wrote to him such news? "Many wearing rapiers are afraid of goosequills," she recited to herself from William Shakespeare's masterpiece. Let the men dream of battle, whether in Washington or on the frontier. Family and friends instead would bolster her strength and courage.

Like Alice, like Caroline, like Miss Farrow and others, Almyra Alexander understood the task to come. Not war, she thought; instead, the unstoppable power of love for one's fellow persons.

*But was it true,* she wondered, *that a woman in the pulpit at the frontier need not give up her calling if she married*? She drew out a fresh sheet of paper and began a letter.

*"Dearest Alice and Caroline."* There was a great deal to tell them and to ask about. So she would save that final question for the end of her reply.

*"If you please, ascertain this for sure. I find that I have an urgent need to know. Yrs always, with the fierce flame of friendship and honor.*

*Almyra."*

# EPILOGUE

Almyra tried not to hurry. She'd spoiled her page with an ink blot and now copied the sentences carefully. This letter to the Springfield Wesleyan Seminary, requesting admission, needed to be perfect. Or as close to it as she could manage.

Uncle Eliphalet still hadn't returned from the gathering of men at the general store. The news from the convention in Montpelier had raced around the village yesterday. Almyra recalled her uncle's voice reading aloud to her aunt from the newspaper. "We say—get the friends of freedom together; secure their co-operation and consequent organization, to carry out the principles on which they agree."

Later, she had re-read some other portions. "Resolved, That the institution of Slavery is a great moral, social and political evil; that it was so regarded by the fathers of the Republic, the founders and best friends of the Union, by the heroes and sages of the revolution." Heroes and sages. How right and good that seemed.

And at last: "Resolved, That henceforth all compromises with Slavery are at an end, and our rallying cry shall henceforth be the repeal of the Fugitive Slave law, and of the inter-state slave trade, the abolition of slavery in the District of Columbia, the prohibition of slavery in all the Territories of the United States, and the admission of no more Slave States into the Union."

Surely Vermont's stand would lead the nation into righteous action. Almyra felt some relief, that this issue must be settled at last. She could settle herself into her upcoming studies, knowing the freedom they'd worked for was about to become a reality at last, in all the nation.

Yet, there might still be efforts to be made, here in the village of North Upton. Did she still dare to leave? Aunt Charlotte, Miss Farrow, Mrs. Sanborn, they knew what was right and fitting. They would write letters, make arrangements, bind good-hearted people together in the necessary efforts.

Still, someone must be willing to take risks. To leap onto a horse if needed. To carry the word with her.

Would Susannah have too much on her shoulders? Almyra worried, as she folded her letter and inked the seminary's address on the paper.

# About the Author

Beth Kanell's focused attention to eccentric, quirky, and just plain unique Vermont lives laid the grounding for her award-winning writing, from novels to feature articles to gloves-off in-depth investigation. Her novels have probed the state's unique Northeast Kingdom (*Cold Midnight*, *The Secret Room*, *The Darkness Under the Water*, and the Winds of Freedom series: *The Long Shadow* and *This Ardent Flame*). Beth's writing earns awards from the National Federation of Press Women, SPUR recognition from Western Writers of America (for her frontier fiction), and the Break the Bechdel With Strong Female Characters Syndicate. She is also the author of three books of adventure exploration, two of history, and hundreds of poems and feature articles. Beth Kanell lives in rural Vermont, with a mountain at her back and a river at her feet.